432

PINCH GUT ROAD

To Ashton

Enjoy

(handwritten signature)

432

PINCH GUT

ROAD

A NOVEL

By

KENT HUGHES

MIKE PARKER
EDITOR

ACKNOWLEDGEMENTS

I've met so many people along my writing journey that I now find it almost impossible to name everyone involved in my development. If by chance I remembered to put your name in *4th Sunday: In the Dirty* or in my novel *Three Lies*, your acknowledgment still stands good for *432 Pinch Gut Road*.

I truly need to thank Jesus Christ, my Lord and Savior, for my life, my gift, and my family. I would like to thank my mother and father, Jesse and Maiseville Hughes ... thank you so much. To my siblings ... Theresa Figgs, Jesse Jr., Elvese McLean, Jannitfer Sykes, Sheila Williams, and Sherick: thanks, being my best friends. Even in my storms, you made my light shine and only God knows how much you all mean to me.

To my in-laws, Charles Sykes, Dora, Terry McLean, and Megan ... You are more like my sisters and brothers. In an effort not to leave out all my nieces and nephews names, I will just say thanks for being such great nieces and nephews.

I must give thanks to Tiffnii Hughes, Tiffany Stancil, Mike Parker and to Mrs. Dawn for their great jobs. And thanks to Lydia Parker who assisted with the final proofreading and editing. I would also like to thank Prinn Deavens, Darryl and Lashawnda Key for helping me to stay sane while out promoting my work.

DEDICATION

To my wife Tiffnii Hughes

I can't imagine my life without you. I also dedicate my life to you, for without you to live for, I can't really say I've lived. God bless our family...Monster, P.J, Dizzle, Mike, Young Mookie and our Grand boo...Harms!

Love you,
Hubby!

TABLE OF CONTENTS

CHAPTER	1	Particular Night
CHAPTER	2	Pitch a Fit
CHAPTER	3	Now… Let's Eat
CHAPTER	4	Private Detective
CHAPTER	5	Watching
CHAPTER	6	Like a Jackrabbit
CHAPTER	7	SHUT UP, TEENY BABY
CHAPTER	8	This Stuff Had to Happen
CHAPTER	9	Ten Miles of Ugly Road
CHAPTER	10	Pinch Gut Road
CHAPTER	11	In Elizabeth City
CHAPTER	12	Overwhelmed
CHAPTER	13	Fool hurt my feelings
CHAPTER	14	Quem deus vult perdere, dementat prius
CHAPTER	15	Haints
CHAPTER	16	I think I'm pregnant
CHAPTER	17	The Damage Was Done
CHAPTER	18	4th Sunday
CHAPTER	19	Faith and Hope combine
CHAPTER	20	Something Unimaginable
CHAPTER	21	The Madness Stops
CHAPTER	22	Straight to Therapy
CHAPTER	23	The Michael McDuffy Youth Center

Preface

By

Kent Hughes

432 Pinch Gut Road *F.S.I.T.D pt. 3* is a spin off my previous novel Three Lies *F.S.I.T.D pt. 2*.

After Donnie's execution there was a plethora of questions to be answered. The book he wrote while in prison 'Three Damned Lies," seemed to preserve all the mysteries behind the three lies or murders that took place. When writing the book Donnie befriended a young officer that worked on death row, Officer Stanley Miles. Officer Miles vowed he would get the book published. The one promise Officer Miles had to keep was that nothing would alter the outcome of

Donnie's demise. Little did he know, Three Damned Lies held way more secrets than he first thought. There was another sinister happening that was about to take place in the small country town of Camden NC, that would shake this small community to its core. Stanley would need the help of Donnie's closest friends and family members to solve the mystery of Pinch Gut Road, through the passages and clues left Donnie's book.

His first contact was Beatrice and Beany Harold, who Donnie spoke about in his book and the abilities Beany had that would leave him amazed and curious. Together they would unlock history of the Cantos family and reveal more than enough secrets. The secrets down an unpaved road in Camden, somewhere on Pinch Gut Road.

While writing 432 Pinch Gut I had no idea where I was going to take it, but luckily the characters took over and lead me on this crazy journey. This was one of the hardest projects I have ever attempted to do being I had to tie the two stories together and make it make sense, yet one of the most rewarding. After completing the story, and going back to read it several times, I tried keeping it as down-home southern Camden as possible. It was a task of its own. I tried to use less profanity as possible but there were situations in the story the characters chose profanity stating, "that's just how we talk." So, I had to write as they gave their story.

It is a mystery, but it's also a story about love, family, close friends, first times, and heartbreaks. Not going to lie…I never in my history of reading my work, have I read something that covered every emotion like Pinch Gut Road…I laughed out loud and got chills while reading this book…that, 'I' wrote…Thanks everyone for giving me the courage to keep writing…See you on 4th Sunday in the Dirty(F.S.I.T.D Pt 1)…The beginning!!

To Be Without

To fly without wings
And to soar without caution
      Is to believe
To love without preparation
And to care without condition
      Is to be blessed
To find without looking
And to seek without answers
      Is to be patient
To have without wanting
And to request without needing
      Is to be thankful
To be with or to be without
      Is to live...
      To be...
      And to dream

CHAPTER 1

Particular Night

As the rain and crowd slowly dissipated, Beany stood wishing she could have done something. For the first time in her life, she wanted to understand her gift and have control over it. Her biggest problem ... all she could do was warn people ... appear in their dreams and ... warn them.

She was in love with Donnie Johnson as a little girl even though they were cousins, and although she'd never told him or even knew that it was love. But she would appear in his dreams to try to guide him.

His execution made her wish she knew nothing about his innocence. She even thought about dying ... maybe ending her own life, so she would not have to suffer with each tragedy that followed her psychic vision. Yet ... that was not the order of things ... an order of things she could not control or understand.

Beany remembered the stories her mother, Beatrice, had told her of how she warned her father, Harry Harold, of his death. Each time Beany remembered that day, each time she played the story back in her head, she felt vexatious and addled.

By age five, she had known she was different. The dead were her friends.

Grand Ma Amy, Ma Elise, her father, and a few other dead children who wandered around, lost, from Pinch Gut Road, would come around to play with her and share their secrets.

Beatrice knew about Beany seeing dead people. Beatrice thought she knew all her daughter was seeing. But Beany never told her mother about the others because Beatrice was never willing to listen unless Beany spoke about her late husband, Harry.

When Beany was a little girl, Beatrice told her the TV was going out the window if Beany were to get stuck in it. As a child Beany became afraid to give out too much information about what she saw. She actually believed she was going to get stuck in the TV like the little girl on the movie *Poltergeist*. Beany would leave the room whenever her older brother Alex would turn on the television. In fact, Beany never watched TV until she was in her late teens for fear her mother was right about her getting stuck and having to follow the light.

After her father Harry's death, Beany always considered Harry her real father, she learned that Tavone was her biological father. Since the father she loved was in the ground and she felt disconnected from the father who sired her, she figured she was better off claiming no father.

Rev. Tavone McKnight seemed to be a nice enough man, and he tried to be there for her growing up, something about him just was not right. Something about Tavone's presence at Donnie's execution didn't seem to fit the order of things. Something always happened when he was around. That something was never good. Beany stood outside Central Prison waiting for Beatrice and Tavone as more of the crowd started to leave.

Donnie had requested to spend his last few hours with Beatrice. She was the only family he knew. Tavone was also there to be Donnie's spiritual guide when the state of North Carolina took Donnie's life. Tavone knew an even deeper relationship existed between Donnie and him – but only the two had a need to know.

When Tavone and Beatrice finally came out of the prison gates, Beany ran to hug her mother. They began to sob. After a few minutes, the sobs subsided.

"Mom, are you okay?" Beany asked.

"Yes, I'm okay, but I never in my life want to experience anything like this again ... ever! This was just too much for your mother. I cannot believe that Donnie took the blame for his brother – died for his brother's crimes. I love you and Alex to death, but if you ever go astray and feel like you want to kill someone, you are on your own."

Beatrice paused.

"I don't drink, but I could sure use a shot of something after all this," she said.

"Well, Mom, you don't have to worry about me or Alex harming anyone. And you don't have to worry about Donnie's brother bothering anyone again. The crows are going to take his ass away from here tonight."

"Beany!" Beatrice said, "I do not feel like hearing that shit tonight. Just drive my black ass home.... Damned crows.... You can come up with some of the craziest shit sometimes."

Tavone walked out of the prison gates, a few steps behind Beatrice.

"Hey, Beany. How are you?" asked Tavone. "Aren't you going to slow down enough to say hi?"

"Hi, Tavone," Beany said. She continued to walk with her mother. Beany didn't feel like carrying a conversation with him. She still wondered what part Tavone had played in everything that had been going on in Camden for the last twenty years.

When Beany was a little girl, Beatrice usually advised her to be a little nicer to Tavone. As Beany got older, Beatrice stopped hoping Beany would accept Tavone. Beany's love for Harry was just too strong. Beatrice also knew Beany had the gift to read right through people. Beany must have detected something about Tavone that did not fit.

Beany's dismissive response didn't stop Tavone from trying to carry on a conversation with them.

"Hey – the book *Three Damned Lies* that Donnie wrote was pretty good, wasn't it? It brought back a lot of good and bad memories. I wish I had known all that was going on with Donnie and his brothers. I would have paid a little more attention to those boys."

"Like you did your own, right?" Beany said icily.

"Beany!" Beatrice said. "You may not remember, but the man did try at one time."

"Well, he didn't try hard enough. And I don't care if he did."

"Right or left?" Beany asked Beatrice. In the darkness Beany had lost all sense of direction as she tried to return to their car. Still, she picked up her pace a little, moving farther from Tavone.

Beany knew that Tavone was a bad person. She just couldn't figure out how she knew or why she could not get a clear sign. Maybe ... she thought ... maybe it was because he was her biological father or maybe he too ... was hiding behind something. No matter, Beany didn't care or want to be around him.

"Do we make a right?" Beatrice asked. "I'm not sure."

"It's a right, Mama. I've got my bearings now. We parked by the light with the letter G on the pole." Tavone felt an urgent need to head back to his car. He felt uncomfortable with Beany walking beside him. Still, he made an insincere offer.

"If you guys want me to, I will walk with y'all to your car. But my car is back that way."

"No thanks," Beany said quickly. "We've got it from here. Go on ... run on your way."

"Beany!" Beatrice said. "Why are so you mean to the man?"

"Mama, he was so ready to get back to his car anyway."

"I would be, too, if you talked to me like that."

"Mama, there's something about him that ain't right."

"There's something about you that's not right, Beany."

They both started to laugh as they walked the black, icy-looking pavement to their car.

"Suit yourself," Tavone called over his shoulder, already heading to his car.

The moon was at its fullest, taking center stage as clouds moved across the midnight sky. The ashy light shimmered bright enough to help them navigate the traffic. Fighting the blinding headlights from vehicles driven by spectators and protesters, Beany finally made her way onto the main road that led to Interstate 40.

Beatrice was burned out from the grief she had endured watching Donnie die. She reached for a pillow from the back seat, plugged her headphones into her portable CD player, and fell quickly to sleep. Beatrice did not like listening to the radio when Beany was driving because she didn't like the music Beany listened to. Beany only listened to opera. Beany complained that the monosyllabic words used in music today gave her a headache. She swore today's music was filled with subliminal messages that spread the devil's curse on the world.

The drive from Raleigh to Camden would take four and a half hours. For the first hour, Beany let Beatrice rest. This solitude would give Beany time to figure out just what about Tavone she did not like. Why didn't she trust him? There were so many things that her mother didn't share with her about Tavone being her father. Who was this man … really? She'd never met Tavone's mother ... her grandmother, or Tavone's father, or heard anything about them. Ultimately, Beany wanted to know if love had bonded her mother and Tavone together … and brought her into this world.

Every now and then, she glanced at her mother.

"What was going on with Mama and Daddy that led her to sleep with Tavone?" She had never really wanted to question Beatrice ... until now.

Beany, now twenty-one, was starting to feel as though she was old enough to ask a few questions. She allowed her mother to sleep until they exited on Highway 64. She had so many questions she wanted to ask. Perhaps those questions could give answers about Tavone.

As Beany pulled off the exit ramp onto US 64, she turned the radio as loud as it could go. She unplugged her mother's headphones from the CD player.

"Beany! What the hell are you doing? You damned near caused me to have a heart attack."

"Mama, you have been asleep for about an hour, and I have been doing a lot of thinking. I have a few questions about my daddy."

"I told you everything you ever wanted to know about Harry. What else do you need to know?"

"I'm not talking about Harry. I am talking about Tavone, supposedly my real father ... my birth father."

"Okay. What do you want to know?"

"Let's start with how you hooked up with him, and why you cheated on my daddy to do it?"

"Beany, I really don't feel like this is the right time to be talking about this. You know what I've been through today. Why do you want to put me through even more stress?"

"Damn, Mama, was it all that bad that it stresses you out when you talk about it?"

"Look, Beany. Tavone and I were good friends in college. When me and your father had problems, Tavone and his good for nothing ass was there to take advantage of the situation. I never meant for all this to happen."

"So! I was a big mistake. Is that what you are saying?"

"No! I did not mean it like that. I meant that I did not want you to be Tavone's. I wanted you to be Harry's child, not the kid of that bootlegged preacher."

"Okay. Still, that doesn't explain much of nothing. I guess you don't owe me any explanation. Other than this unwanted ability I have, my life has been somewhat normal. I got you to thank for that."

Beany really felt a little sorry for asking her mother how she met Tavone. She knew that Beatrice was never proud of her fling with Tavone. But that was not the end. Beany still needed to ask the most important questions.

Beany took her eyes off the road for a split second to glance at Beatrice and then placed her right hand on her mother's thigh. She stared back at the road. Focused as ever.

"Mama, who is he really? Where is he from? I know you met him in school, and I still hear Mrs. McDuffy talk about that fourth Sunday in the dirty south thingy at church. I know that's how y'all found out he was running around with almost every woman in the congregation. And ... I know that he lives in Norfolk. But where is he from? Who are his parents? Suppose I get sick and need bone marrow or a lung or liver or something. I don't know anything about him, other than him trying to be a fake-ass preacher. Mama, the truth is ... I don't trust that man."

Beatrice always had a way of making Beany laugh and feel good even about bad situations. Beany thought it funny that Beatrice scared so easily.

With all the questions being thrown at her at once, Beatrice didn't have time to answer not a one.

"First of all," Beatrice said, a little playfully, "you need to get your hand off my thigh. I'm not that type of lady."

"Mama!" exclaimed Beany as she smiled.

"Well, you asked too many questions at one time. Now, I'm not exactly sure where he comes from, but I do remember him saying that his mother was from Lenoir County. He never really talked a lot about his father. All I know about him is that he was a white man."

"A white man?"

"Yep, that's what he said. He wouldn't say too much about him. It's like he was ashamed of that or something. I used to tell him that he should be proud of who he is and where he came from."

"So that's where I got these funny looking eyes from. You always told me that I got them from God."

"You did."

"Yeah! By way of Tavone's father, right? Why didn't you tell me the truth?"

"Look at how you are acting now, Beany. Hell, you can't handle the truth."

Beany sat a few minutes. Finally, she broke the silence.

"So, if that's the case, how can he go around preaching if he can't even handle his own demons. If he can't accept his father, then there must be a lot of himself that he doesn't like too much, either."

"Beany," Beatrice whispered. "Why don't you get together with him sometime and ask him the same questions you are asking me? I'm sure you will have a better chance of getting the answers you want from him. ... I know you could get them better than I could. Hell! Back in those days, I didn't want to know anything except when I was going to get some help from him."

"Mama, don't you think that something is kind of strange about him?"

Beatrice put her index fingers to her temples.

"Hmmm ... now that I think about it, I do. When you were a little girl, we had what we used to call Harry and Son's Bar and Grill. It was something Harry and his crazy friends used to do during the college basketball championship game."

"I remember those games," Beany said.

"Well," Beatrice said, "anyway ... Tavone came over the night I decided to let Alex oversee the party. It was the first-year anniversary of Harry's death, and everyone was trying to have a good time. The fact that Harry wasn't there brought such a gloomy feeling to the garage that night. Then, for some reason, the music went off and then back on, but not before Harry's old eight-track tape played loudly in the shed. All of a sudden, Tavone came knocking at the door from nowhere. Hell! I'll never forget that night. He looked like a car had run over him. That was so strange."

Beany was confused.

"What was so strange about that?"

"You, Beany. You were so strange about that. Normally, you would jump right in and say what was going on and who was doing what. You know, using that ESPN psychic stuff you use. But you acted just like you did not know a thing. You even acted like you were scared a little. Your being frightened of anything was a little unusual. That particular night I felt like Tavone was ... well, something didn't feel right about him. It's funny to hear you saying this about him now ... years later."

Obscure green marks highlighted the gas gauge. They needed to fill up. Beany drove for another ten or so miles looking for an exit. Once the red light started to flash, Beatrice panicked, thinking that they might have to push the car to a gas station. Beany continued to drive and talk as if nothing was wrong.

"I hope you are smiling like that when you're outside of the car pushing, and I'm steering," Beatrice said.

"Mama, we got enough gas to go another twenty miles."

Soon they drove up to an Exxon Station with gas to spare. Again, Beany was having a little fun with her mother. Beany knew that every time she predicted the right outcomes, and she was always right, her mother would get crazy-mad.

They filled the car, got a few snacks for the road, and headed back to the highway. With only about fifty miles to go, Beatrice wanted to drive the rest of the way. Beatrice was tired of answering all of Beany's questions.

The rule was whoever drove could listen to whatever she wanted on the radio, and Beatrice was ready for some good old-fashioned R&B. She fumbled through a few radio stations until she found her favorite, WOWI 103.

We cut into your regular scheduled programming, to bring you the following newsbreak:

Maurice Johnson, brother of convicted murderer Donnie Jackie Johnson, was found dead in his condo, an apparent suicide.

Latest reports indicate that Private Detective Teddy Warden, along with Wake County police officers, were at his apartment to question him about the murders of the three women his brother was executed for killing.

Donnie was put to death at 12:01 a.m. for those murders.

Police have not disclosed what evidence that they have, but a spokesman said the evidence justified holding him for questioning. We will have more details as this story develops.

Beany and Beatrice were all ears as the news broadcast horned across the airwaves. Just weeks before, a young man, Stanley Miles, a prison guard at Elizabeth City State Prison, had stopped by their house asking questions on Donnie's behalf about the murders. Stanley wanted to know about the book Donnie had written while in prison and how he believed Maurice was the murderer. Beany, in almost a paralyzed state, began to flux with acridity.

"Mama, could you please turn that off. That's why I didn't and don't like listening to those kind of radio stations."

Beatrice turned it off, but it was not because she was trying to please Beany. She started thinking about Donnie's manuscript *Three Damned Lies* and how it was now in the hands of the authorities. She thought about all the information in it. She needed to talk to Officer Miles as soon as possible.

Officer Miles was the officer that Donnie had turned his manuscript over to before he was executed. She wanted to make sure that her family wasn't in any kind of danger.

***

Camden County had a population of about six thousand people and was the fastest growing county, not just in North Carolina but in the United States. It consisted of close-knit families who had called Camden home, for over two hundred years. Gossipmongers continued to rule how the truth and lies were spread throughout the community.

Beatrice knew that if the truth got out about Maurice being the real killer, it meant everyone in the country would know of Beany's weird behavior as a child. The book talked about Beany's abilities and how as a little girl she was able to tell Donnie what was to come. Beatrice knew that it would put Beany and her cousins, the Johnson family: Stacy, Donnie, Maurice, and David out there for the country to talk about. She did not want to make a circus of all that had happened to her family or have the newspapers and TV to make a mockery of the town.

Especially the black folks.

***

Back in the late eighteen 1800's, Camden was built on the backs of the black slaves and later sharecroppers. The blacks in Camden took pride in being hard working, respected citizens.

Potato, corn, and cabbage fields were their main source of income. And they worked from sunup till sundown, making sure the farmer's crops were ready by season. Even though the county was quiet, there was a vice that had a grip on the people of Camden ... an unwritten rule ... don't cross the tracks after dark.

The tracks of Belcross, like most small southern towns, separated the whites from the blacks.

Separate but equal.

Meaning, as long as you stayed on your side of the tracks and you were black, you might have an equal chance of living a full prosperous life. If you were black and crossed the tracks, you better have a good excuse. If it was dark, you might have to wait until sunlight – if you didn't want the Klansman hanging you or burning a cross in your yard the next night.

Although times had changed, Pinch Gut Road was not a road you wanted to be on at night – even in the 21st century. Some say that the spirits of the black men, women, and children who had been hanged still lingered on. At any given time, one might show up and cause you to have a heart attack. The only black family with enough courage to live off Pinch Gut Road ... was the Johnson family, and the last of that family had killed himself tonight.

***

The phone rang as Beatrice drove past the road sign indicating they had just crossed the Pasquotank County line, twenty-five miles from North River Road in Camden County.

"Beany could you get my cell phone out of my bag? Hurry girl before it stops ringing."

"Okay ... okay! It ain't nobody but Alex."

"Hey! Bro," Beany said knowingly. "What's up? Have you heard all the craziness that's been going on with the Johnsons?"

"I'm not even going to ask how you knew it was me. I see you are still as sharp as ever," Alex exclaimed with a sense of point-blank wit. He then answered her about the Johnsons.

"Yes. I've been watching the news. I can't believe I'm watching guys that I grew up with have such a horrific ending of life. Didn't you have a crush on Donnie when you were a little girl? What ever happened with that?"

"How did you know that I had a crush on him?"

"By the way you used to go to his room when they had to stay with us."

"I did not go to his room. It was my room, and they were sleeping in it. And anyway, I don't remember going into their room."

"Well ... he told me that he saw you standing at the door, and you were saying something crazy," Alex said, knowing Beany had no idea what he was talking about.

Whenever Beany acted as medium or spirit and made contact with someone living or dead, she didn't remember anything about it. Alex knew this because other than their grandmother, Ma Elise, he was the only other person that listened to Beany and cared about the special gift she had. He also informed her of each time she went into some type of paranormal state, which would leave her unconscious and outside of her body for long periods ... hours even. Alex never knew where Beany was – when she was out there in sleuth mode – and was afraid to bother her, fearing fulmination if she was awakened before she was done. He often tried to help her remember where she was and what happened, but she could never remember.

For years, Beany had been seeing what she called shadow people. These people seemed to follow her during the daylight hours. It was like they were playing hide and seek with her. She felt like they were keeping an eye on her for some-thing or someone. Alex just wanted her to be safe and wanted her to get some type of help. Beany didn't want to end up in some psychiatric ward and turned down any offer made to her by Alex.

"Alex, you never mentioned that he told you that," Beany said with a little shyness in her voice.

"Well! I didn't want you to trip out or anything. Anyway, he's, our cousin. Couldn't nothing of happened with you two anyway, plus you weren't old enough to even think about liking someone."

"That don't mean I didn't want to know what he said."

"Okay ... whatever," Alex said, cutting off the subject and starting a new one. "Where is Mama?"

"Right here, calling herself driving. You want to speak to her?" Beany asked quickly, handing Beatrice the phone. Beany was a little upset with Alex.

"Hey, boy! Where are you?" Beatrice asked. "Why didn't you come out to the prison with Beany and me? You were so close to Donnie and his brothers growing up, I just knew you would be there."

"We weren't that close. All I ever did was play ball with them. I'm not going to lie. I was a little scared of Donnie. Back in those days, he was known as a gangster. Anyway, I didn't want to be out there with all those clowns standing in the rain. I saw it all on TV. That was close enough for me."

Another thought zoomed across Alex's mind, changing the direction of the conversation.

"Hey, did you hear about Maurice killing himself?"

"Yes, Beany had already told me about some damn crows coming to get him earlier, so I figured that something was going to get him."

"Crows?" Alex said, snickering.

"Hey! That's what she told me."

In the background you could hear Beany saying, "Y'all shut up! I know y'all are talking about me. I'll let some crows get one of you ...you two keep on messing."

"And before they get me," Beatrice said, "I'll make sure you have gotten a well whipped ass before they get here."

Alex was on the phone laughing madly, as were Beany and Beatrice.

While Alex went on talking to Beatrice about Maurice and Donnie, Beany thought to herself, "Alex, why don't you tell Mama the truth. You know you are not at school."

"Mama," Beany questioned, "Why don't you keep straight and cut through Pinch Gut Road instead of going to Belcross, which is all out of the way?"

"Girl, I haven't been on that road in twenty years, and I damned sure ain't going to drive on it tonight."

"Why?" Beany asked. "I drive through Riddles all the time. What's supposed to be the problem."

"I tell you what," Beatrice said with the will of a bull in her voice. "When I'm not in the car, you can drive through Riddles on Pinch Gut Road all you want. Tonight – it ain't gonna happen."

As they turned right onto Belcross Road and crossed the tracks, Beatrice began to explain to Beany the stories her mother used to tell her about crossing the tracks.

"Years ago, you'd better not have been seen on the opposite side of these tracks. That would be like a chicken dancing around a deep fryer. I remember when I was a little girl, my friends and I would sneak across the tracks at night just to see what would happen."

"What happened? Did you get caught? No ... Let me guess. Someone got hung ... Right? I know there's some crazy story to go with it," Beany said, like she was tired of hearing all the sad ... bad ... white people stories.

"Well," Beatrice said, "you better close your ears 'cause that's exactly where I'm going with this."

Beatrice paused for a few seconds and began with her tale.

"As we crossed the tracks and walked along the wooded trail, ... where those houses right over there are now... it was the first time I saw a KKK meeting. Once we saw what was going on, we took off running back across those tracks and back to our houses. You never had to worry about us going somewhere we weren't supposed to be. Never again."

"It might have been my grandfather having that meeting," Beany said jokingly.

Little did she know that joke would be the key to all the answers to the questions she would be asking.

As Beatrice turned onto North River Road, they could see their house.

"Beany, did you leave all those lights on in the house?" Beatrice asked.

"No."

"Well, I know darn well I didn't leave them on. The light bill is already high enough."

As they got closer to the house, Beatrice saw Alex's car in the driveway and started to laugh. She knew that Beany must have known that Alex was home and just didn't tell her.

Beany got a kick out of watching her mother freak-out when Beany played her little games.

Once they parked, Alex came out of the house and into the garage to help get the bags, and to greet his mother and sister. It had been a long ride, and both Beany and Beatrice were tired. Beatrice asked Alex how long he had been home and what's with the big surprise. He always let her know when he was coming home so that she'd have enough food to feed him.

Alex had always been big for his age. At six-four, he was like a walking garbage disposal when he came home. All he did was walk around and eat. He got a full ride to the University of North Carolina at Wilmington on a baseball scholarship. Not only was Alex a good athlete, but he also always kept his grade point average at 4.0. He had promised his mother that if he didn't do well in school, he would quit sports and pay his own way. To his way of thinking ... that pledge helped motivate him academically and in baseball. He did not get drafted after he graduated and was now in grad school at Central State getting his law degree.

Alex also wanted to help Beany develop and control her psychic and paranormal abilities. He took elective courses on mediumship, psychic readings, channeling and releasing emotional blocks – whatever he could find in hopes that he would stumble across a way to reach Beany. Alex feared something horrible would happen to her one day if he did not intervene in some way.

Rev. Felicia Milado, an ordained Spiritualist Minister, served at an interfaith church. She began her studies as a clairvoyant medium and intuitive, Reiki practitioner/healing channel, spiritual counselor, and facilitator. She had been a frequent guest psychic on many nationally syndicated radio shows. Alex remembered seeing her on The Montel Williams Show. One semester, Alex attended one of the classes she offered.

After class one day, she came over to Alex and told him that a family member was in great harm and that he would be a medium's assistant.

Alex had never told Milado about Beany or indicated anyone in his family had any kind of ability. He often shared the information with Beany that he learned from his classes. Yet, he never told Beany of the great danger that Milado shared with him. All he knew was that if any trouble did come Beany's way, he would be right there to help.

Beany knew that she could count on Alex and knew that Alex counted on her. Beany was holding something else about Alex's visit from Beatrice.

CHAPTER 2

Pitch a Fit

"Hi, Mrs. Harold."

"And just who are you," Beatrice said, a look of surprise frozen on her face.

"Oh... oh... mama... this is my girlfriend, Rosemary Martinez," Alex said, stuttering a little.

"Boy! You can't be bringing any women into my house without me knowing about it first. Beany, did you know about this too?"

Beany looked at her mother.

"Mom, I'm afraid so."

"How long are you here for?" Beatrice asked.

Alex quickly took charge.

"We will be here for two weeks," he said.

"Okay. Now where are WE going to be sleeping?" Beatrice inquired more deeply.

"Come on, Mom. Where else but in my room, of course," Alex replied.

"And where are you going to sleep ... outside? Well, I'm tired and I'm going to take a shower and go to bed. Sweetheart, nice to meet you. I guess you can sleep with Beany, and we can finish this in the morning," Beatrice said as she walked out.

Beatrice took a shower but didn't feel that she could fall right to sleep without winding down a little. She decided to cut on the TV to help her end the long day. Before she walked fully into the bedroom, she leaned back stretching her neck, turned toward the living room, and yelled out to Alex and Rosemary.

"Remember the sleeping arrangements I made for you two."

Beatrice walked into the bedroom and started to smile.

Alex laughed to himself because he figured it wasn't going to last long. He had already told Rosa, his nickname for Rosemary, about Beany. When it came to ghosts and the supernatural, Rosa was even more frightened than Beatrice. Still, she was willing to give it a try.

Even though Beany was tired from the trip, she was so glad to see Alex and to meet his girlfriend, so she was not about to go to bed. Beany took a shower and rushed back into the living room to get to know Rosemary.

"So, Alex," Beany said excited, "what gave you the balls to bring Rosemary home? You knew Mama was going to pitch a fit."

"Girl, I'm twenty-three years old. I am not worried about your old tired-tail Mama. She'll get over it. I bet by tomorrow morning; she will be so glad to see me that she won't even mind."

"I sure hope so for your sake," Beany said uncertainly.

"Beany, you act like Mama is going to kill us or something. Mama is just a lot of talk. You know she loves everybody," Alex replied.

Rosemary sat with a nervous smile. She was hoping that she wouldn't have to leave early. She was very much in love with Alex, and they were not here merely to visit. Alex was there to tell his mother that he was planning on getting married sometime in August, maybe on his father's birthday.

He and Rosemary hadn't worked out all the details, but they knew for sure they were going to tie the knot.

"Alex," Rosemary asked, "Are you sure everything is going to be, okay?"

Beany smiled.

"Don't worry. Alex is right. Mama is already over it and lying-in bed right now smiling in her sleep."

"Is she for real Beany," Alex asked cheerfully.

"Yep! I think Mama is ready for some grandbabies," said Beany.

"I sure hope so," replied Rosemary.

"I knew I heard two hearts beating," Beany said. "Girl, you are three weeks pregnant and it's a..."

"Whoa! Who-a-a-! Beany we don't want to know right now," said Alex.

Excited that Beany could really tell her the sex of the baby, Rosemary said, "You can really do that? I want to know."

Beany could tell that Alex did not want her to give away the baby's sex, so she just said she would have been just guessing. She changed the subject.

Beany stayed up for about two hours talking and getting to know Alex's newfound, pregnant love. Beany was happy for Alex and wished she could find someone to love. The problem was that she could read right through any guy she met.

Beany was drop-dead gorgeous, and she knew what guys wanted without them ever having to say a word. When it came to men, Beany thought her gift was more like a curse.

About 3:45 a.m., Beany figured it was time to get some sleep. She had one thing that she wanted to discuss with Alex before she went to bed. Beany politely asked Rosemary to please excuse her and Alex for a minute. She handed Rosa the remote control and told Rosa to watch whatever she wanted.

Beany pulled Alex into her room.

"You know that she ain't going to sleep in here with me ... right?"

"Yes. Is that what you called me back here for?"

"No!"

Beany got quiet for a few seconds, took a breath or two, and then asked Alex what he knew about Tavone.

Alex explained that he thought Tavone was a real cool dude when he was younger. He said it wasn't until he got older that he found out what Tavone had done to his father."

"His cheating and lying made me lose all respect for him," Alex explained.

Beany wanted to know badly if Alex remembered anything strange about her and Tavone's relationship. She asked what he remembered that would make her hate him so much as a child.

Alex sat stagnant, paralyzed in thought.

"There was this one thing that happened at Daddy's funeral."

"What?" Beany asked, ready to hear the story Alex seemed to remember all of a sudden.

"At the funeral ... Daddy's funeral..."

"Alex y'all come here quickly. Yaa' mamas on the TV," Beatrice yelled excitedly.

Everyone ran into Beatrice's bedroom to see what had gotten her so excited. On the late-night news, there was coverage of Donnie's execution. As the reporter was talking with one of the victim's parents, you could see Beatrice coming out of the prison, head down and sobbing.

"Mama, I know you didn't call us in here for that," Alex said. "I thought you saw something good."

"Well, I did. I saw me on TV," said Beatrice with a gleam of movie star. Beany and Alex waved Beatrice off and went back into the living room.

"I think you are very pretty on TV," Rosemary said, trying to get on Beatrice's good side.

"Thanks, baby. Would you like to sit with me for a little while and talk so I can get to know you a little better?"

"Sure," Rosa said as she sat on the edge of the bed.

Alex and Beany went back into the living room. With Beany pulling Alex onto the long sofa beside her, she pleaded for him to finish telling her the story he was about to share with her.

"Alex, now what was you saying about the funeral?"

"Okay, Beany, listen … because I'm not going to keep telling you the same thing over and over again, after this. When we were at Daddy's funeral – I think you were about five years old –, Tavone was preaching at Dad's funeral. You just sat there and stared at him. You didn't blink. You didn't cry. You didn't do anything but sit there and stare at him. Mom said that Tavone told her that it scared him to death."

"Why was I staring at him like that?" Beany asked.

"I don't know why you were looking at him like that. Your guess is as good as mine."

"Well, I don't remember him being at Daddy's funeral too well. I do remember going, but I don't remember him being there. I remember taking a seat beside Mama, but I can't remember seeing anyone preaching. I guess it was just so long ago I don't remember."

"Why do you want to know about Tavone anyway?" Alex asked, frowning a little. Pausing for a second, he said. "What ... Did he do something to you? If he did, I can sure straighten him out for you."

Beany knew Alex was very protective of her, so she just smiled.

"No. I was just trying to know more about him. You better go find out if Mama has killed your girlfriend or not."

Alex got up to rush back to his mother's bedroom to make sure Rosemary was still alive. When he got back to the room, Rosa and his mother were fast asleep.

"Beany! Come look at these two lying on the bed like a couple," Alex said, laughing.

Beany immediately went to see what was surprisingly funny to Alex. Once she saw Rosemary lying snuggled on top of the covers and Beatrice breakneck to sleep, Beany turned to Alex and smiled. Beany took a blanket off the old rocker, placed it across Rosemary, and cut off the TV. She and Alex eased out of the room with light, animated smiles.

"Doesn't look like you're getting any tonight, buddy," Beany whispered to Alex.

"Who said I wanted some?" Alex replied.

As Beany said good night to Alex and headed to her bedroom, she knew that Alex was going to have a lot of explaining to do when the sun came up.

CHAPTER 3

Now... Let's Eat

The shutters in Beany's bedroom allowed the sun climbing over the golden soybean fields and evaporating the dew drops in its path to bathe the room in a soft glow. Everyone in the house was fast asleep from the wee morning family reunion. The occasional F-150 Ford farm trucks, lawn mowers, and tractors-cracked the morning silence and replaced the night noise from the crickets, frogs, and locust.

All were tired, but sleep purification would not be what rejuvenated the lifeless bodies nestled between the warmth of their covers. The way Beany smiled at Alex before he went to bed told him Beatrice must have guessed that Rosemary was pregnant. Alex could not sleep deeply because his mind struggled with on how he was going to explain the situation to his mother – explain why he'd brought a girl into her home – a pregnant girl at that. All he could hear in his head was his mother saying, "Why did you bring her here?" Beatrice would explain … again … why she did not want to be a grandmother before the age of fifty.

Around 11 a.m., Alex heard someone coming out of the restroom. He wanted to jump up to see if it was Rosemary, but he didn't move just in case it wasn't her. By 11:30 a.m. Alex could hear all kinds of feet moving on the floor. He'd rather stay in his room and play dead until his mother made her call for his presence. Her call would be like a summons to death row.

Suddenly, he heard a soft knock on the door. A pecan-tan angel peeped in.

"Come in, Rosa," Alex said, relieved to see her. "Girl! I could not sleep worth a rat's ass last night. All I could do was think about what Mama was going to say this morning."

"Are you sure that's all you were thinking about last night," Rosa said, batting her eyes.

"Well ... you know I was thinking about that too, but I was really-really thinking about that crazy-ass mama of mine and what she's gonna say or do about us."

"Rosa!"

"Yes, ma'am?"

"You tell Alex to get his long ass up and come eat breakfast, and you bring your little fast butt back out here."

"Coming, Mrs. Harold!" she called back. Then she turned her face to Alex and whispered.

"Alex, I just love your mother. She is so funny. I told her I had to get some clothes and take a shower. You know I fell asleep on her bed, don't you? I awoke and went into Beany's room and fell back to sleep. I better get out of here, and you better get dressed, too."

After Rosemary left the room, Alex got up, slightly hesitant with his movements, trying to prolong his visit into the kitchen for brunch. Beany even stopped by his room, banged on the door once or twice.

"Alllleeex ... come out and playeeeaaa."

Beany walked off laughing, telling Beatrice that she might have to call the police to get Alex out of his room.

Alex didn't mind the teasing from Beany. He knew he was kind of wrong for bringing Rosemary home. He remembered his father, Harry, sitting down talking to him about making the right decision when he was little. Alex was ashamed that he found himself in this position. He wished he had Harry's guidance right now to walk him through this. Those fishing trips he and his father used to take always seemed to make sense of everything and iron out his problems. It had been almost twelve years since those precious moments were available for him.

But Alex knew he could not stay in his room forever. He got himself together and walked out of the bedroom and into the kitchen to face the hammer of judgment ... a harsh verdict from his mother.

"Alex don't make me come back there, boy! You better get a move on it before this food gets cold."

As he walked into the kitchen Beatrice had the most beautiful Saturday brunch table setting ever. Alex knew something special was going on because she used her best china plates and highly guarded silverware. Beatrice never brought the good china out of the cabinet unless it was a special occasion. It had been so long since the family sat down at the dinner table that everyone was as sparkling as the silverware. Alex also knew that there was going to be a lot of conversation taking place.

"Alex," Beatrice said, sounding like God when He was talking to Moses at the Burning Bush, "come take a seat here beside your beautiful girlfriend so you can bless the food."

When Alex was a little boy sitting at the table with his father, Harry always led the grace, so for a flashing moment he felt as though he was really the man of the house. Alex asked that everyone hold hands and bow their heads.

"Lets us pray:

"God, I want to thank you for bringing us together safely,

"I want to thank you for blessing us with the healthy meal that was prepared by my loving mother. We offer this prayer in Jesus' name. Amen."

As soon as Alex finished, Beatrice butted in:

"Lord, I know my son thinks that he is finished, but he forgot to cover a few things. I just want to thank You ... and cover some things he forgot to mention. Lord, thank You for giving me the strength to not kill Alex when he brought his beautiful, pregnant girlfriend into my house. Lord, you know when I saw her standing in my living room this morning, I tried everything in my power to hold back from kicking his butt out on the street. It's You, Lord, that told me that just wasn't the answer. I again want to thank You, God, because after Rosemary and I talked last night, I found that she is a good woman and ... good for my sorry son. In Jesus' name, I thank you. Amen."

"Now let's eat."

Rosa and Alex sat in fearful silence, but Beany was laughing so hard that tears ran from her eyes. Beatrice couldn't help but join in the laughter as well. After a few seconds, Rosa began to break out in the loudest laugh of the three. Alex sat with his head looking towards the ceiling, asking God to help him.

Beatrice heard the alarm go off on the stove. It was time to take the buttermilk biscuits out.

Alex soon thanked God again, but this time it was for the biscuits his mother made.

As soon as everyone got his or her plates full and settled in, it was time for the topic of the day.

"So, Alex, how far along are you and Rosa's pregnancy?" Beatrice asked smiling.

"She's about three weeks."

"No! It's ... we ... we are about three weeks. Get it right, now. You helped to make it, so it's ... we, not she. Now, let me ask again: how far long are you two?" Beatrice repeated.

"We are about three weeks along, Mom."

"Are you sure it's yours?"

"MOM!" Beany said in shock.

"Mrs. Harold," Rosemary said with more of a "I'm going to die" look on her face.

Alex was so exhausted from the harassment Beatrice had bombarded him with earlier that morning, that nothing coming out of her mouth surprised him.

"Hey ... y'all can sit there like dumb bells if you want to. I watch that show and I'm not letting my son go out like no sucker. No offense to you, Rosa. I think you are a nice girl and cute as a button, but ever since Alex got his first piece of tail, you can't tell him nothing."

"Mama, do we have to talk about this right now?"

"Yes. Now keep eating and be quiet."

"Well, I don't mind him taking a paternity test as soon as the baby is born," said Rosa.

"Now that we've got that out of the way, what are you two planning to do to take care of the baby? I can tell you right now, I'm too young to be a grandmother and way too young to be sitting around the house with a baby."

Alex was feeling just a little bold.

"Why not? It's not like you have a whole lot to do anyway."

"Alright now, don't get too sassy for your own good. Plus, little do you know. I passed the state board teachers' exam and am taking a job at Camden High this year. So, that's how much you know about my life."

"Mama, that's great," Beany said. "You go ahead with your bad self."

"Congratulations, Mrs. Harold. I want to be a teacher also," Rosa added.

"Well, you'd better stop popping out those babies."

"Yes, ma'am."

"Anyway ... let's get back to how are you going to take care of that baby?"

"Well," Alex said, "in two more years I will have my law degree. I've been working with a firm in Raleigh, that's already paying me sixteen dollars an hour. I'm thinking about working full time so that Rosa can finish school. I think we can work things out."

"As long as you've got a plan that does not include me, full time, you both surely have my blessings."

"Well, I want to keep the baby as much as I can," Beany said. "Proud Aunt" seemed stamped on her forehead.

Alex sat smiling, thinking that his mother wasn't as hard on him as she could have been. He knew most of what she had been through with Tavone and his father. He figured that she just wanted what was right for him, Rosa, and the child.

"At this time, I'd like to give a toast to my beautiful ... mother ... to be ... Rosa Martinez."

Everyone held up glasses and toasted the occasion.

After everyone finished eating, Rosa offered to wash the dishes and clean up the kitchen, telling Beatrice that, if she wanted, she could go and relax.

What was thought to be a relaxing mid-noon day turned out to be a phone-ringing frenzy.

Beatrice's cell and home phone rung simultaneously. She knew, at some point, Teeny Baby was going to call because she was concerned with Beatrice's being at Donnie's execution.

When they were growing up, Teeny Baby always thought she was the strongest and the most stable of the two. Beatrice knew Teeny Baby was not the brightest best friend a girl could have.

Since the time she'd found out that Teeny Baby had slept with her husband, Beatrice had always kept Teeny Baby at arm's-length. After listening to the twisted reasoning Teeny Baby had given for sleeping with Harry, Beatrice understood that Teeny had a few thousand screws loose.

Beatrice started to screen her calls.

Most of the numbers were from people she did not recognize or from people that she did not care to talk with.

Except one in particular ... Lucy Gray.

After Lucy Gray watches the news and reads *The Daily Advancer,* she always tries to go straight to the source and get first-hand information. Once she gathers all her information, she spreads her news to the whole neighborhood, giving them an even better story. Her news was often better than anything you could see on the six o'clock news or read in *The Daily Advancer.* She was never too far from the truth.

The phone started to ring in five-minute intervals.

"Mama, Mrs. McDuffy is on the phone. Do you want me to pick up?" Beany asked her mother.

"Yes, let me talk to that crazy fool. I'm about scared to see what she wants."

"Hello," Beany said.

"Hey, sweetie. Where's your Mama? You didn't leave her on death row, did you?"

Beany loved Teeny Baby and thought she was about the funniest lady she had ever known in her life. She laughed, said "Hi," and handed the phone to her mother.

"Hey, Fool! I know you said something stupid. Got my baby laughing. What's been going on with you? I haven't heard from you in twenty-four hours."

"Look. Don't make this call all about me," Teeny Baby said. "You know I called to talk about Donnie. Girl! What did he look like when they put him to sleep?"

"Honestly, Teeny Baby, he looked just like he was going to sleep."

"Hell, he was … wasn't he?"

"You know what I'm talking about girl. ...You know what? I really think Jr. Cefuss has really got you going crazy."

"Girl, you don't know the half of it with that man. But that's another story. Go on, now. Get to the good stuff."

"Teeny Baby, I don't really feel like talking about this right now," said Beatrice.

Teeny Baby said in a sympathetic tone, "I know you probably don't, but I'm sure you need to talk with someone ... so, it might as well be me."

Beatrice knew that in some ways Teeny Baby was right. She did need to talk to someone, but she knew Teeny Baby was the wrong one to share something so serious with. The only thing

Teeny Baby could do to help was listen and be a friend. Beatrice also knew Teeny Baby could make her laugh, so she decided to try her luck and embrace the free therapy … like a hug from a grandparent.

"The hardest part for me, besides eating the last meal with him, was listening to his last words. Girl, that man had me crying like he was my son lying on that gurney. The parents of the girls that were murdered sat there like they were watching a good movie. One family even had the nerve to do their own little silent clap like they were cheering for a football team. I can't believe someone could get that kind of satisfaction from something like this."

"Girl! I talk a lot of smack sometimes, but I don't think I could do what you did. I would have been up in there yelling like I was at a funeral," Teeny Baby said grunting.

"Believe me, Teeny, I wanted to … bad."

"So, how did Tavone take the whole thing?" Teeny Baby asked.

"He did okay, I guess. I didn't really say that much to him afterwards. He was right in there with Donnie when Donnie was lying on that bed. He prayed with him and then stood back as they put the needles in his arms. I tell you girl … I wasn't any good after that. I tried to close my eyes, yet I kept looking for some reason."

As Beatrice was giving all the details, Alex, Beany, and Rosemary pretended to be busy cleaning. They were more listening in on the phone conversation instead. As Beatrice was giving Teeny Baby all the details that took place that day, Beany and Rosemary began to cry in the background. Alex saw that Beany and Rosa were crying and went over to console both. Beatrice looked up and saw Beany and Rosemary crying. She walked into her bedroom so she could talk to Teeny in private.

"Teeny Baby, my children were sitting in there listening to my phone conversation. They are crying like they were watching 'Passion of the Christ.' I swear, I don't have any privacy in this house. By the way, let me tell you about your little sweetheart Alex."

"What? Got a baby?"

"How did you guess?"

"Girl, I knew he was going to get somebody knocked up … as fine as he is. I started to try and be his baby's Mama," Teeny Baby said jokingly.

"Stop playing. This is serious. That fool." Beatrice paused to cut on the radio. "Let me cut on the radio in case they are trying to listen," Beatrice whispered. "He had the nerve to bring her home, and didn't even tell me, or ask me a damned thing. What is wrong with teenagers these days?"

"B.B. – that boy is hardly a teenager. Alex is twenty-three years old. What? You thought he was going to keep it in his pants forever? Girl, when I was his age, I was trying to bring home the bacon with my bird."

"Well, he brought home more than the bacon. He brought the eggs and the pancakes."

"What does she look like? And she better not be ugly. I can't stand to see a nice-looking man with a tore-up looking woman pushing a half-ugly baby around."

Beatrice started to laugh.

"She is a very cute girl. I think she is Puerto Rican or something. Her name is Rosemary Martinez. She doesn't have much of an accent. She was probably born in the States."

"You mean to tell me that you don't know where the woman is from. Girl you better find out more about that girl before she cut y'all's heads off while you are sleeping."

"Teeny Baby, you can come up with some of the most foolish shit."

"Well, I'm going to find out just who she is and where she comes from! What do you have planned for today?"

"Nothing. Why?"

"Let's take her and Beany for one of our little Wal-Mart trips. We can give her the third degree and find out as much as we can about her. I don't want my godson to be put in a jam."

Beatrice was for finding out as much as she could about Rosemary without seeming like the bad guy in the process. She and Teeny Baby talked for another ten minutes, putting together a few pertinent questions.

After hanging up, Beatrice went back into the living room to ask the girls what their plans were for the day. Both answered nothing and asked what she had in mind. Beatrice explained that she and Teeny Baby were planning a Wal-Mart trip and asked if they would like to tag along. Beany said that she was sick of going to Wal-Mart because it was always too crowded. She would go only if they could eat at Madison Palace afterwards.

Rosemary, trying to be polite and wanting to fit in, agreed to go along for the ride happily.

Alex, thinking that he was included in the plan said, "I think I need to get something from there, anyway."

Beatrice snickered and looked at the girls.

"You might have to get what you need some other time. This is a girls' time out. Plus ...we might go by Little Times; Teeny Baby wants to pick up a few things for Jr. Ceffus to celebrate their anniversary."

Beatrice knew Alex did not want to go in a lingerie store. Alex told her that he had some friends that he hadn't seen in a while and for them to go ahead. He then winked at Rosemary.

"Pick up something for me while you are in there."

"Okay, Baby, I'll get something real sexy for you," Rosemary said, shyly.

The phone had not stopped ringing. Beatrice had cut the answering machine off because she didn't want to hear the mouths behind the rings.

"Mama," Alex asked, "aren't you a little curious who some of those call are? Why don't you cut on the answering machine to at least listen to the calls? Some of them might be important. Someone from school might be trying to call me."

"Why? Don't you have your cell phone on?" Beatrice asked Alex.

"He ran his phone bill up," Rosemary answered out of turn. "If he didn't make so many phone calls to all those other girls, maybe he would still have minutes on his phone."

Alex gave a look that would have drowned a fish.

"I haven't been calling other girls ... thank you."

Beany jumped into the conversation.

"Well, as long as it's you he loves, I think he can have other friends," Beany said defensively.

Beatrice tried to end the argument brewing.

"Well, now that you both have that baby on the way, y'all can't be wasting money on a bunch of foolishness. Daycare isn't going to be free, and they sure aren't giving diapers away these days. You better start saving."

"That's right," Rosemary said, feeling she had a little back up from Beatrice.

As the girls got ready to leave, Alex got his keys and headed out. He didn't want the ladies to leave before him. He wanted them thinking he cared about being left behind. Alex knew that Rosa did not understand that she was in for a rude awakening once they picked up Teeny Baby. Teeny Baby had a habit of saying anything and was going to ask Rosemary whatever was on her mind. Alex felt that Teeny Baby's brain was a little too offshore to ask questions that would make it all the way inland.

The girls were dressed and heading out the door when the phone started to ring again. By this time, it was 5:30 in the afternoon. The phone had been ringing for most of the day.

"Mama, do you want me to get the phone?" Beany asked.

"Just see who it is."

"It's Mrs. McDuffy."

"Don't answer it. We are on our way. Hell, she'll keep calling until we get there. Teeny Baby is so impatient. She'll be calling my cell phone next. Beany ... while you're over there ... leave the answering machine on so I can listen to what the hell these people want with me."

Beany did as Beatrice asked and soon followed her mother and Rosemary out the door. Beatrice knew that the television stations were going to call for interviews. She did not want to be put on the spot and did not want all the attention. She thought that maybe even one of the victims' parents might want to call to ask how she could be in the room with Donnie during his last meal. Beatrice thought, they might have considered Donnie a beast and her one as well ... for supporting him.

All Beatrice knew for sure was Donnie was innocent and that he went through too much as child. She also knew that Donnie's execution was a big mistake. She wasn't sure that putting anyone to death for any crime was the answer. She wondered how it could make someone feel as good as Loretta

Johnson's parents seem to be feeling as she sat beside them and watched.

Donnie was Beatrice's younger cousin. If his father, her uncle, had lived, Donnie and the other boys would have turned out differently.

***

Donnie's mother, Stacy Johnson, never stood a chance from the beginning. When she crossed the tracks and married Reeo Michaels, the town of Camden was divided even more. She was the first white lady known in Camden to marry a black man. It wasn't too long before that marrying outside a person's race was a crime.

Stacy was only seventeen when she got pregnant by Reeo. Being that she was from up North, she didn't quite understand why people got so rowdy about her being with her husband.

Reeo was born in Camden and folks from Camden said that he knew better than to bring Stacy back with him. But he wasn't the kind of person to listen to what others had to say. He proudly went wherever he wanted to go, not caring at all what people would say nor about the long stares he and his family got.

When Stacy was pregnant with Maurice, the youngest of the three boys, her life soon changed for the worst. Reeo left for work at the shipyard in Norfolk, where he was a longshoreman. He never returned. The last time he was seen, he was stopping at the Border Store to play the Virginia lottery. No one really knows what happened to him after that. Most of the black folks in the area said that the Klan got a-hold of him. It was not proven and not a soul seemed to care about Reeo that much ... even his own family. Beatrice felt like the family pushed him away, fearing he might cause them trouble. They didn't want to be harassed by the powers to be, whoever they were.

Not one of Reeo's family members helped Stacy with the boys. She did it all by her lonesome, except for help from Beatrice.

If raising three little boys anywhere in the United States wasn't hard enough, being a white woman from New Jersey and raising black boys in the South didn't make it any easier. The biggest problem most of the blacks, including Beatrice had, was when Stacy moved on Pinch Gut Road with that dirty ass James Earl.

A tragedy was already in the making when she married Reeo. Having three biracial children and moving in with a former Ku Klux Klan's grandson was a script made for *Lifetime Television*.

He owned most of the land on Riddles, which his father bought from black farmers who could not pay the taxes on it. Actually, the real situation was more like the county stole the land and sold it for pennies. After Stacy married James Earl, the boys started going through the abuse. Some say she stayed because she loved James Earl. Others say she stayed because she had nowhere to go. Whatever her reasoning was, in the end it was not good for Stacy or the boys.

Donnie did what he could to make sure James Earl would not hurt any other young boys, but James Earl would not be a permanent fixture in the prison. Some recall the trial and how Beatrice was in court supporting Donnie when he helped put James Earl away for molesting Donnie and his brothers. Back then, the community praised her. Now, each time the phone rang Beatrice felt as though the enemy was calling, ready to banish her from the community or do away with her altogether.

***

As Beatrice walked toward the car, she could still hear the phone ringing in the distance. Rosemary wanted to know what Beatrice was going to do about all the phone calls she was receiving. Beany told Rosemary that most of them were from people in the neighborhood just trying to be nosey.

"Mama, what are you going to do if people start coming up to you at Wal-Mart asking you a lot of dumb questions?" Beany asked worriedly.

"I'm not even worried about that," said Beatrice. "You know I'm going to have that crazy Teeny Baby with me. You know ain't nobody gonna come up to me talking stupid."

Wanting to be a part of the chatter going on Rosemary eased in.

"I heard that Teeny Baby was a very pretty lady. Alex said that he would have married her if she hadn't married Jr. Cefuss. He also said that you ... Mrs. Harold and Teeny Baby beat up two old ladies at his father's wake. I can't wait to meet her."

"We didn't beat up anyone," Beatrice shouted as she laughed. "Alex was just telling you a story. And trust me, you ... capital letters ... CAN ... wait to meet her."

Beany cracked a small squeak of laughter, covering her beautiful smile with her hands, verifying what her mother said.

Rosemary tried to fake a little smile, but she was starting to feel uncomfortable. Even though she thought Beatrice was a very nice lady and loved to hear her fuss at Alex, Rosemary remembered Alex saying that Teeny Baby was a fireball.

As they pulled up the dirt path heading to Teeny Baby's house, silence filled the gap in the conversation. Beatrice tried to hold in the laughter she knew was coming. Beany looked back at Rosemary and smiled to comfort her a little. She could tell by the look on Rosemary's face that Alex had told her a little bit more than she'd shared about Teeny Baby.

With Beany driving and Beatrice in the passenger seat, Rosemary slipped over as far as she could to the right, to make sure that Teeny Baby had enough room.

When Teeny walked out the door, they could smell her before she even got to the car. She had on enough perfume to kill a baby bird. The red pumps she had on matched the blouse that Beatrice swore Teeny Baby wore in high school.

Beatrice and Beany were laughing as Teeny Baby walked toward the car. Rosemary was so worried about what Teeny was going to say to her that she was afraid to laugh, thinking that she may not be able to stop in time. One thing Rosemary knew for sure was that Teeny Baby was the most beautiful lady she had ever seen.

As Teeny Baby got in the car, Beany and Beatrice quickly rolled down the window to breathe in the fresh country pine.

"Hey, everybody. How y'all doing up in this piece. Girl! I look good today, don't I?" Teeny Baby asked.

"Yes, ma'am you look very good."

"Ooooh, child, I like you already. What's your name?" Teeny asked.

"My name is Rosemary Martinez, but everybody calls me Rosa."

"Well, my name is Sara May Cobb Taylor McDuffy. Everybody calls me Teeny Baby, except that smartie pants Beany. She has to call me Mrs. McDuffy."

"Any body that's old enough to be my mother, I will put a handle on their names." Beany said with a sassy tone. "So, after all these years you need to get use to it ... Mrs. Taylor."

Teeny Baby didn't mess with Beany too much, although she loved her like a daughter and wasn't hesitant to say what ever came to mind.

"As long as you don't use that witchcraft shit, call me whatever you want," said Teeny.

"Teeny, I have told you a thousand times: my baby doesn't know anything about any damned witches and shit."

"Mama don't tell her anything. When I shove a broom up her behind, she'll stop."

Everyone started to chuckle as Beany wheeled the car around to head to the main highway from the dirt path.

"Teeny Baby," Beatrice asked, trying to hold back a serious giggle, "when are you and Jr. Ceffus going to fix this path? It's almost the year 2020. This path been here since Chicken George was a baby."

"When you get a man."

"How you know that I don't have a man?"

" 'Cause I smell you every day. You smell just like women. You suppose to smell like a man sometimes, you know – FUBU or Calvin Klein cologne melting into your brown skin. You're always smelling like Dial Soap."

"Shit, you can't smell nothing but that 'grandmother going to church' perfume you always wearing."

Rosemary had gotten so comfortable that she forgot she was sitting beside Teeny Baby, laughing up a storm. What Rosemary didn't know was that this trip was planned around a fact-finding mission about her. Both Beany and Beatrice knew it was only a matter of time before Teeny Baby would begin.

"I see you are back here just having a good old time," Teeny Baby said. "You're cute and everything, but that still doesn't mean you are all right with me ... yet. I need to know a little more about you and my Alex. How did you meet him?"

"I met him at school," Rosemary said, a faint tremble in her voice.

"And."

"And I fell in love with him. He was a very nice gentleman. He used to walk me to class and just talk, talk, talk. He was the nicest man I had ever met."

"Well, if he was all that nice, why didn't you make him use something so he could finish school first, get married, and then you and him could have some babies."

"Trust me ... it was a mistake. We didn't mean to get pregnant. I'm in school, too, you know. I want to have a career just like he does."

"Well, what do your parents think about you being pregnant?" Teeny Baby continued to drill Rosemary.

"They were a little upset at first. After they met him and got to be around him, they started to like him. They just told me to make sure I finished school and not to depend on any man."

"Well, at least they told you right. ... Speaking of your parents: Where are you from and where are they from?"

"I am from Florida. My father is from Mexico and my mother is from Cuba. They were both migrant workers in Florida. My father moved to Camden and worked in the potato fields. My mother stayed in Florida. I had an older sister who went to school at Camden High. She came here to help my father in the fields. I was too young, so I stayed with my mother."

"Where did they live in Camden?" Beany asked.

"Somewhere in a place called South Mills?"

"What was your sister's name? I might know her."

"Velma Martinez."

"How old is she?"

"She is thirty-one."

"Okay. I wouldn't know her."

"She told me that she graduated with Donnie Johnson."

Teeny Baby felt she was trying to drift away from the question at hand and began to ask her more.

"Are you sure that the baby is Alex's?"

"You are a little late with that one," Beatrice said. "I already asked her, and she said she would take the test."

"Well, shit then. She's all right with me. I'm going to leave her alone. Slide your pretty self over here and give me a hug."

Rosemary felt like she had passed the test. At least the first test, she thought. Beany looked at her through the rear-view mirror and winked, letting Rosemary know that she'd done well so far.

After Beany found a place to park, everyone grabbed belongings and moved towards the store. Like always, the place was crowded. Just like most of the time, Beatrice and Teeny

Baby didn't want anything in particular. They just wanted to walk around and bring up old times. Rosemary and Beany decided they were going to go in the opposite direction to have their space. Beatrice and Teeny Baby went their way, talking nonstop.

"Hey, Beatrice," Teeny Baby said. "I've got a great idea. Why don't we have a get together at my place."

"Girl, ain't no one gonna want to drive down that long-ass dirt path for any party you want to have. Plus, you know people don't like going to your house, especially with that crazy jealous husband of yours."

"Good," Teeny said. "We can have it at your house. Wouldn't it be great to have all the old gang around again? I haven't seen Lips or Bucky in years. I can't believe that Bucky and Lucy Gray aren't married yet.

"Me neither, girl!"

"Do you remember the night you called me and told me about those two fighting?"

"Yeah, girl. That was the night that I was pregnant with Alex. I swear – I hadn't laughed so hard in my life."

"How about the time at my wedding?" Teeny Baby asked as she grinned.

"No-no," Beatrice said. "How about the time Lips came over to my house trying to break in after Harry died. I thought your crazy husband was going to kill him. Jr. Cefuss was mad as hell that night."

Each brought up times in the past that made them laugh. It made it even more necessary to have a party ... for old time's sake. It would be like a reunion. A neighborhood reunion.

"So, when do you want to do this?" Teeny Baby asked.

A light went off in Beatrice's brain.

"Let's have a party for Alex and Rosa. He says that he is going to be here for a week or two. That will give us ample time to plan everything."

"Ok, it's settled. We going to have a party at your place."

CHAPTER 4
Private Detective

After leaving Wal-Mart, the girls stopped by Little Times. Teeny Baby wanted to get what she called her special under panties. Rosemary wanted to pick out something to wear for Alex. All the girls got out of the car, except Beany. She loved lingerie. Wearing it was like an aphrodisiac to her. A man would complete her hunger for sex and be the cigarette that calmed her craving.

"Beany," Rosemary said with sadness in her eyes, "aren't you coming in with me just to look around?"

"No, thank you. I think I'm just going to sit this one out."

"Beatrice, don't you think that girl needs to find some young man and at least go on a date?" said Teeny Baby.

"Girl, I tried to get her to go out and meet someone. She doesn't have any close friends that she likes to hang with. She just hangs under me. It's kind of my fault that she is like this because I have always tried to over protect her."

"Maybe I can help," said Rosemary. "Alex and I were thinking about going out tonight. He said on Sundays they have oldies night at the Hut. We were going dancing and then get a room ... oops ... sorry."

"There's no need to say sorry," Beatrice cut in. "The damage is done. I know that the stork didn't get you two in this predicament."

"Beatrice," Teeny Baby said, not minding her business, "you don't let them sleep together."

"Not until they get married. I don't care what they do in their own house, but in my house ... how can I put this ... It ain't gonna happen."

"I know you are going to sneak a piece the first chance you get," Teeny Baby whispered in Rosemary's ear. "Don't worry about that old bat. She's just uptight because she ain't getting none."

"All right now. Don't cause her to get a beat down in my house," Beatrice said to Teeny Baby.

Once they got what was needed, they put their belongings in the car and headed for Madison Palace to eat. No one had approached Beatrice at Wal-Mart, although she did get a lot of stares.

"Beatrice, if you don't mind, I think I'm going to your house to chill for a while. I'm letting Jr. Cefuss keep Michael, and I'm going to give myself a time out."

"Sure. That's fine. Maybe you can help me screen some of those phone calls I've been getting for the past twenty-four hours."

Once close to home, they saw a car sitting in the driveway — a car they hadn't seen around before.

"Beany, do you know whose car that is?" Beatrice asked worried.

"No, I haven't seen that one before."

Beatrice told Beany to keep past the house and circle around a few times, hoping the car would be gone when they got back. Teeny Baby told Beany to keep driving until they got to her house, and maybe they could get Jr. Cefuss to check it out. But before they got back to the house, they saw Alex turn up in the driveway. They all figured Alex could handle the situation if it was out of hand. Alex was like Harry in the fact that he allowed no one to mess with his family. As Beany turned in the yard and stopped the car, everyone got out and rushed toward whoever Alex was talking to.

"Mama," Alex said, "this is Private Detective Teddy Warden."

Hesitant, Beatrice finally said, "Hi. How are you doing detective? My name is Beatrice Harold."

"You can call me Teddy, and nice to meet you."

"What brings you here today?" Teeny Baby said, like she lived in the house. "My name is Ella Sara May Cobb Taylor McDuffy, by the way."

"Nice to meet you as well, Sara," said Teddy.

"Mrs. Harold," Teddy said with a firm voice, "may I speak with you in private?"

"You can say whatever you got to say in front of all of us," Teeny Baby said, frustrated.

"Don't pay her any mind. Sure ... do you want to come in?"

"Well, I'd rather us sit in my car, if you don't mind?"

"That will be just fine," Beatrice said. "I just have to use the bathroom, and I'll be right back."

Teddy went to his car and waited for Beatrice.

As Beatrice went inside the house, Teeny Baby met her at the door.

"What did he want?"

Beatrice told her that she wasn't sure exactly what he wanted, but she was going to make it her business to find out. Teeny Baby then made a remark about how handsome Mr. Warden was ... and how Beatrice might try to get his number while she's at it. Beatrice gave her a nonchalant look and kept walking towards the restroom.

When Beatrice got into the bathroom, she put on a light coat of blush and checked under her armpits to make sure she was fresh. Once she felt she had it all together, Beatrice when back outside to talk with the detective.

"Here. Let me get the door for you," Teddy said politely.

"Thank you," Beatrice said.

After closing her door, Teddy went back around to get into the car. He handed Beatrice a folder with Donnie's manuscript in it.

"What is this?" Beatrice said before opening it.

"This is a manuscript Donnie Johnson wrote while in prison. He gave it to an officer before he was sent to Raleigh to be put to death. This is what we used to find out that his brother killed those women, including Donnie's wife. By the looks of it,

Donnie didn't feel like he had much to live for, and you could tell that he really loved his family. I guess he had his own way of how he wanted this to end."

"Yes, I guess he did," Beatrice said. "But why do you want to talk to me? What does any of this have to do with me?"

"Well, he used your name and your daughter's name a few times in the book, and I just wanted to talk to everyone in the book before I consider closing this case. How much do you know about the book?" Teddy asked, knowing she must have known something.

"Well, I haven't read it or anything. I do remember the young officer coming over here and telling me about it. Stanley Miles was his name if I'm not mistaken. He came over here about a few weeks before I went to Raleigh for Donnie's execution. I still don't understand what this all has to do with me."

Detective Warden went on to explain that some very important evidence was pointed out in this book.

"My team and I went back to check and found that Donnie was telling the truth about everything that he wrote."

"Like?"

"Like when his wife, Loretta Johnson, was murdered. He was on his way to visit her. Because of the time of death, there was no way he could have been there at the time of the murders. We even checked on the other murders, and it was proven that he was nowhere in sight when they happened. With the forensic evidence we used, it even proved that the clothes they found had been worn by his brother, not him. The only thing that put Donnie to death was his fingerprint on the knife used … and his admitting to being guilty."

"Okay," Beatrice said. "What you are saying is that if this book gets published, people will know that I used to help Donnie, and that my family and I might be in some kind of danger."

"No, not you ... but your daughter."

"Why my daughter?"

"Well, you know how crazy some people are?"

"Yep, I do know that."

"In the book, Donnie talked about Beany. She is your daughter, right?"

"Yes."

"I'm thinking that maybe if this book gets out, folks from every where will be coming here to see and talk with her. I don't know if you want that kind of company. I came over here to tell you to be careful about how you answer your phone. You may even change your phone number to make sure you get no unwanted calls. I just wanted to warn you to think safety."

"Is the book out yet?" Beatrice asked with concern.

"No, I don't think it's out yet. I don't really know what he's going to do with it, but I do know that the officer promised Donnie that he would publish it. If everything else is true, I think the officer will make good on that promise. Have you seen the news lately?"

"No," Beatrice answered. "My daughter, our friends and I have been out riding around and shopping a little."

"Well, it's all over TV about Maurice killing himself. Neither the police nor I have released just how he was found to be the killer. We made a deal with Officer Miles that we would not release how we got the information. But as soon as he gets ready to publish the book, which I know he will because it's a hot topic, it's going to blow up and I just wanted to let you know."

"Well, thank you so much for stopping by and if there is anything that I can do for you, let me know."

"There is one thing I'd like to ask."

"Yes."

"I'd like to know if I could speak with Beany?"

Before Beatrice had a chance to answer, Breanna came walking out the door towards the car.

"I think you got your answer," Beatrice said. She paused. "If that's all, I think I'd better be going. I have guests in the house."

Beatrice's heart started to pick up speed a little, wanting to ask for his phone number, maybe even wanting to know if he was single, but her mouth refused to open.

"Here's my card, if you need anything," Teddy said smiling.

"Thank you, Jesus," Beatrice said to herself as she thanked the detective.

Beany held the door as Beatrice got out of the car. Beatrice did not want to look Beany in the eyes, fearing Beany would catch a glimpse of the lust mixed in with the blush on her face.

As soon as Beatrice got in the house, she called Teeny Baby into her bedroom, leaving Alex and Rosemary to watch TV. Teeny Baby hadn't changed since her back breaking days and she was ready to hear everything she could get out of Beatrice.

Detective Warden twitched with nervousness as Beany entered the passenger side of the car. He was trying to remember where he had seen her before. For Teddy, it was like Deja vu. He sat, almost star struck. He remembered in *Three Damned Lies*, Donnie spoke of Beany seeing a man in a raincoat and saying the phrase, "Cripple cries." Teddy was almost afraid to speak, but he knew he had to talk with her to see what she thought of all that was going on.

Beany, feeling the vibes coming from Teddy, spoke calmly.

"Don't worry. I'm not going to bite you."

"Oh, sorry. Was I staring or something?"

"Kinda."

"Please forgive me. It's just that it seems like I have seen you before somewhere."

The detective knew he had to be honest with Beany because of the things he'd read in *Three Damned Lies*. He wanted to know about Donnie seeing her in his dreams. He wanted to know why and how Donnie saw the man dressed in the raincoat and hat dripping with water. Teddy was wearing the same thing just days later when he found Maurice slumped over in his chair after Maurice ended his life. He wondered whether it was a coincidence that Donnie kept seeing images of him. Teddy then asked was there anything that she knew about Donnie or Maurice that could help put closure to his case.

Beany told him that she did not know the family that well.

"Other than what Donnie wrote in his book and what you know about it, I couldn't tell you too much more," Beany explained.

"How do you explain the things he wrote about Maurice and what I thought I saw happen when I found him?" Teddy asked.

"Like what?" Beany asked. "I haven't seen or read the book, so I don't have the slightest idea what you are talking about."

"Well," Teddy said. "At the end of *Three Damned Lies,* Donnie wrote something about crows coming to take Maurice away and how Donnie must follow the blue birds. I usually stay with the facts, but several people say they saw a blue mist or light coming from the room after Donnie's execution. Minutes after I found Maurice's lifeless body ... I could have sworn I saw something that looked like a crow going inside his body, taking him away, right through the walls. I just wanted to know if you remember anything."

"No, I don't. I can't control what happens outside of my body. I wouldn't remember anything. Some things I can control and some things I just have no control of. This is just the order of things for me. Sorry!"

"Is there anything you want from me?" Teddy asked.

"Yes, could you do something for me ... please?"

"Sure ...What can I do?"

"I don't have any money to pay you right now."

"I will do it *pro bono*. Now what can I help you with?"

"Would you check up on my father? I want to know more about him."

"Okay ... this probably won't be too hard. I tell you what: just give me the information on him and when I have a little spare time, I will check on him for you. What do you want to know about him? You know who he is right?"

"Yes, I know who he is. I just want to know where he is from. Who are his parents ... and anything that you can find out about him?"

"What is his full name?"

"Tavone Phillip McKnight."

"Are you talking about the preacher that was at Donnie's execution?"

"Yep."

"Donnie wrote about him in his book. He talked about how he thought so much of the preacher. I didn't know he was your father. Small world, isn't it?"

"Yes, it is," said Beany. "He's, my father. He didn't raise me, but I must claim him. I guess it's something that he and my mother came up with that slipped me into the equation somehow."

After the detective agreed to help Beany find out about Tavone, he warned her of the changes that the book also may cause in her life … if it was published. He then assured her that he was going to check back with her. He couldn't give an exact date but assured her as soon as he got all the information together, he would call. He gave her a business card and took her number, writing it in a black notebook that he took from his glove compartment.

What the detective didn't know was the real reason why he was there. Beany had willed him there. He thought that he was there to warn Beatrice and Beany of the problems they might encounter if the book was to be published ... but they knew that already.

As Detective Warden drove off, he began to wonder. Why had he come to see the Harold's. After thinking about it for a while, he knew he was caught up in something out of his control. With the strange things he'd read in *Three Damned Lies* about Beany, little did he know that finding out about Tavone would become a top priority for him.

Beany knew more about Detective Warden than she let on. One of the dead children of Pinch Gut Road had mentioned his father's name.

***

Teddy came from a long line of policemen and detectives; his family tree ran deep in law enforcement. His father was a detective, and he tried to help the children back when he was a rookie working with ... his father. His father also kept a secret about David, Donnie, and Maurice that he took with him to the rest home where he was still holding on to his last days.

CHAPTER 5

Watching

Peeping out the window, Beatrice saw that the detective had left the yard. She waited to see what Beany talked about with the detective. Beany walked in smiling. Teeny Baby was dying to see what was going on. She was the first to ask Beany what she was so happy about.

Beany looked at Teeny Baby.

"I'll let you know when I find out."

Teeny Baby looked at Beatrice with a smirk.

"I don't mean any harm, but I just can't stand your smart-ass child."

Beany answered for her mother.

"And I know she can't stand your ass either. Now come over here and give your goddaughter a kiss."

Beany whispered in Teeny Baby's ear, "You know you love me," and then walked out of the room to hang with Alex and Rosemary.

Beatrice sat down in her tan glider rocker next to the phone. She looked at her answering machine. The light was blinking like a stop light after midnight at Camden Crossroads. Beatrice decided that with Teeny Baby there she would have someone to discuss each call with. She hit the button to listen.

After the beep came the messages:

11:47 p.m. ... "Beatrice, this is Lucy Gray. Call me when you get in."

11:48 p.m. ... "Yes, this is Ruby Oliver from *The Daily Advancer*. Would you please return my call at 919-555-7734? I would like to do an interview with you about your experience sitting in on an execution. Call me at any time. Have a nice day."

12:00 a.m. ... "Girl, I'm sitting here watching all those people outside the prison crying on TV. Call me ... this is Lucy Gray ... call me. Now!"

"Girl," Teeny Baby said, "Ms. Lucy Gray can't wait to get her hands on some information so she can start calling around the neighborhood."

"You know I'm not calling her back. Before the night is over, she'll call me again. I'll bet you," Beatrice said with assurance.

Two more calls passed as they had their brief conversation. Then the focus was back on listening to the calls.

12:56 a.m. ... "This is your girl. Call me. ...Bye!"

4:39 a.m. ... "This is Tavone. I'm just calling to make sure that you made it home safe. Give me a call back when you get this message."

5:30 a.m. ... click.

6:00 a.m. ... click.

6:10 a.m. ... "This is Nancy Bergin of WAVY-TV NEWS Channel 13. Give me a call. My number is 757-555-3364. Thanks."

8:00 a.m. ... "Beany. This is your uncle. I will be seeing you soon. This is our family's 20th anniversary, and I have something special for us."

"Beatrice, who was that?" Teeny Baby asked.

"I don't know," Beatrice answered. "Play it again. Let me see if I can catch the voice."

Teeny Baby played the message over about three or four times. Neither could figure out who it was. For a minute they thought it was her two fat crazy aunts on Harry's side of the family playing a trick. Beatrice figured that couldn't be. They had never had a man in their lives that liked them enough to make a call like that. They called Beany into the room to listen to the call. They wanted to see if she could identify the caller. Beany came into room with Alex and Rosemary. They all listened to the message, but they could not come up with anyone that would leave such a message.

"Mama, I don't know who that could have been. Maybe it was someone from school just playing a prank."

"Mama," Alex asked, picking on his mother a little, "why don't you get rid of that old 1920's answering machine and get one that tells who called, what time, and the phone number? If the number is private, they won't get through."

"That's a good idea. Why don't you pick me up one the next time you are out?" said Beatrice.

Beatrice had ten more calls to screen but decided that if they were that important, the callers would call back. She erased the remaining calls, and Beatrice and Teeny Baby talked about the calls for the next several hours.

CHAPTER 6

Like a Jackrabbit

The early morning rain pulled the sun behind, leaving a massaging like warmth about the air. It was time for Beatrice and Teeny Baby to sit behind the house in their favorite spot and make plans for the party for Rosemary and Alex. Whenever Teeny Baby could get away from the house, she would often forget where she lived and stayed away for hours.

At 7:30 a.m., Rosemary remembered the oldies night that she was supposed to invite Beany to with Alex and herself. She went into the bathroom, trying not to look suspicious. She then called Alex in pretending to look for something she needed. Once Alex was in the room, Rosemary asked him if Beany could come with them tonight.

Alex thought inviting Beany was a great idea. The only problem he had was ... how he was going to get Beany to agree to come. Beany had never been dancing. In fact, Beany never did any of the things normal girls her age do. He figured that the only way he could get her to go to anywhere was to see if he could convince Beatrice to go with them. After plotting how to get Beany to go, Alex and Rosemary went outside to ask Beatrice.

"Boy, you know I am not going out any where. I haven't been out to the Hut since I ... Beatrice paused for a minute and soon completed her thought, "since... I lied about going."

"Not even for Beany? It may do her some good to get out for once in her life."

Teeny Baby, eager to get out from under Jr. Cefuss, said, "Beatrice let me go home and get dressed. I'll go with them if you won't. I haven't shaken my booty on the dance floor since Popeye was a baby. I'll go with you three dummies if you don't mind an old lady going."

"We would be more than happy if you would come," said Rosemary.

"Yeah. We wouldn't mind at all. Come on, Mama. Let's all go. It's oldies but goodies night. Lots of folk will be there ya'll's age."

"Ya'll's age?" Teeny Baby snickered. "I don't want to see any men my age. I'm going to be out dancing with the young guys. I got an old man at the house barely moving around."

Beatrice finally agreed to go. The only thing they had left to do was convince Beany to go along.

Alex ran in the house and yelled for Beany.

"Mama wants you!"

"Coming!"

"Yes, mother dear," Beany said, cracking smiles a bit.

"We are thinking about going out to the Hut for oldies night. Do you want to come with us?"

"You are going, too?"

"Yep. I think I could get out tonight and shake a leg."

"Wel-l-l-l."

Everyone paused.

"I guess if you are going ... and Mrs. McDuffy, too?"

"Yes, I am ... thank you. Got a problem with that?" Teeny Baby asked.

"No," Beany answered. "I don't have a problem with that and ... I guess I'll go."

All looked at Beany with shock. The only thing left was for Beatrice to help Teeny Baby to get out of the house. Being that she had been gone all day she knew that it would be hard, but if it was one thing those two ladies could do, it was scheme.

Teeny Baby figured it was about time to go home to see if she could get her husband to let her hang out with her friends. Since Harry had died, Beatrice had not been too much of a bother to Teeny Baby. Beatrice knew that if she asked Jr. Ceffus to let Teeny Baby come out with her, he would more than likely say yes.

Beatrice told Teeny Baby she would do the talking and that would be their plan.

Before leaving, the ladies went into Beatrice's bedroom to help Beatrice pick out an outfit for the dance. Each time Beatrice picked out something that she liked, the others started to laugh.

"Girl, we are going to a night club, not a funeral," Teeny Baby said. "Here ...Why don't you wear this? This would look good on you. I wish I had a big butt like that. Looks like you have been riding a bull."

"Is my butt that big?"

"No, Mama, you have a nice shape. I wonder where I got my behind. Hmmm, never mind," Beany said.

"Mrs. Harold, they say that I have a big booty, also, but your son loves it," said Rosemary.

"I bet he does," Teeny Baby said. "Does he like hitting it from the back?"

"Teeny Baby, let me take your crazy tail home. How are you going to ask my son's girlfriend something like that? I bet your man can't even find your back 'cause you are always sleeping on the couch. What are you ... on strike?"

"No. That man just sleeps too hard."

"You ought not to work the poor man so hard and go get a job."

"I have a job taking care of him and his son. We need to stop all this jaw jacking and get me home so I can dress."

As Beatrice and Teeny left for Teeny's house, Beatrice reminded Alex and the rest of the gang to be ready when she got back.

They had to stop to pick up Teeny on the way to the Hut, and she didn't want to spend all night waiting for them to get dressed.

When Alex saw the car finally pulling off, he called Rosemary back to the bedroom and explained to her that they had about fifteen minutes to get their groove on before Beatrice returned.

"What?" Rosemary said. "I'm not about to get caught doing the nasty in your mother's house."

"Well, what are we going to do? I'm not going three weeks without being with you. You are the one that had the great idea to invite everyone and their mother to the Hut."

"You two can go ahead and get your groove on," Beany said as she stood by the door listening. "I'll let you know when time is up. But now if you two fools keep on going when I let you know time is up, well, then you are on your on. If I timed it right, you have ten minutes, Rosa, to get your groove and five minutes to take a shower and be dressed by the time Mama gets back."

"Thanks, girl, 'cause I really need a piece myself," Rosemary said, already taking off her clothes.

Beany rushed off to take her shower. Once out of the shower and dressed, she went to knock on the door. She stood there for a minute just to be nosy.

Alex and Rosemary were still in the room, moaning and grunting. Beany stood at the door almost in a trance, caught in their rapture. More than ever, she longed to make love just once. She wanted to see what it felt like to hold a man and feel him inside of her. She wanted to be in love and get married. But for her, it all seemed like only something to dream about.

Beany soon snapped out of her daydreaming and banged on the door to warn Alex and Rosa that if they wanted to have a long life, they better stop and get a move on.

"Whatever," Alex said, still trying to reach his peak. Rosemary jumped off Alex, grabbed her things, and left him on the bed as she ran through the hall butt naked to the shower. As soon as she finished her shower and got dressed, she could hear Beatrice's car pulling up in the yard.

"Thanks, girl," Rosemary said to Beany. "I swear it was just getting so good that I almost forgot where I was."

"Was it?" Beany asked curiously. "What does it feel like?"

"What? You have never done it before?"

"No, but I want to. I just haven't found anyone that I like."

"Trust me. Take your time. It isn't what it's all made out to be. I remember my first time."

"Please tell me about it," said Beany.

"Ok ... I was only sixteen."

"Only sixteen?" Beany said in amazement.

"Yes, sixteen and too young to know what I was getting into."

"Who was he? Where did you meet him? Tell me everything."

"It's not clear to me how we met. I just know we did. I think his family lived near my grandparents, so I would see him around sometimes. His name was Brandon. He would call me on the phone almost every day. We called ourselves girlfriend and boyfriend."

"Yeah, yeah, yeah. Get to the good stuff before Alex or Mama comes in."

"Okay ...okay. I really liked him, kinda sorta, my first official boyfriend. He would leave to stay with his family in Washington D.C., and I would miss him. When he came back, we planned to see each other, but he had something else in mind. Brandon thought that we should make our relationship official. The next thing I knew, God help me, we were in my parents' house. watching like a jackrabbit, he was ready to start.

"We went to my bedroom, kissed a little, and with not much warning, my clothes were off, and he started in. Not very gentle I might add. He pushed his way into me with a little force, a little bit at a time – at first. But it was clear to me that this was his first time, too. It hurt badly, and I wanted him to stop, but he kept assuring me it would be all right as he kept pushing.

"My tears were flowing, and all of a sudden being in love was not what it was cracked up to be and neither was this ... having sex thing. I knew then that sex was overrated.

"It didn't last much longer after he popped my cherry. I lay there in pain, hurting, scared and used ... and that was only my heart. My body felt worse than that, and he left right away. I had to clean up and didn't know how much longer before my parents were coming. Oh, God, look at those sheets and what's that white stuff? ... And, oh, I'm bleeding. I did, later after the trauma, tell my cousin Stephanie and vowed never to have sex again and never to see him again."

"So where is he now?" asked Beany.

"I broke up with him and never spoke to him again. Oh, and Mom did find the bloody sheets before I got a chance to clean them."

"Damn!" said Beany. "I don't think I'll ever want to give it up now."

"You will," said Rosa. "You just have to be in love with that person when you do."

"Alex told me that you attend Elizabeth City State," Rosa added. "I know that there are some nice-looking guys out there. And you are a very attractive girl. I know those guys are hounding you like a dog. If you were at Central, you would be like a queen. Especially with those green eyes."

"Yeah, well I don't think that I'm that fine. Ain't nobody knocking my door down to get with me. Plus, most of the guy's act like they are scared of me. Like I'm some kind of freak or something."

"I'm sure there's someone you like out there."

"There is, but he is married."

"Married?"

"He will be there tonight."

"Ooh. That's why you said 'yes' so fast? Alex just knew we were going to have to drag you out."

"Yes, but don't tell anyone."

"I won't tell if you don't tell on me."

"Tell what?" Beatrice asked as she walked in the door.

"Nothing, Mama. We were just talking girl talk."

"What ... Ev ... Ver. Let me get back here and get dressed so we can get back to pick up Teeny Baby. She is so excited that we are going out."

"I bet she is," Beany remarked.

Before Beatrice walked out, she looked back at Beany and thought to herself how beautiful her daughter looked in her little outfit. Normally, Beatrice would not go out anywhere, especially when she hadn't been to church in a few Sundays.

Tonight, was special. She was going to spend a night out with her daughter, son, son's girlfriend, and best friend. She almost felt like she was helping release Beany into the world.

CHAPTER 7

SHUT UP, TEENY BABY

Everyone was dressed.

They all got into the car and left for Teeny's. When they got to Teeny Baby's house and blew the horn, it took Teeny Baby ten minutes to come out. They figured she had to give Jr. Cefuss a piece of loving before she could get dressed. She called Beatrice's cell phone to let them know that she was on the way out. It was another five minutes before she got to the car.

"Woman, what took you so long? I thought that he had tied you down and wasn't going to let you go," Beatrice said as everyone in the car laughed.

"Girl, that man was tripping. He wanted a piece of tail, talking about he just wanted to make sure I wasn't lacking anything while I was out. Girl! I put it on his old butt."

"Teeny," Beatrice said, "I'm not going to lie – you look like you are twenty-five years old. I hate to admit it, but you are one nice looking woman. If I wasn't strict-ly dick-ly, you might be in trouble."

"Mama! You and Mrs. McDuffy are the dumbest two women God ever put on this green earth. Y'all will just say anything in front of anyone."

"Sorry, but you know we ain't right."

"That's an understatement," said Alex.

As Alex drove, he decided it was his rite of passage to lay down some rules. His father had always made the rules when he was alive to make sure that nothing got out of hand.

Rule one: No fighting.

Rule two: No slow dancing, except for Rosa, Beany and me.

Rule three: Don't stare at me when I'm drinking a beer.

Rule four: We come together ... we leave together.

Rule five: If any of these rules is broken, I'm kicking somebody's ass.

"Alex, your rules are good, but there is only one thing wrong with them."

"What's that, Mama?"

"Whose ass are you going to kick?"

"Nobody's. I just wanted to say that because Dad used to say it."

"I remember Harry saying that mess right before they got drunk, and that crazy Lips and Bucky would start to fight. Boy! Your daddy was a fun man. ... I sure miss him."

"Me, too," said Teeny Baby.

"ALL TOGETHER, EVERYBODY," yelled Beany. In unison, Alex, Beatrice, and Beany yelled:

"SHUT UP, TEENY BABY!"

After arriving at the Hut, Alex rode around trying to find a place to park. They had this event only once each month to give the older people somewhere to dance. It was an event held by the Eastern Sisters to raise money for the elders in the community.

Once Alex parked, everyone got out of the car in record pace ... all except Beany. Just hearing the bass from the speakers vibrating through the walls and causing the leaves in the trees to shake was enough to make Beany feel light-headed. She knew if she didn't get out, everyone would start to plead for her to come. With her legs rubbery and her heart pounding like she had been running from Pit Bulls, Beany stepped out of the car and drew in a deep breath.

"I'm ready," she said. Then she hollered, "Let's go party!"

They moved toward the crowd. Teeny Baby couldn't help but talk about each person she passed.

"There sure are a lot of church folks out here tonight. Look at Caroline and her ugly-ass husband. I can't believe that she goes out in public with that man."

"Why are all these people staring at me?" Beany asked. "They act like they haven't seen a real woman before."

"Beany," Rosemary said, "I told you that you are a pretty girl. Look at that guy over there with his tongue hanging out of his mouth."

"He was checking me out, wasn't he, Rosa?"

Beany started to smile and felt her confidence rise with each gazing eye that chased her lime green mini skirt. Even though the night had just started, she was already wishing she had tried this before.

Teeny Baby and Beatrice enjoyed standing outside and waiting in the long line to get into the Hut just as much as they would enjoy themselves once inside. A few of their old high school friends met and greeted them. Both got compliments on how good looking they were. Beatrice returned the compliments, but Teeny Baby couldn't stop talking about other people she saw to stay focused on anyone greeting her.

Finally, they were all inside. Alex walked around until he found a table with enough seats for them. The waiter came over to ask what everyone wanted to drink.

"I'll take a club soda."

"I'd like a bottled water."

"Same here."

"And you, sir?"

"I'll take a Rum and Coke on the rocks," said Alex.

"Same here," said Beany.

"What do you mean, 'Same here?'" said Beatrice.

"I mean, 'Same here,'" said Beany. "I didn't come here to sit around and look at you and Mrs. McDuffy. I am going to get my party on. Now, if you want me to leave then ... plus Alex's rules were no asking about what others drink."

"No, the rule was not to ask about HIM drinking beer ... not you," said Beatrice. "But go ahead. You are grown. Just don't overindulge and don't be crying to me in the morning."

"I won't, but if I do, I know that you have my back."

The waiter took everyone's orders and moved to the next table.

"Alex, I know that I'm going to get the first dance," exclaimed Teeny Baby.

"I think Alex wants to dance with his mother first," said Beatrice, staking her claim.

"No, Alex don't. Alex is going to dance with his Rosa," said Alex. "And I think this is the song we are going to dance to."

Alex grabbed Rosemary by the hand and introduced her fresh legs to the dance floor. Someone soon tapped Teeny Baby on the shoulder and asked her to dance, leaving Beatrice and Beany at the table. A few seconds later Beatrice found herself on the dance floor, leaving Beany to guard the purses and to wait for the drinks. From across the room, she noticed a very handsome young man that kept looking at her. She wanted to get up and move a little closer to see him, but she could not leave the table.

Soon the song was over, and the dancers returned.

The waiter returned with the drinks.

As the music played loudly, they sat talking in an even higher pitch over the agreeable sounds. Beany tried to look around Beatrice to see if her mystery man was still in her view.

"What are you looking for? See something you like out there?" Beatrice asked loudly.

"As a matter of fact, I did – until you sat down and blocked my line of sight."

"Excuse me, Alex," said Rosemary, "Beany and I have to go to the ladies' room."

Rosemary and Beany got up and worked their way around the crowd as they tried to make their way to the restroom. Before they reached their destination, Beany was tapped on the shoulder by the guy that she had looked at from across the room. Afraid to look back, she kept walking towards the restroom ... even picking up her pace.

Grabbing her heart and throwing her back against the wall, letting out a big gasp of air, Beany asked Rosemary:

"Did you see who tapped me on the shoulder?"

Rosemary said that she did not see anyone because she was too busy trying to get to the restroom without someone touching her stomach. All Beany knew was that when he touched her, she felt a bolt of lightning ... provoking a delicate part of her that she wanted to be ignited. She didn't know if it was the alcohol or what. All she knew was that she was ready to find this guy and see if he could be the one to satisfy her appetite.

"Beany are you okay?" asked Rosemary.

"Yes, I'm fine. I'm just ready to get back out on the floor to see who the guy is that touched me. I think I know who he is."

"Is he the married man you were talking about?"

"I think so. I'm not for sure. I've got to find out though. Are you ready?"

"Just let me freshen up a little and I'll be right with you ... or you can go a bit ahead of me in case you meet him, and he wants to talk. I'm not trying to be a blocker."

"A blocker? What's that?" Beany asked.

"You know ... a cock-blocker. Guys used that term when another guy is trying to prevent them from getting with a girl. It's usually the guy that can't find a girl of his own that's doing the blocking."

"Oh, I see. I guess I better get moving. I don't need that to happen."

As shy as Beany usually was, she said OKAY and walked out of the restroom ahead of Rosemary. When she opened the door and took two steps, there he was standing, as if waiting for her to come out.

"Excuse me ... Beany Harold ... right?"

"Yes, and you are?" Beany asked, knowing who he was at first sight. He got as close to her as possible, to make sure she could catch his name.

"My name is Miles ... Stanley Miles. You may not remember me, but I stopped by your house."

"Yes – yes, I remember you," Beany yelled over the thumping music.

"Where are you sitting ... like I haven't been watching you since you walked in. Ya mind if I join you and your mother?"

"You remember my mother, too?"

"Hey! It wasn't that long ago. And your mother is a nice-looking lady. I couldn't forget that."

"Thanks. She will be glad to see you," Beany said, thinking about the book that her mother wanted so much to talk to Stanley about.

Stanley walked in front of Beany easing his right arm back and outward, gesturing that she takes his hand as he navigated the crowd. Beany held on as they walked back to her seat. Beany began to wave her hand at the table and point at Stanley in front of her showing them that she had made her catch. After making their way to the table, Stanley pulled Beany's chair out for her to sit. Then he took a seat beside her.

"Let me introduce you to everyone," Beany shouted.

"My brother, Alex."

"My godmother, Mrs. Sara McDuffy and ... wait. Here she comes. This is my sister-in-law to-be, Rosemary Martinez."

After the greeting, Beatrice's favorite song started to play. Beatrice didn't wait for someone to ask her to dance. She got up, grabbed Teeny Baby, and ran out to the dance floor. It was the "Stepping" song by R Kelly. No one really needed a partner to dance with. It was more like a group thing.

Rosemary and Alex soon joined Beatrice and Teeny Baby on the dance floor. The entire dance floor was in unity, heads bobbing to the rhythm. Beany and Stanley decided that they would sit and talk while everyone was dancing.

Alex came over and pulled Beany out of her seat and onto the floor.

Beany looked back at Stanley as Alex pulled her on the dance floor. She waved for him to come also. Stanley finally got up and joined in on the fun.

After the song ended, The Funk Master, a popular disc jockey in the area, said in his best Barry White voice:

"It's time to take that special lady in your arms and hold on tight. It's time to slow it down a little. If you don't have a special lady, this is the time to find one and make her ... your special lady ... if only for one night."

After The Funk Master helped fill the dance floor, he started to play Luther Vandross' song, "If Only for One Night."

Alex held on to Rosemary as the song began to play. Beatrice and Teeny Baby walked to the table to make sure that their purses were still in place.

Beany turned to walk off, but Stanley had other plans. He lightly pulled Beany towards him and asked if he could get in one last dance before he had to go. Beany felt her heart punching her chest as "yes" slipped out of her mouth like fresh air. She had never slow danced with anyone – never been that close to a man in her twenty-one years of being alive. The closest she'd ever been to a man was her father when she was a little girl.

As she pressed against Stanley, she felt a weakness that moved quickly down her legs, causing her to step directly on Stanley's shoes.

"I'm sorry. I've never slow danced before and I'm kind of nervous," Beany explained.

"That's okay ... no, really, that's okay. I haven't danced with anyone in a while myself. Let's just hold on to each other and figure this thing out as we go along."

"I'm holding on."

It wasn't long before they caught their groove and began to move with the changing rhythms. Beany didn't seem to mind the words in the song. Normally she would not have liked any song with a lot of singing but this song seemed almost perfect. She was so caught up in the magic that she couldn't hear anything but Stanley's heart as she laid her head on his chest.

Over at the table, Beatrice, and Teeny stood watching in disbelief as Beany and Stanley slow danced. Beatrice started to shake her head and almost came to tears as she watched. She was so elated to see her daughter doing something that she felt was normal.

Teeny Baby looked at Beatrice.

"You better get ready for another grand baby. Beany is up there twisting her little butt like she knows what she's doing."

"Could you just shut up so I can enjoy the moment? Damn, you can mess up a wet dream," Beatrice said, moving away from Teeny Baby.

"Don't get mad at me because your daughter is out there like she is in a rap video."

When the song was over, Stanley informed Beany that he had to go pick up his little girl from the sitter. He asked her to walk out to the car with him and she agreed.

"Just let me go over here and tell them where I'm going."

"Ok, I'll wait right here for you."

"I think you better come over to say goodbye. My brother is funny about who I talk with. He'll just follow right behind us if you don't. He'll think something is strange or wrong or ... something stupid. Not to mention my mother's friend. She's crazy as a bat."

"OK, I'm right behind you," Stanley said.

"Mama, Stanley has to go, and I'm going to walk with him back to the car. I'll be back in a few minutes. Ok?"

"Nice to have met everyone," said Stanley.

"Same here," they all replied.

After saying their good-byes, Beany and Stanley headed out the door. As they walked outside, Stanley pointed in the direction of the car. He told Beany he would drive her back to the club after they reached the car.

"So, Beany, tell me: as nice looking and as nice as you are, why haven't you got a boyfriend?"

"Who said that I didn't have a boyfriend?"

"I was just assuming you don't."

"Well, you assumed right," Beany said, as she looked at him and smiled. "I guess that I haven't found anyone that interested me ... until you came along."

"I'm glad you found me … interesting. The first time I saw you, I was mesmerized. You are, at the least, the most intriguing person I have ever met before."

Beany knew he was married, but she wanted to hear from him why he didn't pursue her if he thought she was all that. So, she asked.

"If you felt that way, why didn't you come back?"

"Well, I was married at the time, and I consider myself a one-woman man."

"Was married?" Beany said, confused.

"Yes, this is the first time I have done anything since my wife died six months ago."

"Oh, I didn't know. I'm sorry to hear that. Please forgive me for asking. I just thought you were seeing if you still had it or something. I'm so sorry."

"That's okay. I still have a hard time believing it myself. I still miss her so much. My mother is the one who suggested that I get out and go somewhere. She even volunteered to keep the baby tonight. I really don't have to go this early, but I'm not used to being away from my little girl that long."

"What's her name?"

"Chasity … Chasity Tiamia Miles."

"That's a beautiful name. I would love to see her."

"Thanks. Maybe we can all go out for dinner or something sometime."

"Maybe so. How old is she?"

"She's six months old today. My wife died having her."

Beany grew silent. She could tell Stanley was getting downhearted as he talked about it. She decided to ask him about the book.

"Stanley, what are you going to do about the manuscript Donnie wrote? Are you going to try and get it published?"

"Yes. I was going to start working on it tomorrow. I have to get an agent. I've already had six publishing houses calling me to get the rights to publish it. Why do you ask?"

"Because my mother doesn't want to see it published. She's afraid that our business will get out and everyone will think that we are crazy or something. She is especially worried about me. You know what he wrote in there about me?"

"Yes. I know."

"And you are not afraid of me?"

"No. What is there to be afraid of? You've never hurt anyone, as far as I know. ... Have you?"

"Of course not. I would never hurt anyone if I could help it."

"Well, then, I'm not the least bit scared of you. As cute as you are, I'm willing to take my chances."

Beany smiled and said thank you. But she soon focused back on the book.

"Why do you feel a need to keep a promise to Donnie about a stupid book? He's dead now and that book can't bring him ... or Maurice ... back."

"It's not just that. I do want to keep my promise to him, but I also have a child that I need to take care of. I'm so tired of working at that prison that I don't know what to do. That place can really take a lot out of you. I'm really tired of going to work and taking a chance on not making it back home to my daughter."

Beany was getting ready to comment on what he'd said until she saw Alex walking out of the nightclub looking around.

"That's my brother standing out there. I told you that he was overprotective. Let's go drive up there so he can carry his ass back inside. I don't know why he's worried about me. ... He has his own problems to worry about."

Stanley started the car and pulled in front of the Hut.

"Here. Let me give you my number, and you give me yours and we can talk more. ... And Beany, don't think twice about that book. I'll be here for you ... that's if you want me to be."

"We'll see," said Beany, blushing.

As Beany got out of the car, Stanley called her name out.

"Hey! Did anyone ever tell you that you have the most amazing eyes?"

"Not anyone I wanted to hear it from," Beany said, as she walked off with an extra swagger in her hips. Then she turned toward him.

"Goodbye, Stanley."

"Holla back!" Stanley yelled out, as he slowly pulled off.

Beany waved.

"Hey! I ain't no 'holla back' girl." She then looked at Alex standing like he was guarding her and said, "What are you looking at? Don't you have a girlfriend in the club? I bet she is dancing with someone right now. ... Some nice-looking guy."

Alex looked at Beany, shook his head, and rushed back into the club.

After dancing and socializing for two hours, all decided that it was time to head for home. On the ride back everyone talked about the people they saw and who was doing what. Beany was the most talkative of the five. Beatrice was curious to know if Beany talked to Stanley about what the detective mentioned earlier that day.

"Beany, did you talk to that man about the manuscript?"

"Yes."

"What did he say?"

"Well, I didn't have time to really get into it, with Alex standing out there looking around for me. But I do know that he's planning to get it published. He said that he was going to start tomorrow."

"Didn't you tell him what I thought about him publishing the damned thing?"

"Yes, I did. He had other reasons why he thought he needed to get it published ... besides the promise he'd made to Donnie. He told me a little, but I really didn't have time to talk a lot about it. He gave me his phone number and I gave him my cell number. Hopefully, if he calls, we can talk more about it."

"Well, I sure hope he doesn't, but if he does, I hope he knows what may start happening around here."

"I'm sure he knows what he's doing."

"Well, I damn sure hope he does!" Beatrice said sarcastically.

Being that Beany had a little to drink, Beatrice did the driving. Beatrice pulled onto the dirt path leading to Teeny Baby's house. Teeny Baby slept all the way home. At the club, she'd started out with club soda and ended up drinking a few too many gins and juices.

"Girl, wake your drunk tail up and get out of my car. You ain't as young as you thought you were."

"Who's drunk? I'm not drunk. I'm just tired. I haven't danced this much since I was single."

"All I know is that you'd better get yourself together before you get in the house. I don't want you to be calling, telling me to come back and pick you up because Jr. Ceffus done kicked your ass."

"Ha! I wish that fool would lay his hands on me. I'd be calling you to call the hospital for his ass."

"Ole girl, go on in the house. I'll call you tomorrow. ...Bye."

"Ok. See you girls later ... you, too, Alex."

They gave Teeny a hardy good-bye, waited until she got in the house, and drove off.

"Hey! Why is it so quiet in here? I know you three haven't gone to sleep on me, too."

"I'm not sleepy. I could have stayed out all night," said Beany.

"You would have been out there by yourself," said Alex.

"I think I have started something," Rosemary said.

"Yep, you sure have," said Beany. "I'm going to be out there every chance I can get now." Then Beany raised up her hands.

"I'm free at last," she shouted. "Thank God Almighty, I am free at last."

"If you are that free, you might want to start paying rent or helping with the groceries," said Beatrice.

"I'm not that free yet, but I'm going to start working on it," said Beany as she leaned the seat back in total chill mode.

As they turned on to North River Road, a car sped past them going the opposite way almost running Beatrice off the road. Beatrice tried to look through the rear-view mirror to see if she could recognize the car, but no luck. It was speeding so fast she only saw the red taillights. She wondered if they were drunk drivers or high or something. Beatrice soon after thought of how blessed they were not to have run in the ditch or head on into the car.

"Mama, what is that up ahead?" Alex said as they got closer to the house.

Beany, Beatrice, and Rosemary soon saw what Alex was talking about.

Something seemed to be burning.

As they got into view of the house, they saw it was burning there in the yard. As Beatrice pulled in and stopped the car, all jumped out and walked over to what looked like the figure of a man on fire.

Nancy Perkins was standing on her property, next lot over, with phone in hand.

Soon after a few neighbors who lived less than a mile or so down the road, came over to see what was going on. Nancy, with cane in her right hand, walked over once she saw Beatrice's car pull up.

"Did you see who did this, Mrs. Nancy?"

"No, Beatrice, I sure didn't. I usually stay up a little late on Sundays, but I fell to sleep watching the late show and woke up when I heard all of them yelling. You know I can't get around too fast with this bad hip. By the time I got to the window to peep over to see what the noise was about, who ever it was had sped off."

"Have you called the sheriff's department," asked Alex.

"Yes, that was the first thing I did," said Mrs. Perkins, shaking.

***

Being that Camden had a population of about sixteen thousand and most were spread out about the farmland and separated by the tracks, it would take the sheriff's department twenty minutes to get to the house.

The Harold's house was on the opposite side of the tracks, it would take another fifteen minutes, because these days, it wasn't a good idea for the authorities to be over this side without a good reason. The younger generation didn't take too kindly to police and would give them a hard time.

***

"Mama, do you have Officer Hutton's phone number? If so, why don't you call to see if she is working?" asked Beany.

Officer Hutton worked for the police department in Elizabeth City, but she lived in Camden not too far from Beatrice on Indian Town Road. Because Camden had a shortage at the sheriff's department, Officer Hutton was allowed to work with the sheriff when she was not needed in Elizabeth City. She also knew most of the black folks in Camden. They didn't mind her coming around and would often call her for almost anything.

"That's a good idea. Let me get her number out of the house. Alex, get the water hose and put out that mess," said Beatrice.

"Mama, I think I'm going in the house with you. You don't know if anybody is in there or what."

"Good thinking, Alex. Beany, you and Rosa get the water hose and start putting out the fire while Alex comes with me."

Beany and Rosemary ran around the house. They pulled the hose around front and started to put out the fire, but it was already starting to burn out.

As Alex and Beatrice went to the back door to get Lisa Hutton's number, Beatrice warned Alex to be careful when he opened the door. Alex assured her that he didn't think anyone had been in the house, but he wanted to be careful anyway.

Soon the sheriff's department arrived, along with Officer Hutton, and the fire department. By that time, anyone within a mile of North River Road was parked in front of the Harold's house.

***

Not since the late Fifties or early Sixties had anything like this happened in Camden. And when it did, back in the day, the white folks quickly swept it under the proverbial rug. When integration of the schools began in Sixty-nine or Seventy, the county felt like they had overcome all the hatred and racism that used to plague the county.

Most blacks didn't see it that way.

They still felt the aftermath of what their elders went through. Blacks still had a hard time getting loans to buy homes, still lived in shot gun houses – the same houses once used for sharecroppers – and landlords still had unfair practices as well.

If that wasn't problematic enough, blacks also had to deal with the hidden racism.

Every Tuesday they would go to the courthouse, and all they could see were blacks there for traffic violations. A spot that runs from Camden High School to the Shell Station, about a three-mile stretch, was where anyone black driving after two in the morning would almost surely to get a ticket. Once, blacks even protested that injustice. But because not enough people were willing to show up at town hall, the protest faded like a bad memory.

Most of the blacks who graduated in the Eighties left Camden and only came back to visit. Alex came home to visit and got stopped by a county sheriff ... a guy that he'd played baseball with at school. He was asked where he was headed that early in the morning. Then the officer asked could he check Alex's bags. Alex knew his rights but allowed the deputy to search anyway because he was tired and ready to get home. After checking his bags, he gave Alex a ticket for speeding and sent him on his way. That's when Alex decided to go to law school and to come back home to help others who did not want to leave Camden or lacked the means to move away.

Elizabeth City, only five miles away, was where most blacks from Camden would eventually move. At the least, they had a place to live with running water and it was affordable, being that most jobs were located there.

Even with all such incidents being swept under that same old rug, Camden was still considered a safe place to raise a family. But now the question was – safe for whom?

***

Officer Hutton advised Beatrice that she had already called the State Bureau of Investigation to get them involved in the matter. That would keep the local police from being in total control. Beatrice agreed and thanked the officer for coming by. Beatrice asked if she would spend the night.

"Just let me go home to get a few things, and I'll be back," said Officer Hutton. "I think you'll be safe until I get back."

"Don't worry," said Alex. "I know where Dad's old shot gun is in case, we may need it … and I know how to use it."

CHAPTER 8
This Stuff Had to Happen

After the officer got her belongings she needed from home, she came back to spend the night with the Harold's. She backed her patrol car in front of the driveway, grabbed her things, and went into the house. Beatrice had arranged for Beany to sleep with her. Alex was to sleep on the sofa and Rosa would have Alex's room.

Beatrice stuck to the expectation that Alex and Rosemary were not going to sleep in the same bed.

"Oh, Beatrice! You didn't have to go through all of that. I would have slept out here on the sofa."

"No. Alex knows what time it is. He knows good and well why he is sleeping on the couch and not in the room with his girlfriend."

"Ooh! He's not married?"

"No. She is just a girlfriend right now. Maybe they will get married, and then they can sleep together on top of the house if they choose to."

"Well, I can understand that. I remember when John and I were dating, and I got pregnant with Cecil. I thought my parents were going to kill us. Alex's got it a lot better than I did."

"I wanted to kill them. If you know what I mean," said Beatrice.

Officer Hutton changed the subject.

"Who do you think did this?"

"I don't have the slightest idea. I think maybe some of the people in Camden were a little upset that I was with Donnie when he was executed."

"Yes, I saw that on the news. I felt sorry for that boy. I used to make a lot of stops over at their house. His stepfather and Stacy used to fight all the time. Both would be just as high as a kite when I got over there. Those little boys would be crying and clinging to their mother. After a while I used to bring toys and candy over when I went there for a domestic call."

"Yeah, I still can't understand why she married that man knowing that she had those little black boys. You know who James Earl's father was, don't you?"

"Yes, I remember my mother telling me about him. She said that he was the meanest white man that she ever met."

"That's what Ma Elsie used to say."

"Whoever did this in your yard will be found and prosecuted. You know this is considered a hate crime in North Carolina. When the S.B.I. gets here from Raleigh tomorrow, they will get to the bottom of it."

"I sure hope so."

"Where were you at the time this happened?"

"We went to the Hut."

"Oh, yeah! John and I were planning on going there when we both have a day off. How was it?"

"It was nice. You know I'm not about a lot of foolishness. We had a good time. It's mostly an older crowd, and the music was nice. I had a good time with my crazy friend, Teeny Baby."

"How did you get Breanna to go with you all? I know she didn't like it ... or did she?"

"Girl, Beany loved it! She went there ... had a drink or two ... and found a man."

"Alright now!" said Officer Hutton.

Beatrice and Officer Hutton sat up front chatting as the rest of the crew was back in Beany's room having their own conversation. Although it was about two in the morning, no one seemed sleepy. In less than two days, more had happened to the Harold family than in the last fifteen years.

Every five minutes or so Alex would peep out the window, thinking that he had heard something. Beany assured him that whoever did it was not going to be back any time soon.

"Beany, do you have any clues who may have done this?" asked Alex.

"No ... for some strange reason I'm not picking up on any of this. I'm not feeling any vibes or nothing. And I'm wondering why."

Alex thought about the Rev. Felicia Milado and what she said about the family being in great danger and that he would be a medium and help Beany. Alex wanted to tell Beany and his mother, but he did not want to scare anyone. And he did not want his mother to know that he was taking courses of any kind that dealt with that type of craziness. All Alex knew was he was now the man of the family. He was going to protect them at all costs. Still not only did Beany wonder why she could not pick up on any vibes, but Alex wondered, as well.

Beany and Alex saw that Rosemary had already fallen to sleep. Beany lightly shook Rosemary and told her that she could go ahead to Alex's room. Soon after, Alex took a few blankets out of Beany's closet and headed to the living room.

Beatrice and Officer Hutton were still in the living room talking. Alex asked – if they didn't mind – if he could cut on the TV to see the news. Both agreed because they wanted to see if this burning had made it to the airwaves. Alex got the remote control from the coffee table and hit the power button.

"Turn it to Channel 13," Beatrice said.

Alex flipped the channels until he found Thirteen Morning News.

Beatrice and Officer Hutton continued to talk as Alex fixed a comfortable spot on the couch. Suddenly Alex sat straight and turned the TV up.

"Mama ... Lisa ... listen to this."

The news broadcaster began to talk about the incident. They showed what they described as straw stuffed in man's clothing, burning in the yard. They went on to state that no one was home at the time of the incident. After showing that segment, they began to talk about what they thought may have led to the burning.

Patricia Brown, a publicist for Tyron Publishing, released a statement a few hours ago that the book, *Three Damned Lies*, written by Donnie Jackie Johnson, would be published.

"Donnie, as you remember, was executed a few days ago, for murdering three women ... one being his wife."

Patricia stated that in the book Donnie described in detail the person who was responsible killing these young women. Donnie had given his book to an officer at Elizabeth City State Prison and made the officer promise he would get it published. The book led police to question Donnie's brother, Maurice Johnson, for the murders. The brother, Maurice Johnson, was soon found dead, an apparent suicide. Donnie claimed in the book, his brother killed all three women. Donnie also told how a young woman who lives in the house that had the burning early Sunday morning had tried to warn him by using some sort of psychic powers.

Ms. Brown said that this book would be one of the of best true crime murder mysteries of the year. *Three Damned Lies* was slated to be released sometime in October.

"We will definitely keep you posted with the latest information as we get it. For WAVY-TV news, I'm Michael Leesburg, bringing you up to date on ... your up-to-date news."

As soon as the news short was over, Alex cut off the TV and pulled the covers over his head as if in shame.

No one said anything. Beatrice got up and asked to be excused and left for her room. Officer Hutton soon followed to comfort her.

Alex rolled over on the couch to sleep. He knew he'd have much explaining to do when he returned to school in three weeks. The newscaster did not say his name, but when the book was published, he knew it would be in there somewhere. The only thing he could think to do was to get Stanley to convince the agent that he would be working with not to use real names.

Before long, what sounded like dump trucks pulled near their house. Officer Hutton asked Beatrice if she could use the phone to call the station. She wanted to call to let her captain know that they would need to provide round the clock coverage at the Harold's until daybreak and that she was already spending the night at the house. She wanted to make sure that the news cage forming outside was controlled. She then went back to console Beatrice.

"Beatrice, I'm so sorry that this stuff had to happen. But just wait. It will all blow over like a big wind."

"I know it will," Beatrice said. "I'm not going to let this get the best of me and my family. I do know at some point; I'm going to have to talk with the media about Donnie's book. I'm not going to say anything until I find out what is in it. I want to know exactly what the book says in there about Beany and me."

"That's a good idea. I'm sure that they must have an idea themselves, or they wouldn't be out there in front of your house."

In minutes the doorbell was ringing. Beatrice and Officer Hutton went back into the living room. Alex got up to answer it, ready to curse out whoever was ringing the doorbell this early in the morning. He was thinking that if it was the press, they should have gotten what they needed the first time they were here.

Before he reached the door, Officer Hutton warned him not to answer. She told him that he had to be careful how he handled the press. They could quickly turn this into a freak show. Beatrice advised Alex to let Officer Hutton answer.

Officer Hutton went to the door.

"Yes. May I help you?" Officer Hutton asked, with a microphone stuffed in her face.

"Yes. I'm Sherelle Mosely with WITN News. I would like to speak with Beatrice Harold."

"I'm sorry. We have had a busy day and everyone's tired. We would just like to get some peace right now. Please give the family a chance to recover from the tragedy that they had to deal with. I'm sure Mrs. Harold would be willing to talk with everyone as soon as she gets a little rest."

As Officer Hutton was trying to explain to the news reporters about the family's situation, a deputy from the sheriff's department came up and politely escorted them back to their cars. The deputy let Officer Hutton know he would be hanging around until seven.

Beany and Rosemary came out of their rooms to find out what the commotion was all about. Alex told them about the news broadcast and how, within minutes, a slew of news folks showed up outside. Officer Hutton suggested to everyone that it would be a good idea if they all went to bed and got a good night's sleep. No one argued.

"Mama, I think I'm going to have to sleep with Rosa," said Alex.

"Shit ain't that crazy around here. You better catch that couch you made."

Rosemary and Beany went back to their rooms as Beatrice and Officer Hutton talked about how to meet and deal with the press in the morning. Not long after, the two decided they could best come up with better plans after a little rest.

"Lisa, I was just thinking about something. Do you remember when I called you to check on Ma Elise when she was living? Boy! She put a cursing on me that night when I finally got in touch with her."

"Yes, B.B., I remember that. Your mama was such a sweet, but crazy lady. I know you miss her."

"Yes, I sure do. Well, I'll see you in the morning. There are more blankets in Beany's closet if you need them."

"Thanks, but I don't think I will need them. Not as hot as it's been today. ... Well, goodnight."

"Good night or good morning, Lisa. Take your pick."

Officer Hutton returned the end of the day greeting and went to sleep in Beany's room.

Officer Hutton, like most people close to the Harold's, wondered why Beany did not see any of this coming. Officer Hutton stayed with the facts, but since she had lived near North River Road all her life, she, too, was handed down the stories about the supernatural events that happened around Camden. She wasn't too fond of sleeping in Beany's room, but she did. She was a praying woman and felt that nothing could harm her. She took off her plainclothes uniform and put on a jogging suit she had brought from the house. She took her .45 caliber pistol, checked to make sure it was on safe, and put it under her pillow. Lisa kept her flashlight beside her under the covers just in case she needed it. She wanted to make sure that if anyone came into the room, she would be able to recognize him or her before she shot them. Beany's room was the perfect temperature. Officer Hutton decided to lie on top of the bed using only a thin sheet for cover. Other than an occasional car starting and driving off, everything on North River Road was quiet.

Officer Hutton dozed off. It was close to 4 a.m. before all was calm in the house. As Officer Hutton lay with the thin sheet across her legs, she started to feel an ice-cold chill cover the room. She just pulled the covers over her shoulders and slept even harder. The room soon got so cold that she got up, went into the closet, and got a thicker blanket to put over her. She fell quickly back to sleep.

Everyone was sleeping except Beany. She woke up and walked to the entrance of her bedroom door. The dead always made their entrance by coming through her room door. Beany stood wanting to know why the dead children from Pinch Gut Road had appeared in the house suddenly. She wanted to know if they knew what was to come and would anybody be harmed. They never answered her. They only stood chanting and pointing at the wall behind Beany.

"Over there. It will happen over there."

"Beany, will you Double Dutch. ... Jump rope with us like you used to? We never play anymore."

"Yeah, why are you so big now?" said another voice.

"Play with us."

Beany, wondering why they had come back after all these years, stood frozen and confused. The oldest child handed Beany the rope, but Beany was too afraid. They didn't look like the dead children she used to play with from Pinch Gut Road. Still, Beany knew they were the same children. They acted strangely and began to whisper among themselves. They had never excluded her before, they use to tell her all the secrets they knew about Pinch Gut, now they whisper amongst themselves.

They started to sing cantankerously the song they'd taught Beany when they used to play with her when Beany was just a little girl:

Cripple ... cries
Dancing ... lies
The truth shall come at ... night

Lonely ... walls

Tear that ... falls

When guided by the light

Dead man ... sick

Still, he's set ... free

Gonna burn you ... if you cry

His blood is ... yours

Under his basement floor

He's gonna get you before he dies

Beany now wondered what the exhortation meant. Was the cry a cry for help? Was the cry a warning not to tell the others?

She wanted to question them, but they seemed to become angry. Their faces started to look disfigured and gross as they began to fade away. The sun was coming up, and they couldn't play in the daylight.

The daylight took them away.

They did not like the daylight.

Beany also didn't want to wake Officer Hutton.

Although the officer could not hear the children playing, she would have heard Beany if Beany were to have talked to them.

In seconds they were gone, leaving Beany jolted. Beany turned, went into the living room, and fell back asleep in the glider rocker.

Officer Hutton found that she was getting hot with so much cover over her. She quickly kicked it off as she turned and went back to sleep.

CHAPTER 9

Ten Miles of Ugly Road

At 9:00am Beatrice got up to get breakfast started. She peeped out the window and saw that the TV crews were still out there. Beany soon woke and was urging Alex to do the same. She wanted to talk to him about the children. Alex just rolled over and slept even harder.

"Beany, what did you and Mr. Stanley Miles talk about last night?" Beatrice asked from the kitchen.

"Nothing much. We really didn't have time to talk, with your son standing outside watching over me like a hawk."

"Did you even talk to him about the book that Donnie wrote in prison?"

"Yes...I mentioned it."

"What did you ask him?"

"I asked him was he going to publish it. I told him that you did not want it published. Didn't I tell you this on the way home from the Hut?"

"Well, I want to hear it again. Now, what did he say?"

"He told me that he had to ... for obvious reasons."

"Being?"

"Money more than anything. He tried to go in depth, but I had to leave. My bodyguard was waiting. I did get his number and gave him mine."

"Will you call him and ask him to come over?"

"When?"

"Now. We need to discuss some things with him," Beatrice said, seriously.

"I'll call him in a little while. This seems a little too early in the morning to be calling someone. Anyway, I'd rather for him to call me. It's not right for me to call him first."

"It's not right, only if you like him. Is that the case? Are you planning on dating him? Isn't he married anyway?"

"He was but his wife died. He does have a little girl."

"Well, if he doesn't call you by noon, I'm going to call him myself. On the news last night, they talked about the book Donnie wrote and they mentioned us. They didn't say our names, but I believe someone has leaked something to those reporters outside."

Beany agreed to call Stanley if he didn't call her by noon. She felt caught up between her feelings for him and the way she knew her mother and Alex felt. If anyone needed someone in her life, it was Beany. She took only minutes to figure out that she was going to date Stanley no matter what happened. In some way she felt drawn to him. She was happier when she thought about calling him to come over. If he didn't call, she knew she had a reason to call him anyway.

Beatrice set the table for breakfast while Beany went to shower. As Beany passed by her room, Lisa said good morning. Beany returned the morning greeting and asked her how she'd slept. Officer Hutton claimed she that she'd slept like a rock and told Beany thanks for letting her use the room.

"Any time," said Beany and thanked the officer for sleeping over.

Soon everyone was dressed and at the table for breakfast. Officer Hutton called her husband to let him know that she would be home in an hour or so. She told Beatrice breakfast looked good as she sat down at the table. Alex led the grace, and they began to pass food and conversation.

"So, how's everybody doing this morning?" asked Rosemary smiling like she was at a sleep over.

Alex looked at her.

"Next question," he said.

"Ah, shut up, Alex," said Beany. "We are doing fine, Rosa. And how are you?"

"Fine, Beany. Thanks."

"So, Mama," asked Alex, "what are we going to tell those reporters out there? I know we can't stay in here all day."

Officer Hutton looked at Beatrice for permission to answer Alex's question. Beatrice nodded.

"I talked to the SBI this morning. They said that they would be here to go over a few things and handle a few questions that the press outside may ask. Until then we'll just sit here and wait."

"What time will they be here?" asked Beany.

"They were on the road when they called, so they should be here in an hour."

"So, Beany, are you going to call your little boyfriend?" asked Alex.

"He's not my boyfriend ... yet. And, yes, I think I will ... thank you very much."

"Well, I think he's nice looking," said Rosemary.

"Thanks."

As they were eating, the doorbell occasionally rang. Beany rose from the table and turned the radio to her favorite station, a station that played what Alex called "elevator music." She returned to the table.

"Now we can really tune them out."

Office Hutton's phone rang. The SBI agents were at the door, a voice said. Beatrice went to answer the door.

"Please do come in," Beatrice said, extending her hand to greet them. "We were just finishing breakfast. Would you like something to eat or drink? I have some freshly brewed coffee."

"We ate already ... on the way up here, but we would love to have some coffee."

"Sure," Beatrice said. "Beany, could you fix these gentlemen some coffee?"

"Yes, ma'am. Two cups – coming up."

"I take mine black," said one of the agents.

"I'd like a spoonful of sugar – no cream," said the other.

Beany fixed the coffee and carried it to the investigators. They both thanked her and introduced themselves.

"I'm Agent Bill Fisher," said the older man, who looked about Beatrice's age. "Just call me 'Fisher.'"

"I'm Agent Rodney Clark," said the other man. Beatrice thought he looked to be in his mid-thirties. "I'm just plain Rodney," he added.

"Well, Fisher and Plain Rodney, thanks for coming," Beatrice said.

"Our job is to get to the bottom of this burning," Fisher said. The agents began to explain what they thought may have occurred. They opened a briefcase and passed out copies of Donnie's *Three Damned Lies* to Alex, Beany, and Beatrice.

In the manuscripts, the agents highlighted each chapter that contained anything about the Harold family and names of family members. They asked Beatrice, Beany, and Alex what they remembered about anything Donnie had written about them. After going over everything, the investigators asked who would be speaking for the family.

Early that morning Beatrice and Officer Hutton had already agreed that Alex should be the one to speak to the crowd. The investigator talked with Alex and had him read the outlines in the book. He then asked Alex if he was ready to put his game face on and talk with the reporters.

"Alex, before you go out there, you'd better go put something on much better than what you're wearing," Beatrice demanded.

"What's wrong with what I have on?"

"Boy! Let me tell ya. If it's one thing I can't stand ... it's seeing black folks around here on the news looking like ten miles of ugly road. It's like the reporters find the worst looking person in the neighborhood to interview. You are trying to be a lawyer, so you need to start practicing. Now go."

"Alex, baby ... you know that your mama's right," said Rosemary. "Now put something on pretty for your baby." Alex surrendered.

"Oh, all right."

Alex asked the investigators if he could take a few minutes to freshen up.

"Sure," Fisher said. "Let 'em wait."

After ten minutes, Alex reappeared in a coat, tie, and dress shirt. With Beatrice, Beany, Officer Hutton, and Rosemary by his side, Alex walked outside with the investigators to answer questions.

The phone rang as they were heading out. Teeny Baby was on the other line trying to contact Beatrice to find out what was going on. She had just seen the news at noon and didn't know about the burning.

"I'll call you later," Beatrice said shortly.

Once Alex read the statement Officer Hutton, Beatrice, and the agents had prepared, he answered a few questions and handed the platform over to the agents. Most of the reporters wanted to know about the connection between *Three Damned Lies* and the murders. Only a few asked about the burning in the yard. Most seemed determined to connect the burning and the book.

After the press conference, Teeny Baby came into the house as loud and as crazy as ever.

"Why didn't somebody call me? Now, ya'll know that I would have come back to make sure you all were alright. The real question is why did I have to find out about this on the TV? I'm up cleaning my house and the next minute; I'm looking at your house on the tube."

"Look, Mrs. Thing, stuff around here was happening so fast that I didn't have time to call anyone but the police. If I had called you, I would have talked for a half-hour trying to explain it all to you. We all knew you were going to find out … and come around here … anyway. And, bah-da-boom, here you are. So, what's up buddy?" Beatrice asked, smiling like she knew she was wrong for not calling.

Officer Hutton gathered her things and headed out the door. She thanked Beatrice for the hospitality and told her to call if she needed her.

Soon, the crowd outside of the house started to disperse, leaving only the sheriff's deputies standing around. Beany went into the room wishing that she had taken her mother's advice and called Stanley. After reading what Donnie had written in the book, she wanted to explain how she thought her special gift worked.

With everyone in the living room talking about all that had happened, she decided to take the initiative and call Stanley while she had some privacy. She dug through her purse looking for her cell phone and his number. She dialed, let it ring two times, and then hung up. After attempting to call several times, she finally got enough nerve to go through with it.

"Hello."

"Yes ... Stanley, ... this is Beany!"

"Hey, Beany! I was just getting ready to call you. I saw what happened on TV, and I was worried about you and your family. Are you guys alright?"

"Yes, we are fine. It was a little nerve racking, but we pulled through it. I don't really want to talk about it over the phone."

"Yea, I know what you mean. Hey. I was thinking that maybe we could spend the day together."

"You don't have to work at the prison today?"

"Girl, that's another long story that we can't really talk about over the phone. We really need this day to ourselves."

"Ok," said Beany. "What do you want to do? Do you want me to meet you somewhere, or do you want to come picks me up?"

"I prefer to come pick you up, if it's ok with you."

"It's fine with me," said Beany. "But I have to warn you that my family ain't so happy about you getting that book published."

"Yeah, I figured that. … If you'd like, we can meet somewhere," Stanley said thinking he might be better off meeting her than going to her house.

"No, I think it will be better if you came here to pick me up. If you start dodging them now, you'll be running from them forever. I'll take care of them. You just make sure you'll be here," Beany said in a sweet, seductive voice.

"What time?" Stanley asked. He had to make sure he could make arrangements for the baby.

Being this was his first date with Beany, he wanted to make sure that he got to know her well before he involved his daughter.

"What time would be best for you?" asked Beany. "I'm flexible. I know you have to get Chasity Taimia dressed."

"You remembered her name? … Yes, I do have to get her dressed, but I'm taking her to my mother's this time around. I figured that we need some time to get to know each other before we put her into our little mix. It's one thirty, so let's say that I'll be there at around three o'clock."

"Three o'clock is fine."

"Then three o'clock it is," said Stanley.

Beany closed her phone and went back into the living room, all smiles and glowing like the sun was shining on her face. Rosemary was the first to notice.

"Why are you so bubbly?" Rosemary asked Beany.

"What are you talking about? ... You can see right through me, can't you?"

Everyone listened as Beany answered Rosemary. They all began to notice the swagger in Beany's attitude as well.

"You must have just talked to Stanley," said Beatrice. "Hope you told him what I think about that book."

"I think he knows. He is coming over to pick me up. We are going out on a date, and I don't want no one messing this up for me. I will be able to find out more about him and why he got the book published if y'all don't give him the third degree."

Being that this would be Beany's first date, her family was more excited about her having a date than they were about all that had happened the night before. Although Alex did not agree with Stanley publishing *Three Damned Lies*, even he promised to keep his mouth closed.

"Beany," said Alex, "I'm not trying to be funny or anything, but could you get as much information out of him as you can? Find out what he learned from Donnie and what he is planning on telling people once he starts his little book promoting tour. Tell him that he needs to be careful about what he says about us."

"Don't worry," said Beany. "I don't think he's planning on saying too much about anything. He already feels like this is being taken out of context. Well, I better go get ready for my man."

Beany walked out of the living room with everyone in the room talking. She knew that all didn't agree with her dating Stanley. She only hoped she could make a good impression on him. She also hoped her gift didn't become a curse and cause something weird to happen while they were out. Although no one said anything about it, this uncertainty was as much of a concern for the family as it was for Beany. Teeny Baby was sure that Beany, at some point, was going to send Stanley into a comma with some paranormal event. Not being able to hold back her mouth, as usual, Teeny Baby just had to say something.

"What are you going to do when your damned head starts to spin around in the car while he's driving? Now you know you have done some crazy shit over the years that has halfway put your mama and me in the nut house."

As Beany walked toward her room to get dressed, she shot back at Teeny Baby.

"What did Jr. Cefuss do when he found out about you sleeping with my daddy ... and my biological father? He stayed married to your fast butt, didn't he? I'd rather be a freak than a super freak."

"Ya mama," Teeny Baby said back, knowing that she could not top Beany's last remark.

"Teeny Baby!" Beatrice said. "You sound like Lips when we joked about his fat ass lips. All he could say back was ... 'Ya mama.' That reminds me: we have to talk later about that ... you know what we are planning?"

"Mama, Rosa and I are going for a ride. Do you or Teeny Baby need anything while we are out?" Alex said.

"No, go ahead. We are fine."

Alex and Rosemary left, leaving Beany waiting for Stanley. Beatrice and Teeny Baby sat in the living room gossiping about everyone and everything they could think of, as well as going over the plans they were making for the surprise party for Rosemary and Alex.

CHAPTER 10

Pinch Gut Road

Beany came out of the room dressed in an extra short jean mini skirt and a see-through lime green halter blouse that did little to hide a revealing but fashionable bra. Her bra matched the panties she wore underneath. Her long, silky, curly black hair hung over her shoulders. When she sat down in the living room with Beatrice and Teeny Baby, she knew they would both have something to say about what she had on, but neither said anything negative.

"Beany! You look like a super model," said Teeny Baby. "You are absolutely beautiful. My God! You look like a pure angel. Come over here and let me finish you off," said Teeny Baby. Teeny Baby went into the kitchen and got her purse and came back into the living room. She asked Beany to sit on the stool by the island in the kitchen.

"Don't you have my baby looking like a clown," said Beatrice.

"I'm not, Beany. Don't worry about your mother. If there's one thing I know, it's how to attract a man. Now sit still."

Teeny Baby pulled out some sparkling lip-gloss and some dark brown eyeliner. She explained to Beany that a man loves to see sexy lips and beautiful eyes. With Beany having natural green eyes, Teeny told her that a light coat of liner would bring them out.

"Now, go look in the mirror," said Teeny Baby. "Tell me what you think." Teeny Baby paused. "See! Doesn't this compliment the green shirt you have on?"

Beany got up and hurried back to the bathroom to look at her newly made face.

"Mrs. McDuffy, this is very pretty. I like this. You sure know how to turn a ho into a housewife, and I am not even a ho," said Beany.

"So is that a compliment, because if it is, I'd just rather hear thanks," said Teeny Baby, laughing and proud to be a part of Beany's first date.

Beatrice just sat back with tears blurring her vision. She was glad to see Beany so happy, especially with all the strange and hurtful things that had been taking place in her short life.

"Beany, you look so cute," Beatrice said.

Before long, the doorbell rang.

"I'll get it," said Teeny Baby, like she lived there.

Beany and Beatrice stood nervously as Teeny Baby answered the door.

"Stanley, come in," Teeny Baby said. "Beany's been waiting for you."

Once in, Stanley spoke to everyone. He then looked at Beany.

"Hi," he said nervously.

Beany wasted no time. She grabbed her things and quickly walked toward the door, telling Beatrice and Teeny Baby not to wait up for her and that she would call them if she needed them. As soon as they got out the door, Stanley looked at Beany and told her that she had looked like she just stepped out of a beautiful dream.

"I'm real, and this is definitely not a dream," Beany said. "Where are we going?"

"I thought we'd go to Virginia Beach and walk along the board walk and maybe chat a little bit. Maybe we'll find out a little more about each other."

"That's a good suggestion," said Beany. "Let me just call Mama to tell her where I'm going since it's out of town."

"So, you don't work at the prison anymore?" Beany asked.

"No. As soon as I decided it was time to get with the publishers, I resigned. If I hadn't, they probably would have fired me anyway for accepting the manuscript from Donnie."

"Would you have gotten in any trouble for taking it?"

"I think so ... because the book had so much information in it about the crimes. The way I turned it over to the police, I think they worked out some kind of deal to let it slip through the cracks."

Since Stanley was from Elizabeth City, he didn't know much about Camden. He asked Beany for the shortest route to Highway 64 to get to Virginia.

Living in Elizabeth City, all Stanley had to do was hit Highway 17 and travel through Dismal Swamp. He hated traveling that narrow road. But it was the closest route, and taking it only made sense to save time.

Beany suggested that he go through Pinch Gut Road. It would put him on 258 and would take him straight to the state line and run into Highway 64 East.

Stanley didn't know anything about Pinch Gut Road ... or its rumors of ghosts, its Klansmen, and the pure hatred that plagued the small town within a town.

In his book, Donnie never spoke of where he lived, or about the other problems he had. He only talked about looking out for his brothers and staying to himself. He didn't want his story to be one about ghosts and racism. He only wanted to stay focused on his innocence and how he got placed in such a bad predicament.

As they traveled through Riddles on Pinch Gut Road, Beany pointed at a house that was for sale. She informed Stanley that it was the house Donnie grow up in a child. Stanley asked if they could stop and look in. He said he wanted to see how Donnie lived. Beany suggested that they keep going, but Stanley insisted that they stop. He said that he just might want to buy the place.

Beany insisted that if he did want to buy that house, he should rent it out to someone – not to live there. She told him the history of the town and the folkloric stories. Stanley told her that he didn't believe in that kind of stuff and that it's only true if you believe it. He then asked her whether she believed.

Beany did not want to tell him that she saw the dead children that lived on Pinch Gut Road. She did, in fact, believe the stories because the dead children with whom she played as a child had told her the stories.

Beany smiled.

"Ok, if you think you can handle it," Beany said with an air of mystery.

"I can handle it – if you can," said Stanley.

He slowly pulled into the yard and stopped, keeping the car running. He opened the door and asked Beany if she wanted to come along to look around and maybe peep in a few windows. Beany said that she would pass and waited for him in the car.

"Don't be too long," Beany called as Stanley walked towards the house. An edge of fear accompanied her words. Stanley looked back, smiled, and waved his hands to assure her he would not be long.

As Stanley went snooping around the house, Beany turned the radio to her favorite station to calm her shaking hands. She then looked in her rear-view mirror and noticed the three young boys sitting in the back seat ... three dead boys. The dead children of Pinch Gut Road never came out in the daylight, so Beany knew something was terribly wrong.

"Why are you here? You cannot be here," one boy said.

"Yea! This is not a place for you to be anymore. They don't like you. You won't play with them anymore."

"He is coming back and..."

"No! You can't tell her that," the first boy said angrily. *"He will try to get us again."*

Beany tried to pose a question, but her voice was skipping like a scratched CD.

"Who … is coming … back and … what is he … going to do? Please … tell me," Beany cried.

"He says your baby boy belongs with us. … He's going to be down here with us."

Beany turned to look at the boys, trying to get them to tell her what they had meant. But their faces began to melt like candles. Beany began to panic. Beany had never panicked before when she dealt with the dead, but this time she scratched the door panel, trying to find the handle to open it and get out.

Stanley heard her screaming. She looked like she was fighting someone. He ran to the car to see what was wrong. He got to the car and snatched opened the door. Beany reached over, grabbed his shoulders with her hands, and dug her fingernails into him.

"Please … can we just get the fuck out of here? I told you that this was not a good idea."

"What happened?" Stanley asked.

Beany stopped yelling, looked Stanley straight in the eyes, and said in an almost demonic tone:

"Just start the fucking car and let's get the fuck out of this place."

Stanley looked at Beany. Sweat drenched her face so heavily that her shirt was soaking wet. Although the air-conditioning was on in the car, the car was as hot as it was outside. But when he touched Beany's arm, she was ice cold. He quickly started the car, backed out of the yard, and spun off.

Looking back at the house, Stanley thought he saw someone standing at the door – an older man who was waving good-bye.

"Are you all right, Beany?" Stanley asked. He suddenly felt bad. What had he put her through?

"I'm ok, but let's get off of this road. They are getting angry with me, and I don't know why. Something is wrong with the order of things, and I don't know what to do."

Beany continued to rattle off broken phrases that even she didn't understand as Stanley drove as fast as he could. Once off Pinch Gut Road and on to Belcross Road, Beany asked Stanley to stop the car so that she could get out and get some fresh air. Stanley pulled over at the old Belcross filling station and opened the door for Beany.

"They were worried that something like this would happen," Beany cried.

"Something like what?"

"Don't pretend that you didn't see me acting like a freak."

"Well, I didn't see you acting like a freak. I saw you frightened about something … and I want to help you. Do you remember when I said that I was going to be with you throughout this book thing? Well, I want to be with you through it all. I think you are a super fine and super sweet young lady. If I can work in a prison with a bunch of real live monsters, I can sure deal with whatever you think is out here."

"I just feel so embarrassed."

"Don't. I should not have stopped there in the first place. I guess curiosity got the best of me. ...What happened?"

"Let me get myself together. We can talk about it when I get back in the car."

Stanley opened the trunk of his car and got out his old prison jacket to place around Beany's shoulders. He held her close, not saying a word, just letting her pull herself together.

"I'm ok. We can go now," said Beany.

Stanley opened the door, and Beany eased back into the car. He asked her if she just wanted to call it a day and go back to the house. Beany would not have it any other way than to spend the rest of the day with him. She had thought about this date with Stanley in her dreams, maybe even planning this date the night before they met. She wasn't about to let Stanley out of her sight. She looked at him, smiling, and told him that she was just fine – if he was.

Stanley reached over and kissed her on the cheek.

For the first time, Beany felt the softness of a man's lips on her flesh. She started to warm up with each glance at Stanley. Beany looked at him and thanked him for being so understanding and sweet.

"You are welcome," said Stanley.

Stanley wanted to ask Beany what she saw but figured he would wait and let her tell him when she was ready. Instead, Stanley decided to compliment her on how good she looked. He began to look down at her pretty tan, brown legs.

"Beany, I don't know any other way to say it than ... I cannot keep my eyes off your legs. I want to reach over and just rub them right now before I start this car up, pull off and have an accident."

Beany was surprised that Stanley was so straightforward. She decided to shoot one back at him just to call his bluff.

"I wore this extra short skirt hoping that you would find these long sexy legs attractive. If you want to rub them, here's your chance. I'm still a little chilly, and I need strong hands to cause enough friction to bring them back to their right temperature."

With no hesitation Stanley eased his hands over and began to rub on Beany's legs – softly, gently, slowly ... going up and down sliding as far as his hands could reach with her sitting. He looked into her eyes and saw that she was begging to be kissed. Beany was breathing in an asthmatic rhythm, almost at a dying pace ... dying to be kissed back to life.

Stanley was about to ask if he could kiss her, but she placed her left hand over his mouth. She then took the palm of her right hand and placed it behind the back of his head and brought his lips toward hers. She began to engage in the most pleasurable and desirable joining of the lips possible by an untouched, un-kissed, love-starved virgin. The gloss on her lips only made Stanley kiss back with an equal passion.

Stanley had not a women's touch in six months and Beany had never been kissed, so both nefariously teased their uncontrollable sexual craving. They wanted to release all of themselves ... right there in the car.

Beany pulled away slowly and looked down at Stanley and smiled.

"Nice. When can I have it?"

Stanley was embarrassed, but he responded.

"When you think you are ready and can handle it."

"I'm ready all right. I've been ready since the first time I saw you."

They laughed and decided that it was time to get going before they were pulled over by the police for indecent exposure. Beany sat thinking: that kiss was a pinnacle in her twenty-one-year-old life. She wanted to thank Stanley for breaking what she thought was a curse on her love life. Stanley started the car, put it into gear, and pulled onto the highway. Beany reached over and gave him one last kiss on the cheek.

"I know how Snow White felt when she was kissed by the prince,"Beany said.

"How was that? How did she feel?"

"Horny, if she felt like I just did."

"You are so funny. ... I think you are so funny. I love to laugh. I guess I didn't expect to see you like this."

"Like what?" asked Beany.

"I have met a few gorgeous women in my day and most of them were ... how can I say it ...were... stuck on themselves. Trust me when I tell you this: you are not only beautiful, but you're also sweet and sensitive ... not to mention ... you have a body to die for...and live for again and again and again...if you know what I mean? I'm so glad I met you in the Hutt the other night."

"Well, thank you. You are not so bad yourself," Beany said, blushing.

CHAPTER 11

In Elizabeth City

Being that the ride to Virginia Beach was forty-five minutes long, both figured they would spend that time getting to know about each other. Beany wanted Stanley to know as much about her as possible. She did not want to surprise him with anything that might run him away later. Although he proclaimed his devotion to her, she figured, sometimes people just say the right words ... when times are going well. She also wanted to know more about him and his family, and maybe she hoped to persuade him to get his literary agent to replace their names in the book and use fictitious ones.

"So, Stanley, tell me about yourself."

"What do you want to know?"

"What is your mother's and father's name? Where are they from? Do you have any brothers and sisters?"

"Ok. Which one do you want me to answer first?"

"All the above."

"Ok. ... My mother's name is Cynthia Maise Miles and my father's name is Stanley Deya Miles Sr. I have two sisters, Jane, and Seth, and one brother, Steven. My father and mother are from Raleigh, North Carolina. My brother is in the military, and my two sisters live right here in Elizabeth City. Did I leave anything out?"

"How did they ... your parents ... end up in Elizabeth City?"

My father's father was from somewhere down this way, but I've never been clear on why he left. I think his father said something about four children that were found lynched. Grandpa moved my father and the rest of his kids away to a safer area. I'm not too sure because my dad doesn't talk about it too much."

"No, I'm sure he wouldn't," said Beany. She paused. "I think you covered most everything. So, how long were you married to ... you never told me your wife's name."

"Sandy."

"How long were you and Sandy married?"

"We would have been married two years in September."

"I can tell you really loved her because each time I mention her name, I can see it in your eyes."

"Yes. She was my soul mate."

Beany began to stroke the top of Stanley's hair. She hoped that one day he could only feel that way with her. She wanted to find out more about Sandy, but she could see his interest in her slowly fade as he thought about his love of his deceased wife. Every mention of her name seemed to take him further from Beany. Beany may have had little experience with dating or men, but she had spent enough time listening to Teeny Baby and Beatrice to know that you never bring up the other women in a man's past. They said it only brings the nonexistence into existence and gives too much power to the other woman.

Beany had learned this love lesson: some things are better left behind. Beany decided not to talk about Sandy ... unless Stanley brought her up. She felt like Stanley needed his chance to ask a few questions of his own.

"So, Stanley, what do you want to know about me? I know you have a bucket of them. I promise to answer what ever I can. So hit me with some of the big ones."

"Ok. ... Here's the first question: Where did you get the name Beany – and why do you let them still call you that? You sure don't look like a 'bean' to me. I think Breanna is a beautiful name. It fits you just perfectly."

Beany paused for a moment.

"My father gave me that name when I was a little girl. Mama said that he used to say that I looked just like a string bean. I kind of liked it, but I think it contradicts these nice firm thighs I have now."

"I was about to say you have the nicest shape I have ever had the pleasure of seeing without looking at a music video."

Beany slid her short skirt up, revealing just a bit more leg. Stanley ran off the road slightly, and then recovered.

"Hey!" Beany chided. "You better keep your eyes on the road, mister."

"And you better stop playing so much," said Stanley with a heart rush.

Stanley asked Beany to tell him about her father. Beany shied from this line of questioning. She did not want to talk about her father.

Still, she understood she had asked Stanley questions about his deceased wife. Although she sensed his pain, she knew Stanley had been honest and direct. So, she began to talk about both of her fathers.

"My dad, Harry Harold, died when I was only five. The evening before he died, Mom said that I told him he was going to heaven to be with my grandmother. I remember him being ... like ... the greatest person on this earth."

"Do you remember him well?"

"Yes. I used to see him all the time after he died. He wouldn't go to his other home until he made sure that my real father took care of us."

"Your real father? What do you mean?"

"My biological father."

"Ok," Stanley said uncertainly.

"His name is Tavone McKnight ... and, yes, he is."

"He is!"

"Yep. He's the Reverend Donnie talked about in the book. And the one that was there when Donnie was executed."

"From the sound of it, you don't really like him."

"No, I really don't. There's something about him that I just can't put my hands on. I'm having a private detective to look into who he really is."

"What do you mean?"

"I really don't know who the man is. I don't know his mother or father, or where he's from … or nothing. I just want to find out about him. If I'm wrong, I will just leave it alone. But for now, I just don't trust the man."

"Well, like they say, sometimes you got to trust your instincts."

Stanley pretended not to care about what happened on Pinch Gut Road, but he was more curious than he let on. He felt this would be the perfect time to ask any questions he had about her paranormal abilities.

"So, when did you realize you could see dead people, and see things, and all that stuff?"

"I guess it would be like me asking you when you first started drinking water. I guess I've been like this all my life."

"Have you ever been scared?"

"Not until today. Today scared me to death. I have never been frightened of them before, but they are starting to be mean and angry." Her voice dropped. "I don't know what's going on."

"You know," said Stanley, "you don't hear tales of black people talking about these kinds of things."

"I know. My mother fears everything. She never likes hearing about this kind of stuff."

"I bet."

"How does Alex feel about it?"

"He used to pick on me when we were kids, but now he is just concerned. He has never been scared. He just hated sleeping in the same room with me when we were little. He's been very supportive. I feel kind of sorry for him ... girlfriend pregnant and all. Mama treated him some kinda bad at first."

"How did he act?"

"Alex? Alex is so crazy he acted just like it wasn't nothing. He swears that he's the man of the house."

"Can I ask one more question? Then I'm going to leave it alone."

"Go ahead."

"What did you see back there?"

Beany shuddered. She did not want to relive that experience, at least right now. But she knew he really wanted to know. He wanted to help. He was not trying to get something to throw back in her face. Oddly, she trusted him and wanted him to love her ... and know everything about her. Then she smiled.

"I saw three boys sitting in back of the car ...three dead boys who've been there since the Nineteen-Forties."

"What were they saying?"

"One was trying to tell me something, but the others wouldn't let him. They looked so menacing that I just couldn't take it. I'm sorry."

"You don't have to apologize. I'm just glad I didn't see anything."

In fact, Stanley thought he saw something, but he dared not to tell Beany. He stuck to his story that he didn't believe in ghosts. He didn't, really. Did he?

"Why me?" he asked.

"What?"

"Why me? You could have any man you wanted. I know this for sure. If you rode around on a broom, guys would still try and get with you. Why me?"

"Your heart," Beany said. "It's your heart. I can tell you really care about me, and sex is not all you want. You really care for me."

Stanley didn't know how Beany knew what she knew, but she was right. He wanted to make good of their relationship. He wanted to find a way to help, too.

With all the conversation going on, they were in Virginia Beach in no time. They spent the rest of the day walking along the beach. Beany could not believe she was falling in love for the first time. She held on to Stanley, thinking of how good it would be to spend the rest of her life with him.

CHAPTER 12

Overwhelmed

As the evening pushed the sundown below the earth, Beany felt it was time to go home. In the back of her mind, she wanted to ask Stanley if he wanted to get a room and just let nature run its course, but she knew that was not the womanly thing to do. Being that she knew Beatrice and Teeny Baby wanted to know how things were going, she told Stanley that she needed to use the lady's room. Stanley sat on the bench near the boardwalk as Beany went to the bathroom. The closest one was at the ice cream stand, so she decided to use the rest room and get them both ice creams on the way back. As she walked toward the stand, she reached into her purse and got her cell phone.

"Mama, what's up?"

"Hey, baby! How's your date going?"

"I'm having a great time. Mama, I think I'm falling in love with him."

"Don't move too fast now, girl."

"I'm not. He's just so nice."

"Well, you deserve someone nice. Just don't do any of Teeny Baby's fast moves."

"I won't. I'm not going to get my 'back broke,' if that's what you are talking about. Although I really want too, I'm not. I know I must get to know him better. I'll give it another two days."

"Two days?"

"I'm just playing Mama. Tell Teeny Baby that lip-gloss and eyeliner really worked. Okay, I got to go. I'll be back home before twelve."

"Okay. But just remember that if you want him to respect you, you are going to have to control yourself … and don't be too aggressive."

"I love you, Mama. Bye."

"Bye."

Beatrice hung up the phone and started to tell Teeny Baby all that Beany had shared. As the two were reminiscing about their dating days, Alex and Rosemary pulled up in the yard. Beatrice had to hide the list they were making up for the party they were planning for them.

Rosemary and Alex walked in.

"So, where have you two been all day?"

"I bet I know," said Teeny Baby.

"I went to TP's house. I wanted to introduce him to Rosa."

"How is he doing these days? I bet he's a nice-looking young man now."

"He is," said Rosemary.

"Trish was around there. We had a good little talk. I was trying to find out information for Beany."

"You didn't go asking her too many questions, did you?"

"No, but she was glad to answer anything I wanted to ask her. She heard about what was going on with us, and she also talked about the book that Donnie wrote. She said that she didn't know Donnie, but she had seen pictures of him and the other boys. She also said that she found a picture that looked like Donnie's step-father when he was younger with a lot of other pictures." She paused. "Tavone used to keep them in an old shoebox."

"Did you ask her what he was doing with a picture of James Earl in a shoe box?"

"Yes, and she said she never asked him because she was snooping around when she found it. Plus, she said it was years ago, and she never thought too much about it. But went she saw a picture of James Earl on the news, she thought that he looked an awfully lot like the picture she remembered seeing in that box. She said he had pictures of a bunch of white folks. Some pictures were of really old white folks too."

"Did you know that his father was a white man?" asked Beatrice.

"Yeah. I found that out today. Does Beany know?"

"I told her on the way back from Raleigh the other night."

"What did she say?"

"She said, 'So that's were I got these green eyes from.'"

"Beany said she didn't feel comfortable around him and that she didn't trust him. I just wanted to get down to the bottom of who this man really is," said Alex.

Alex had promised to do whatever he could to help Beany and he felt that by finding out what he did today was a start.

"So, have you heard from her?"

"Yes. She just called a few minutes ago."

"Did she?" Rosemary asked excitedly. "What did she say?"

"She's having fun. She said that she was really starting to like him and that he was nice."

"I can't wait until she gets back so we can have our girl talk," said Rosemary.

The girls went on talking about Beany and her date with Stanley, but Alex was lost in thought trying to piece together the information he'd gotten from Trish. Being that she was married to Tavone, he felt like she knew him better than anyone. Alex wanted to meet with her again to gather even more pieces of the Reverend Tavone McKnight puzzle for Beany's sake. While they were in the living room talking, Alex decided to get on the computer and look up some names and addresses that would lead him to finding out even more. Because of the pictures Trish thought were James Earl, Alex knew he was on to something. He just didn't know what.

"Alex! Telephone!" Beatrice shouted from the living room.

"Rosa, could you bring me the phone?"

"Coming!"

"I see why Alex loves you so much. You treat him like a king," said Teeny Baby.

"He is my king," said Rosemary, and then turned to carry Alex the phone.

"We'll see about that when that baby comes," Beatrice said in low tone as Rosemary walked out of the room.

Alex took the phone, kissed Rosemary, and said thank you.

"Hello!"

"Alex, this is Dr. Midilo. I felt some very strong vibes, and you were the first person that came to mind. I saw the news. I just wanted to say, you really need to go to work on helping your sister. I'm afraid she or someone close to you and her are in danger. It may not be anytime soon, but just keep an eye out."

"Where are you calling from now?" Alex asked.

"I'm in Pensacola, Florida."

"And you saw us on the news there?"

"I'm afraid so. I think it's everywhere. Look for the Morning Show to contact the family soon. Well, I have to be going. I just wanted to speak with you. Are you coming back to school week after next?"

"Yep. I'll be there."

"See you there. Call me if you need me. You still have my number, right?"

"Yes, ma'am."

"Okay, then. See you later."

"Alright. Goodbye … and thanks," said Alex.

Alex got off the phone and felt the need to call Beany. Even though Beatrice said that she had talked to her, Alex just felt the need to talk to her and hear her voice.

"Hey, Bean Head."

"Hey, Butt Face."

"How's the date going?"

"It's going very well, thank you. Now what do you want?"

"Nothing. A brother can't call his sister to see if she's, okay?"

"Well, I'm fine, thank you," Beany said with an air of annoyance. Then her voice shifted. "And thanks for your concern, but I have to go," she said softly. "Now go tend to your pregnant girlfriend."

Beany hung up the phone and gave Stanley the ice cream she'd bought for him. He told her thanks and took her by the hand and continued the walk along the boardwalk. Time was slipping away and soon it would be time for them to go.

"Beany, I would like to do something before we go," said Stanley with a sparkle in his eye that almost blinded Beany.

"What?" Beany asked, hoping he wanted another kiss.

"While you were gone, I went into the Boardwalk Book Store and found this. I would like to read you something from it."

"Ooh, let me see. ***Black Frame: Life Inspired Poetry***."

Stanley guided Beany onto the shores of the beach and got on one knee. He opened the book and found the poem he'd marked and began to recite it for Beany:

If Asked
If asked to describe my love
I'd say
Warm
Soft
Gentle and slow
If asked how far I would take my love
I'd say ...
Forever ... is how far I'd go
If asked, how do I love thee ...
I couldn't even count the ways ...
I'd
Hope
And wish
For a better love...
And pray for better days.
And when the day that God decides,
to take us far away from here
I'd wait to find my place in heaven
'Because I know I'd find you there

If asked.

Beany was overwhelmed. Any other time she would have been shy, but not this time. She pulled Stanley from his knee and began to kiss him as passersby watched. Some even applauded as they embraced. Beany looked toward the sky and thanked the heavens for raining the blessings of a man into her arms.

Even though Beany was twenty-one, Stanley wanted to do the right thing by getting Beany home early. Beany, caught in the rapture of the moment, wanted to stay longer. Stanley insisted they leave for home. Beany finally picked her heart from off the sands of the beach and walked hand in hand with Stanley back to the car. Stanley opened the door for her. He then walked around to the other side. Beany reached over and opened the driver's side door for him. She thanked him for the most wonderful day in her life. Stanley returned the thank you with his own claim that he hadn't felt so alive in months himself.

Beany cuddled the book in her arms like she was holding a newborn baby. She promised she would cherish it forever. Each time she read from it; she would think only of him.

They talked about the phenomenal day they'd had and what they would do for an encore. Hoping to out do their first date, they started to plan for the next. It didn't seem long before they were back in Camden. Beany decided that she did not want to drive through Pinch Gut Road this time. She turned on Belcross and took the long way back to North River Road.

When they pulled in the yard, they could see the curtains pull away and heads peeping out of the window. Stanley cut off the car and attempted to walk Beany to the house, but Beany suggested sitting in the car for a few more minutes. She wanted to get her last few glances of him. She also knew that everyone in the house would anticipate her first steps toward the door.

After talking for several more minutes, Stanley convinced Beany that he had to go. He said that he wanted to pick his daughter up before it got too late. He promised her that maybe the next time, they would include Chasity Taimia. Beany agreed, but she added that she didn't mind if it was just the two of them again. She figured that she had a long life with Stanley, and she could get to know Chasity Taimia in the future.

Stanley got out of the car and went around to open the door for Beany. As Beany got out, she intentionally exaggerated the need to spread her legs open, hoping to remind Stanley of what he had in store. Beany was inexperienced in dating, but she remembered all the little tricks that Teeny Baby had taught her when she visited and talked about men. She knew it worked because Stanley looked at her and smiled.

"Panties match the bra, niiiicccceee."

"Naughty boy," Beany said, thinking that it had worked just perfectly.

Once they got to the door it was time for the goodnight kiss. Stanley put his arms around the small of her back and brought her toward him in a slow motion. Beany, not holding back, kissed Stanley like she was starring in her first movie. As they engaged in their kiss, Stanley slid his hands down and onto Beany's firm buttocks and caressed it before sliding them back up. They then said their goodbyes, and Beany walked into the house flowing like a soft tone on her favorite radio station.

"Beany, you are just glowing girl," Rosemary said.

"Yeah! Girl, let me tell you about it. Let's go in my room," said Beany.

Beany showed Rosemary the book of poetry that Stanley had bought her. Rosemary took the book and started to read through some of the poems.

"Girl, I like this. Where did he get it from?"

"He got it from the Board Walk Book Store in Virginia Beach."

"I'm going to get Alex to buy me one the next time we go there. See...that's why I told Alex I like it here. It's quiet, but you can drive a few miles down the road and be right there at the beach."

As Beany and Rosemary went back into the bedroom, Alex and Beatrice sat and watched TV. Alex was glad that Beany had a good day, but he was more concerned about Beany's safety. Beatrice was now glad that Alex brought Rosemary home with him so that Beany could have someone her age to share her special moments with.

Before long the two came out of the room and showed Beatrice the book that Stanley had bought for her.

"Look, Mrs. Harold," said Rosemary. "Look what Stanley got for Beany."

Beatrice looked at the book.

"Isn't that a coincidence?"

"What do you mean, Mama?" asked Beany.

Beatrice got up, went into the bedroom, dug around in a closet, and found a box with old letters from Harry. She pulled out the book **Black Frame**. She carried it back into the living room and showed it to Beany.

"Mama, where did you get that? Why haven't you shown it to me?"

"I got it from your ... stupid father ... Tavone."

"Why haven't you shown it to me?"

"Girl, this book got me in so much trouble that I just threw it in a box and put it way back in the closet. But don't get me wrong, it's a good book. I love the poem 'If Asked.'"

"That's the same one Stanley read to me on the beach today. I loved it too."

"I want Alex to get me one," said Rosemary loudly, knowing Alex heard her and hoping he got the hint.

Beany and Beatrice started to flip through the book picking out different poems. Some poems brought back memories. Some made Beatrice breathtakingly happy, and others brought back majestic memories of the pain she went through when Harry died.

The night faded with the family sitting around enjoying each other's company. All seemed normal in the Harold family. Beatrice was slowly getting attached to Rosemary. Beany was, too. They soon realized that they both were going to miss Alex and Rosemary when they returned to Durham for school.

CHAPTER 13

Fool Hurt my Feelings

Alex had spent the last two weeks enjoying his family. Now he was getting his things together to head back to Durham.

Meanwhile, Beatrice and Teeny Baby were gathering all resources to get started on the party they had been planning for the last two weeks. Other than Beany, no one knew what they were trying to pull off. Alex and Rosemary were to leave that Sunday morning, so the party was planned for that Saturday. Beatrice left it up to Beany to figure out a way to get Alex out of the house so they could get it decorated. Beany knew just what to do.

She and Stanley had been seeing each other as frequently as possible. Beany was barely holding on to her virginity. The story that Rosa told Beany about her first sexual experience stuck in her head like Crazy Glue.

The news stations and papers finally stopped bothering the family, but everyone stayed cautious of what they said and what they did while out in public. Stanley, when not with Beany, spent time traveling to book fairs, radio stations, bookstores, and different TV talk shows helping promote his book. To protect the Harolds as much as possible, he convinced the publishers and his literary agent to not use real names in the book and to leave out any real names of actual roads and addresses. Even his best efforts never stopped shows like *Extra* and *Entertainment*

Tonight from making visits to Camden where crews talked with people in the neighborhood trying to get any dirt, they could about The Harolds, Donnie, and the Johnson family. Stanley promised Beany that he would respect her and the family. He kept his promise.

After word got out that he and Beany were a couple, the publishers tried to persuade him to bring her with him sometimes to up the sell, but Stanley wanted to keep his love life out of the public eyes.

The book sold more than six hundred thousand copies in the first week and was slated to sell even more over the next couple of months. Because Stanley was given all rights to the book, he had been paid an advance of $1.5 million for *Three Damned Lies*.

The first thing he did was build a house on the shores of the Pasquotank River. What Beany didn't know was that his second plan was to buy her an engagement ring and ask her to marry him at Alex's going away party.

Alex had also planned to let the family know his intentions to marry Rosemary as well.

Beany thought she knew everything that was going on. While she was scheming a plan to get Alex and Rosa out of the house, Stanley was scheming himself. Alex was helping Stanley get a ring without Beany knowing. Because Alex and Stanley had become good friends, Stanley first talked it over with Alex before he went on with his plans.

Alex felt Stanley had nothing but good intentions with Beany and gave him his blessings. After all, Stanley had lived up to his word by not giving out too much information about the family. Alex was reassured by the pure fact that Beany trusted him. Agreeing to the engagement was easier than Alex thought it would be.

The millions that Stanley received from the book didn't hurt either. He could only warn Stanley about Beatrice. As cordial as Beatrice had been with Stanley, she would definitely give him the third degree. Stanley assured Alex that he knew about the third degree. Beany had told him how Rosemary had gotten it when he'd first brought her home.

"She told you about that?" asked Alex.

"Yeah. That day that we were on the beach, she talked about you and how much she loves you ... and how you were very protective of her. Why do you think I asked you about our engagement first?"

Alex wondered if Stanley knew about Beany's strange behaviors. Alex decided to be as blunt as Beatrice.

"How much do you really know about my little sister?"

Stanley never talked to Alex about the things Beany shared with him, but he knew just where Alex was going with his question.

"What?"

"She never told you about her seeing ghosts and shit?"

"Oh, that? Yeah, she mentioned it to me. Plus, you know that it's been all over the news with the book being out."

"And what do you think about it?"

"I told her that I was behind her one hundred percent."

"Are you sure? She is into some deep doo doo with that stuff."

Stanley wanted to let Alex know just how much he did know in order to assure him that he knew probably as much as Alex did. He decided to tell him about the time he and Beany stopped by the house on 432 Pinch Gut Road.

"What happened?"

"She said that she had an encounter with three boys."

"And?"

"She just said they were being mean to her, and someone was trying to get her ... or else come for her baby boy. Whoever they were talking about said that they wanted her to be with them or something."

"Why were you and her at that house anyway?"

"She mentioned to me that that's where Donnie lived. Since Donnie and I had become good friends, I wanted to see where he lived. She didn't want to stop, but I insisted."

"What happened after that?"

"I got back in the car and drove the fuck off like I was in a Dukes of Hazards episode."

"I don't blame you," Alex said laughing.

"She also told me about Tavone and how she didn't trust him. She asked a private detective to do a little investigating to find out more about him."

"She did? I didn't know that. I did a little researching of my own, but I couldn't find out too much. Every time I tried to find out something, it would cost so much money; I never got too far with it. I hope he found out more than I did."

"He will," said Stanley. "I sent him a right nice check to cover his expenses."

Stanley knew that Alex was practicing for the third degree that Beatrice was going to give him when he talked to her. From the way Alex was laughing when Stanley was telling him about his first encounter with Beany's ghost, Stanley knew that he could withstand the heat that Beatrice was going to give off.

"So how are we going to get the girls to go one way while we go another?"

"Well, Mama and Teeny Baby always go to Wal-Mart just to shop for parties. Why don't we convince the girls to go to Wal-Mart? Once we drop them off, we can go to the mall and buy the rings for them. They will think that we are in the car talking or something, and we can sneak off since the jewelry store is right around the corner. If they start to look for us, we will be there before they can notice we are missing."

"Good idea."

After Alex and Stanley got their plans together, they went back into the house to see if the girls were ready. Even though

Stanley knew they were having a party for Rosemary and Alex, Alex didn't have a clue. Beany was so glad to be planning to have something for someone she loved so much, she was eager to get on the road.

"Beany! Don't forget that we will be setting up the house for the party while y'all are out, so take your time. ... And call me to let me know where you guys are," said Beatrice.

It was twelve o'clock when they pulled out, and Beany had about six hours to waste. She had to make sure that she didn't run into Beatrice and Teeny Baby while they were out at Wal-Mart buying for the party.

Beany decided to go to Military Boulevard in Virginia to shop, claiming she just wanted to ride. Stanley agreed. Rosemary and Alex just went with the program. The only problem was Alex and Stanley needed to get away to get the rings for the girls. Neither Beany nor Rosemary knew that the boys were planning on asking them to marry. Neither Alex nor Rosemary knew a house full of family and friends would be waiting when they got back home. This would be a confusing day for all. Everyone anticipated the adventurous hours leading to the big celebration.

When Beany and Rosemary got to Wal-Mart, they decided they would rather go find something to wear from the mall instead, which worked right into the boys' plans.

"You girls go wherever you like. Stanley and I have some looking ... I mean shopping ... to do of our own," said Alex.

"Don't let me have to knock your eyes out like old man Lucky," said Beany to Stanley.

"That goes for you too, Alex," said Rosemary.

"Don't worry. We'll be good."

As Beany and Rosemary moved out on their mission, Stanley and Alex headed out the door and across the street to Forever Diamonds.

"May I help you?" asked one of the sales ladies.

"Yes," said Stanley. "We want two of the most beautiful engagement rings in the store. Money is no object."

"It may not be for you, but it is for me," said Alex.

"Don't worry, bro-in-law. I gotcha. Just consider it a loan."

Alex paused and then brightened.

"Hey. Like the man said, money is no object."

***

Beatrice got on the phone to call Teeny Baby, to see if she had made all the necessary calls to the gang.

"Did you get in touch with Lips, Bucky and Knotts?"

"Yes. Jr. Cefuss said leave the key in the mailbox and they will come over here to set up the garage for the party. He's already got the grill on the back of his truck and will be heading over as soon as Knotts gets here."

"Well, I will be over in a minute to pick you up. Is Michael coming?"

"No. He wants to go with his daddy. He reminds me so much of Alex and Harry when Alex was a little boy."

"Yeah, yeah, yeah! Well, I have Stanley's little girl. I just love her. She is so sweet. Beany wanted me to keep her while they're out shopping."

"And you said, 'Yes?'"

"I have her here, don't I? And what's the matter with that?"

"Nothing ... Not a thing at all. Just remember I told you that you were going to be a grandmother sooner than you thought."

"Just be ready when I get there. Bye."

"Bye ... Granny."

With Teeny Baby and Beatrice out shopping for the party, and Alex, Rosemary, Beany, and Stanley out shopping, Jr. Ceffus and the boys were over getting the food and other necessities together. Before long the party was on its way. It was almost like old times when Harry used to have the garage looking like a sports bar.

Alex had stopped by the ABC Store to get a few gallons of liquid, thinking that he and Stanley may need a drink before they proposed to the ladies.

Bucky showed up with Lucy Gray. They met and started dating at a party Harry had in the garage years ago. Knotts came with Jr. Cefuss, and Lips came by himself driving the same car he drove thirty years ago. After he parked the car, it was another ten seconds before anyone could see who was driving. They had to wait until the smoke cleared, which came from inside the car and from the tail pipe.

Teeny Baby and Beatrice went all out for the gathering. They had enough food to feed a small army. Jr. Cefuss had the grill smoking like a burning tobacco barn. People could smell the flavor from the barbecue for miles. Beatrice knew there would be a few uninvited guests, so she made sure she had enough of the gang to clear out two acres of potato field workers if needed.

Beatrice managed to get Hiddy, Harry's twin sister, to come up from Atlanta for the occasion. By trying to surprise Alex and Rosemary, Beany would be in for the surprise of her life as well. As much as she loved helping others, now was her time to shine like the sunlight she always wished upon others.

Everything was set. Beatrice called Beany to find out where the kids were and to let Beany know that most of the guests had arrived.

"Hello. Beany. Where are you?"

"We are on Belcross Road."

"Good," said Beatrice, "because we have a house full of guests waiting to see Alex and Rosemary."

"Bye the way, Mama, Rosa and I aren't talking to your son and Stanley. They got missing while we were shopping and can't remember where they were. Until we get some answers we are not talking."

"Ok. Whatever. Just bring my son home. Bye."

Beatrice warned everyone that Alex and Beany were on their way and to get in the garage. As Stanley turned on to North River Road, they all saw the cars parked in the yard. Alex got excited thinking that something had happened. He told Stanley to pick up the speed, fearing the worse. Beany, knowing there was a party going on, played with Alex and Rosemary, also telling Stanley to hurry.

Once they got to the house and stopped, Alex jumped out and ran around the house to see where the smoke was coming from. After seeing that it was a big Adirondack Grill, he walked in the garage. Beatrice, along with the rest of the crowd, yelled out "Surprise!" to Rosemary and Alex.

A large banner was hanging inside to the garage reading: 'WE LOVE YOU AND GONNA MISS YOU ALEX AND ROSA.'

Alex knew that he had been tricked.

Beany was just as surprised as Alex and Rosemary when she saw her Aunt Hiddy and couldn't wait to introduce Hiddy to her newfound love.

The food was ready, and everyone dug in. Bucky, as usual, brought a loaf of bread. Being that he and Lucy Gray were a couple, she brought along some potato salad to make up for all the other times she'd come and not contributed.

Despite the alcohol being served round the back of the house, no one got into any fights. But there were lots of loose lips. Beatrice and Teeny Baby still positioned themselves where they could talk about everyone as they entered. Since they hadn't seen Lips or Bucky in months, they just had to pick on them.

Both eased their way over to the two as they were around back pouring drinks.

"Hey, you two ugly fools: don't drink all the liquor," said Teeny Baby, with Beatrice laughing.

"Don't worry 'bout us. You need to be worrying about that tore up house you and Jr. Cefuss are living in. Don't make any sense. Got my buddy working his ass off, and you're just sitting around in that raggedy-ass house. One more good wind and you'll be seeing the Wizard of Oz," said Lips.

"Give me five," said Bucky.

"That's alright," said Beatrice. "I hope the next time you are riding that lawn mower down the highway; you get hit by a car. I heard you got a ticket for speeding on it. Come on, girl. Let's get back in the house and let these drunk fools be," said Teeny Baby.

As they walked off Teeny Baby gave a sad smile.

"Lips has gotten a little better with the jokes, but the damned fool hurt my feelings talking about my house."

"Why don't you get a job and help buy another one?"

"There you go," said Teeny Baby. Teeny Baby paused, thought about it, and asked, "Is my house that bad?"

"No, girl," Beatrice said, bursting with laughter.

When Beatrice got back inside the garage, Stanley called her and asked if they could talk. Beatrice guided him through the crowd and into her bedroom.

"Yes, what's wrong?"

"Nothing is wrong. I just wanted to ask you for your blessing."

"Blessing for what?"

"I want to marry your daughter."

Beatrice's jaw dropped as her eyes welled with tears. She turned her back and began to wipe her face. Before she could give him any kind of answer, she had to make sure that he knew what he was getting into, just as Alex did.

"Now, Stanley, you know that my baby is special."

"Yes, ma'am. I know."

"And I want her to graduate from college, too. I don't care how much money you have made off that book."

"She's planning on doing that."

"Well, why do you want to marry my Beany? You've only known her for three months."

"Yes, but I love her, and I feel like I've known her all my life."

"Is she pregnant?"

"No, ma'am, … unless the stork's brought one that we don't know about."

"Have you and Beany even...."

"No, we haven't."

"I can say that I really enjoyed talking with your parents. They seemed to be enjoying themselves. Your mother said that she hadn't seen you so happy since before your wife passed away. ... And Chasity Taimia is just too cute. She really enjoyed being with Teeny Baby and me shopping today."

"Do you think that Beany really minds me having a baby and all?"

"Beany loves you so much that she will love that baby like she had it herself. Okay, enough of the stupid questions. Come give me ... your mother-in-law ... a hug. Does Beany know about this?"

"Hey, I haven't told her anything, but you know Beany. You never know what she knows."

"When are you going to tell everyone?"

"I figured right now is as good a time as any."

"Well, come on. Let's do it."

Beatrice walked back into the garage where everyone was eating and enjoying the festivities. She quickly ran to find Teeny Baby to give her the news. Fifteen years ago, Jr. Cefuss had proposed to Teeny Baby at one of Harry's get-togethers.

She picked up an empty glass and a spoon from the table and began to tap the glass calling everyone to order. As all got quiet and gathered around, Beatrice turned the attention to Stanley for his announcement.

"My dear family and friends, we have someone in here that has to make an announcement."

Beatrice then turned the floor over to Stanley.

Stanley called Alex up to the front with him so that he could also make his vows of love.

"Since this party is for Alex and Rosemary, I think it's only fair for him to make his announcement first."

"Rosa," said Alex, "could you please come up and stand next to me? I have something very important to ask you."

Rosemary slowly got up from her chair and walked over to Alex, smiling. Alex took her hand, dropped to one knee, and recited a poem from the book *Black Frame: Life Inspired Poetry*: *Every Moment*

With all the things that we've been through
Our love has kept us blind
And if we should meet on earth ten times over
I would choose you each of those times
I know these are merely words
They may not mean much to you
But with every happy moment I remember
You were there to see me through
Anytime I needed a believer
You were by my side
Whenever I needed a friend
Your arms were open wide

You've given me more than I could ask
Yet asked for little in return
The more you teach me how to love you
The more eager I am to learn

Everyone cheered after Alex finished reciting the poem. He took the ring from his pocket, and Rosemary began to tremble with excitement and nervousness. Alex then looked up into her eyes and asked her to marry him. Rosemary pulled him from his knee and began to hug Alex repeatedly.

"Yes, yes. I will marry you."

Beatrice stood wondering what had just happened. Neither Rosemary nor Alex told her of their plans to get married. Beatrice was not happy at all, but she knew that this was not the time for an argument to break out. She decided that it was only the right thing for Alex and Rosemary to do. She also knew that they both loved each other and were happy together.

Beany stood wondering what Stanley had in store for her. She could see things that happened to others, but if it was something about her, she hardly ever had a clue.

As Stanley took the platform again, it was time for him to propose to Beany. Not wanting Alex to outdo him, he too got on his knee and recited a poem. Stanley recited a poem from the book *Flight of the Blue Birds* that Donnie had written:

Explained in your Beautiful

Explained in your beautiful…

Understood in your tone…Comfort in the smile you wear

Caught in a daze…Your beautiful out weights

My heavens when…God placed you here

Hugging your rhythm… A kissing your lips

You move me without taking a step

In my arms you belong…Be it right or be it wrong

Be it whatever the gods have left

Your eyes… could train my sun to shine

Your smile… my world to sing

We're carrying a tone now… perfect song… and some how

In your beautiful we can do anything

A taste of wine… Rembrandt painting perfectly

You are more… to me…than just you

You are my wish as a child…My perfect smile

You're my… prayer …that somehow came true

The lips, the hair, the skin, the jeans

The way your sexy flows…

Understood in your tone…Can't leave this daydream alone…

All …

Explained… in your beautiful

"Breanna Latoya Harold, will you marry me?" Stanley asked with tears in his eyes.

"Yes, Stanley Deya Jr Miles, I will marry you. Just say when."

The crowd wowed with the answer Beany gave Stanley. Everyone began to whisper in either agreement or disapproval, but no one dared say anything out of the way...out loud...anyway.

Only the two drunks out by the grill were bold enough to say what came to mind. Bucky looked at Lips and belch out,

"Now, I know that I'm one ugly, stupid, butter biscuit and bean eating country fool, but damned if those two children of Beatrice's have done gone and lost every bit of my respect."

"Mine too," Bucky said as they both took another drink.

Jr. Ceffus butted in.

"You two ain't never had any damned respect from nobody, or had no woman, as far as those matters. Now drink to that and keep cooking, ... especially you Lips with your big mouth."

"Yo' mama ain't never had no woman neither," Lips mumbled as Bucky stumbled a little laughing.

Chapter 14

Guos Deus volt perdere prius dementat

Earlier that day not a cloud marred the sky, but suddenly thunder and lightning started. Everyone outside grabbed things and ran into the garage. Music started to play on the old eight-track tape player from the shed Harry had forbidden folks to go in when he was living.

Everyone stopped what they were doing and looked at Beany...even Stanley.

"Where is your son?" Teeny Baby asked Jr. Cefuss.

"Hell! I don't know where he is. He's your son, too."

Soon Michael came running into the garage, soaking wet from the rain.

"Where have you been, boy?" Teeny Baby asked.

"I was just out in the shed playing some music," said Michael.

Michael had a thing for wandering off with no one knowing where he was. He would sometimes ride his bike from his home to Beatrice's to see Beany. He thought that Beany was the prettiest girl that he had ever seen. Even though he was only eleven, he had the biggest crush on Beany. When Alex first left for school, Beany would go around, pick Michael up, and let him ride with her when she had to go pay bills for Beatrice. She called him her little boyfriend. Michael would always beg to differ with Beany, claiming he was a man. Beany knew that he was having a hard time with her getting engaged. She told Michael in front of Stanley that he'd still be her number one.

That still didn't stop Teeny Baby.

"Michael Alonzo McDuffy: the next time you wander off like a nomad, when you get back, your feet and your ass are going to be sore."

Everyone gave a sigh of relief. They remembered that the last time the eight-track had played in the shack no one had known why.

"Let's cut on some music since we have something to really celebrate," said Beatrice as she rushed to the CD player.

"I'll drink to that," said Lips.

"You'll drink to anything," said Alex, picking up where his dad left off when he was alive.

And just like with Harry, no one said anything to Alex.

As Alex walked off, Lips turned to Bucky, giggling drunkenly as Rosemary listened in.

"Where did Alex find that Mexican? I meant to go get me one of them working at the Potato Grader at old man Johnston's farm, clean her up and marry her."

Rosemary wasted no time letting the two know that she was not Mexican and didn't work on a farm.

"Guos Deus volt perdere prius dementat," she said.

"Hell! We don't speak that stuff. ... Speak English," said Bucky.

"Why?" asked Rosemary. "Neither of you speak English either. ... And what I said was, 'Those who God wishes to destroy, He first drives mad.' Meaning you two are two dumb drunk, crazy fools and will be destroyed if you keep screwing with me. Look at you. You are already crazy and half dead."

Rosemary then walked over to Alex and whispered.

"I like those two guys over there. They're funny."

Beany took Michael's hand for the first dance so he would feel a little better about the situation. Soon everyone was dancing to song after song.

With all the dancing going on, Beany and Stanley soon slipped away to Beany's bedroom for a little celebrating of their own.

"Come on in here. Nobody's going to come in my room. And they are all out there having a good time. I just want to give you something."

Stanley, feeling like he had nothing to lose, eased on into the bedroom with Beany.

Beany quickly grabbed Stanley, held him tightly, and began to kiss him. She then asked him in a rough voice filled with desire to make love to her. She didn't give him the chance to answer.

She started to unbuckle his pants and pulled them down his waist. Stanley knew that this was not the right time or place to have sex with his future wife. Since their first-time would-be Beany's first time, he wanted the experience to be a little more special than in her bedroom … at her mother's home … during a party. Still, his hormones were raging just as much as Beany's, and he could not control the bulge in his underwear.

As Beany began to slide them down to his ankles, all Stanley knew to do was to follow his instincts. He started taking off her clothes as well. As he lifted her bra from her perfectly sculpted breasts, he knew the moment was now out of his control. He unzipped her jeans and they dropped freely to her ankles. While Stanley was going through his motions, Beany began to touch his penis. She stroked it the way she had imagined it should be stroked in her fantasy with him. Since Beany had never seen one before, her heart started to race. How was it going to fit inside of her unexplored vagina?

Stanley was breathing like a wild cheetah running sixty-five miles an hour to catch its prey. He guided Beany onto her bed with one deft movement. Beany was in for something she had never known. Stanley spread her legs and began to lick around her vagina until he extended his tongue into her walls. Beany moaned out of control, begging Stanley to please not stop …groaning that she had never felt like this. In the back of her mind, she thought about Rosemary's first time and remembered her story well. She decided that she would do it standing up, letting Stanley hit it from the back so no sheets would get messy.

Teeny Baby came to the door and heard the moaning and groaning. She cracked the door, not believing her ears. The sounds brought out the freak in her. She saw Stanley's ass and

Beany's legs in the upright position, with Stanley's head between them. She eased the door closed and turned back to mind her business. Soon Beatrice was coming down the hall looking for Beany and Stanley to see why the k out they weren't in there with everyone else being they were a big part of the celebration. Teeny intervened before Beatrice got any further.

"Have you seen Beany and Stanley? Everyone is looking for them."

"Yes. They are in her room talking. I went in there to see if they were okay. They said that they just needed a minute to get themselves together."

"I have never seen Beany so happy," Beatrice said.

"Yeah, I guess this must really make her feel some kind of good … inside," Teeny said with a smirk.

"I only wish Harry was here to see this. I know she would have wanted him to be here. That sorry-ass Tavone could have shown up, but Beany just treats him so bad that I can't blame the man for not showing his face."

"Yeah, she was feeling really good, you could say. Come on, girl. Let's go back out here and laugh at those crazy friends of ours."

CHAPTER 15

Haints

As the crowd started to drift away, Beatrice and Teeny started to clean off the tables and sweep up around the garage. Bucky and the rest of the gang began to help load their belongings onto the truck.

Ten minutes later Beany and Stanley came from her room, acting a little distant from each other, trying to play off the fact that they had just made love for the first time.

"Why are you two looking all dumb in the face?"

"What are you talking about?" asked Beany smiling. "Ain't nobody looking dumb in the face. Can't a girl be happy?"

Teeny Baby took up for Beany.

"Yeah, Beatrice. Can't a girl be happy? I sure would be if some handsome man went down on me ...on one knee that is ... to ask me to marry him ... fine and as rich as Stanley is. I would have a crazy look on my face too."

Beany looked at Teeny Baby, knowing Teeny must have heard or saw something. Beany gave her a sneaky frown. Teeny Baby looked at her and threw her hands up at half mast.

"Well, I'm just telling you like it is," Teeny said.

"Beany, I give it to the young man. He is very handsome," said Beatrice. "You better go out there with him before Lucy Gray gets her hands on him."

"Speaking of Lucy Gray, I bet she will tell all of Camden that my two children are getting married. Oh, hell yeah! She's going to do some talking," Beatrice said.

"Didn't you see her? She was on the phone calling someone right while Alex was proposing to Rosa, and she didn't get off until Stanley was done with Beany. You know what old folks used to say: She missed her calling. Well, she sure missed hers because she should have been a news reporter."

"Girl, we need to stop gossiping and finish cleaning up this mess cause I'm tired," Beatrice said. "Alex and Beany done knocked the wind out of me."

The Harolds and their crew completed the clean up and went into the living room to recap the evening's events. Alex and Rosemary had to get up early to leave for Durham. They went to Alex's room to pack for the morning ride back. Beany and Stanley decided that they would go to his place for a while.

Beatrice enjoyed Chasity Taimia so much that she asked if she could keep her until they got back.

"Sure," said Stanley. "We won't be that long. We are just going to my place to hang out for a while. Beany wanted to show me some of the things that I need to change before she moves in."

"Moves in … when?" Beatrice asked.

"We are talking about when we get married, Mama. Don't panic," said Beany.

"That's what I thought."

"We won't be long because I want to get back so that I can get up with Rosa and Alex to see them off in the morning," said Beany.

Beany went back to where they were packing to tell Rosemary and Alex goodbye. When she opened the door, Alex and Rosa were both laying across the bed with their clothes on … fast asleep. She eased the door to and walked back to say goodbye to Chasity Taimia and Beatrice.

"Mama, you know that Alex and Rosa are back in his room on the bed asleep."

"Beany, I can't believe you are trying to get something started," said Stanley.

"Don't pay her any mind. They have been telling on each other for as long as I can remember. That's alright. They are probably so tired that they just passed out. This has been a long day."

Beany, not believing what her mother just said, commanded Stanley to come on with her as she went to the door. Stanley kissed Chasity Taimia once more and followed Beany out the door.

Beany never left home without her phone, but because of her first sexual encounter, she would have forgotten her head if it weren't attached on to her neck. It was ringing where she left it in the bedroom.

***

By the time they got back home, Rosemary was up cuddling the baby in her arms, and Beatrice was back in her room asleep. Stanley gathered Chasity Taimia's diaper bag and bottles as Beany went with him out to his car. They kissed. Beany asked if they would see each other tomorrow. Stanley reminded her that he had to leave for New York and that he would be back on Wednesday. Beany reminded him to call her as soon as he got where he was going. She went back into the house rushing to tell Rosemary what had happened earlier in her bedroom.

"Oh my God, Beany! How was it? What gave you the nerve to do it in your bedroom?"

"I didn't plan on doing it, but I got caught up in the moment. I've been longing to do it for the last two weeks. He was taking his time trying to get a piece, so I just took it in my hands to make it happen."

"And this was your first time doing the nasty?"

"Yep."

"So, tell me about it. How was it? Did it hurt or what?"

"Girl, I was so hot at first, I didn't care how it was going to feel. All I knew was that I wanted him some kind of bad."

"Sooo ... what did he do? What did you do? Tell me everything."

"Well, I asked him to come back into the room. I started to kiss him, then I started to unzip his pants, and I went inside of his underwear to feel his thing."

"And?"

"He started to say no at first because he was scared that someone was going to come in. Then he worried that it wouldn't be special since it was my first time and all. But I guess he was getting so hard that he couldn't control himself either. After that his thing got so big, I started to get a little scared that it wasn't going to fit. Once he had my panties down, he laid me down on my bed and started to lick my stuff. I tell you the truth: I don't remember much after that. All I know was that it hurt so good. I'm still sore. That's why we went for a ride. Although it hurt a lot, I was still ready for some more. That's why we left. We didn't have a lot of time because we had to get Chasity Taimia, so we came back here."

"Yeah, girl, my legs are always sore when your brother and I do it."

"I do not want to hear about you and that knuckle head."

"I don't care. As a matter of fact, I'm getting ready to go back there now and wake him up and sneak me a piece now that you done worked me all up. Good night, girl," said Rosemary.

"What about Mama? What is she going to say if she finds you are in Alex's room?"

"I don't know. I guess I'll have to worry about that in the morning on the way back to Durham."

Beany gave Rosa a hi-five as she passed her on the way to Alex's room.

Beany was tired also and decided to go to bed as well. When she got to the room, she noticed that her cell phone had mail. She entered her password and played the message:

9:37 p.m. Your call back number is: 757 555-0089. Detective Warden left this message:

"Beany, this is Detective Teddy Warden. I have some very important information for you regarding your father, Tavone McKnight. It seems that you may be on to something about him. Please give me a call so that we can arrange to meet to discuss this. My number again is 757-555-0089. Have a good evening. By the way, tell your mother I said, 'Hi,' and to call me sometime."

Beany wanted to call him back, but it was well after one in the morning, so she figured she would call him after Alex and Rosemary left. She was so tired from the long day that she took a quick shower and went to bed. She read a few poems from the book *Black Frame* and slowly faded into a deep sleep.

Sleeping so deeply, she began to have pleasant dreams of her and Stanley together. Suddenly, something tapped her on her forehead. She slowly opened her eyes. In front of her stood Donnie, David, Maurice looking like they were maybe six or seven years old and their mother Stacy as a little girl, with all the children from Pinch Gut Road.

"He's coming for you."

"He will be home soon, and he is coming for you."

"He can be stopped."

"He doesn't want you. He wants your baby boy."

"He loves boys."

*"**Three Damned Lies** will help you find him. Secrets lie within these places. Chains still on child."*

"Yeah," the children said agreeing with Donnie, David, and Maurice. *He's just like his father and his father's father."*

"Stop him. They will help you."

"He can help you."

"He will tell you."

"The shadow people have been following him during the day. They said he will be back."

Beany began to scream loudly, waking everyone in the house. Alex got up from his bed and ran into her room, telling Rosemary to stay in his room. Beatrice heard the yelling, but she was not going into the room until Alex cut on the light to see what was wrong with Beany.

"Beany, are you okay?"

"Yes, I'm okay. I just had a bad dream, more like a nightmare. You can go back to bed. I will be alright."

"Are you sure?"

"Yeah, I'm alright."

After Beatrice heard Beany say that she was having a bad dream, she didn't want to know what it was about. As long as there wasn't anything walking around in the house, she was used to the noises that Beany sometimes made.

After getting over the shock of seeing all the ghosts from Pinch Gut Road, Beany began to wonder who they were talking about. Who was the HE that could help her? She also thought about the baby boy they were talking about. She first feared that they were talking about Chasity Taimia. One thing she knew about the Pinch Gut ghosts, they were never wrong. Beany knew that she had to talk to the detective, and she knew that she had to talk to him fast. This was not the first time in her life that she had seen what Grandma Amy called Haints, what old Southerners called ghosts or nagging sprits. The only thing that puzzled Beany is why Donnie Maurice and David appeared as children…and why she could only see the thing as children. After a while Beany wasted no time falling back to sleep and was out to the world.

CHAPTER 16

I think I'm pregnant

Alex and Rosa were up getting dressed to head out on their four-hour drive back to Durham. Beatrice made sure she was up cooking a good breakfast before they left. Beany was in her room fast asleep, so everyone had a chance to talk about her while she wasn't present.

After Alex packed the luggage and put it in the car, he came back inside to talk with Beatrice and Rosemary.

"Mama, did you hear Beany in her room yelling and hollering like a wolf? I've heard her before, but I have never heard anything like that. I think something is really going on."

"Like what, Alex?" Beatrice said in frustration.

"Like something is coming after her or something. Stanley told me that Beany said she saw children in the back seat of their car when they were at Donnie's old house."

"What were they doing at that house anyway?"

"Something about he wanted to stop and look inside the house to see where and how Donnie had lived."

"What did he want to see that for? He must be obsessed with that book."

"No. He just felt he and Donnie were so close. I guess he was just curious – that's all."

"I told Beany one time before about being down that road. That Riddles area has got a lot of meanness in the winds. I bet you can't find twenty cars a month traveling that road. Only the cars of people that are crazy enough to live there travel that road, and most of them ain't that bright anyway."

"Mama, I take that road all the time, and I never have any problems."

"Well, you go right on, buddy. Your mama's not," said Beatrice.

"Beany used to tell me when she was having these kinds of dreams and seeing scary things, but she won't talk about it anymore. I was assuming that she didn't see that stuff anymore."

Beatrice thought for a few minutes.

"I don't remember her talking about it or having any problems recently until this. I sure hope it has nothing to do with that book Donnie wrote because that's when it seemed to start again."

"You are so right," said Alex. "She's also tripping off on Tavone lately and trying to find out where he is from."

"She was asking me an awful lot of things about him on the way from the prison that night."

"You think he's got something to do with it?"

"You know, Mama, I don't know. She's got that detective who came around to check up on him."

Rosemary sat quietly. She had started to wonder if *Three Damned Lies* had anything to do with her meeting Alex. After reading it the day the detectives brought over the manuscript for them, she'd kept the stories Donnie told in the back of her brain.

When she'd read it, she'd found that Donnie had gotten a hotel with her sister Velma, the night before he left to find his murdered wife. Maybe it was all a big coincidence, she thought. But out of all the guys at school – of all the guys in the world, why did she fall in love with someone that had a connection to her in such a big and mysterious way? She just listened as Alex and Beatrice continued to talk about Beany. She hoped she was not some sort of piece in this puzzle.

Beany smelled the breakfast and came dragging into the kitchen. Alex and Beatrice's conversation shifted to the party and the two engagements.

"So, how does my new bride-to-be feel this morning?" asked Rosemary.

"Just great. And you?"

"I'm fine. I'm going to miss you, Beany. I really had a good time here with you. You, too, Mrs. Harold."

"You can call me 'Mama,' like the rest of them. You might as well get used to it anyway. You make sure you eat right and take care of the baby. I want a healthy grandbaby."

"Yes, ma'am. I will," said Rosa smiling.

Beany stood there listening to the girls talking about the baby and thought about her visit last night. She wondered at the message about someone wanting her baby. She hoped that she wasn't pregnant by Stanley right now even though she wanted to be in the future. She wasn't sexually active but knew that it didn't take but one time to get pregnant.

"What's wrong, Beany?" asked Beatrice. "You are staring into space."

"Oh, nothing. I was just thinking about Stanley and hoping he makes it to New York okay."

"He had to go to New York?"

"Yes. I told him to call me when he gets there."

"Okay, y'all go ahead and set the table for breakfast," Beatrice said as she made the last few pancakes.

"Yeah, we have to get on the road," said Alex. "I have so much to do as soon as I get back. I have to be at work at six tomorrow morning."

After eating breakfast, Alex and Rosa made sure they didn't leave anything behind, gave hugs and goodbyes, and went on their way. Beany and Beatrice stood on the front porch and waved them out of sight. They went back into the house and cleaned the kitchen. Beany then went to her room and cleaned up a little. She found the panties that she had on when she and Stanley made love for the first time. She put them into a plastic bag and hid them in her closet. She then got the phone and called Stanley to make sure he was okay.

"Hey, Baby! I was just getting ready to call you. I just got to my hotel and was going to call you before I unpacked. So how are you?"

"I'm doing fine. I'm just sad because you are not here, and Alex and Rosa just left."

"Well, I'll be home in two days so, you won't be sad for long. How's your mother doing?"

"She's fine. She is back in her room watching TV."

"Tell her that I'll be on Larry King Live tomorrow. We are going to tape the show tonight."

"What time tomorrow?"

"I think it comes on at nine on CNN."

"I'll make sure I'm sitting right here watching," said Beany.

"What else has been going on?"

"I think I'm pregnant."

"You think what?"

"I think I'm pregnant."

"What gives you that idea?" Stanley asked.

"I know this might sound crazy, but the children stopped by my room last night and said that someone wanted my baby boy. How would they know?"

"Maybe they were just picking with you. Maybe they were jealous or something."

"No, they were warning me of something to come."

"Warning you of what?"

"I don't know. They were talking in riddles. They always talk like that. I also saw Donnie, his brothers, and his mother Stacy. They, too, were trying to warn me of something. I'm starting to get really scared."

"Just hold on until I get back. You have dealt with them telling you things before and there is no need to panic. Have they, the ghosts, ever hurt you or tried to hurt you before?"

"No."

"Well, keep trusting them. They will look out for you. Donnie, your father, and all the dead people you see were people who loved you. They will not let anything happen to you. They will lead you to the answer. Trust me."

"See, Stanley. That's why I love you so much. You are always there and always seeming to have all the right answers."

"Well, that's what I'm here for. What do you have planned for today?"

"I have to call that detective back and meet with him. He said that he has some important information for me."

"You call me back to let me know what's going on. Look, I must be going. I love you and I will call you back as soon as I can."

"I love you, too. And you be good."

"I will."

"Okay."

"See you later. Love you. ... Bye."

"Love you, too. ... Bye-bye."

Stanley stood holding the phone in his hands thinking about Beany being pregnant. He thought of what his wife went through with her pregnancy and didn't want anything to happen to Beany. He was so in love with Beany that he wanted to marry her as soon as he got back from New York. He started to call her back to set a date, but he had to get his things together for his interview later that day.

After Beany got off the phone, she played the voice message from Detective Warden to get the number from it. She dialed.

"Hello."

"This is Beany."

"What's up, buddy?" said Teddy.

"Nothing much."

"Well, I've got some information for you. I'd rather not talk over the phone, so if there is somewhere you'd like to meet, it would be just fine with me."

"Why don't you come to the house? I think Mama would be glad to see you. I think she has a thing for you."

"Did she tell you that?"

"No, but I could tell when she got out of the car with you that day. She was all melt-y."

"Okay. I will be there about two. Is that a good time for you?"

"Yes, that will be just great."

"Well, I will see you then."

"Alright."

Beany knocked on her mother's bedroom door. She stuck her head in to see what Beatrice was doing. Beatrice was lying on the bed reading letters she'd found after Harry had died. She hadn't read them since the day they were found, in the shed, in that box.

"Mama what are you reading?" Beany asked.

"Just some old letters that your father wrote me before he died."

"Can I see them?"

"Here. Read this one."

Beany started to read. She never knew that Harry had written any letters to her mother. Beatrice had never shared the letters with Beany because they were always too painful to read. The letters held secrets that she wasn't ready to share with Beany.

From the time Beany questioned her in the car about Tavone, and since Stanley had bought Beany the same book that Tavone had bought Beatrice when they were sleeping around, Beatrice felt it was time that Beany learned what she knew about both fathers.

The real one and the fake one. ...

"Mama, so you didn't even know that Tavone was my real father until you read this letter?"

"Yep, that's about right."

"Daddy must have really loved you. He stayed with you after all those years of knowing that I was not his biological child and didn't kick your tail every day?"

"Pretty much. I'm telling you; he was a good man. But he was no angel. You know he slept with Teeny Baby and gave me a sexually transmitted disease on our first wedding anniversary. That's what started everything."

"Why did he sleep with Teeny Baby, other than she got a nice shape and is pretty? She ain't nothing special."

"All a women needs are tits and a bird and men will do almost anything. Not all men. Some are totally faithful. I blame a lot of what Harry did on myself and that fast ass Teeny Baby."

"Yeah, she is a nasty thing, ain't she?"

"She was ... back in the days, but her old tail has settled down a lot. As a matter of fact, she has changed completely. Being forty-seven helps put a damper on her wildness."

Beany continued to read the letters and asked Beatrice questions. Time was passing. Beany was so into reading Harry's old letters that she almost forgot Detective Warden was coming over.

"Oh! Mama, I almost forgot to tell you that Teddy will be over at about two."

"For what?"

"I had him find out some information about Tavone."

Beatrice didn't even feel like questioning her about anything. She told Beany to take the letters in her room if she wanted to finish reading them because she needed to get dressed before Teddy got there.

"Why do you need to get all pretty?" asked Beany, knowing why all the while.

"Beany, come on now. You know that that man is fine."

"Ma, he's all old."

"Fifty-six ain't old, especially when you are fifty. I'm not getting any younger."

Then Beatrice told Beany to get out and mind her business. Before long the doorbell rang, and the detective was standing with black briefcase in hand. Beany went to the door and asked him to come in. Teddy looked around and commented how nice the house looked inside and out. Beany said thanks and asked him to have a seat. She then offered him something to drink and began to get nervous. She wondered what information he had for her. She was also wondering what was taking Beatrice so long to come from the bedroom.

"So, what do you have for me?"

"Before I tell you what I have found, I must warn you that when I found out some of these things about Tavone, it even freaked me out. Believe me, I was as surprised as I know you will be."

***

Beatrice was in the room talking to Teeny Baby, telling her that Teddy was over. She told her that she was going to make a move on him as soon as he finished talking with Beany.

***

"Okay, so tell me what you've got," Beany told Teddy.

For the detective to explain his findings, he had to start by finding out where Tavone was from. His hunch was that Tavone was from Camden. He was too familiar with the area.

"Somehow when you are older, you seem to always find yourself back home," the detective added.

Since Tavone's father was white, Teddy figured that his mother had taken him and moved to Virginia.

"So, what I had to do was trace back as far as 1927, looking through Camden's old archives trying to find anything that would give me some type of point of reference," explained Teddy.

"What did you find?"

"Well, I tried to find the wealthiest white families in Camden, and that search led me to Riddles and Pinch Gut Road."

"Why Pinch Gut Road ... and why the wealthiest white families?"

"I figured that if Tavone and his mother had to move away, someone had to help them a little with the moving. That person would have to be someone with money, someone who was trying to keep everything a secret. Remember all of this was just theory. I was just playing with what little I had to go on."

"Okay, continue," said Beany.

"A Hungarian family, Csontos – pronounced Saun-tose – moved onto Pinch Gut Road after buying about a hundred acres of land. They bought the land from the county tax office. The tax office would auction off land owned by black families who could not pay taxes on their land. Just by reading the documents, I could tell that some of the black families couldn't read and didn't know that the land they owned was being sold."

As the detective continued telling Beany his theory about Tavone, he showed Beany pictures and photocopies of old documents.

"After the blacks learned that their houses and land were being stolen right from underneath them, they began to fight back. That's when the KKK started showing up. They burned the blacks right off their land. And the leader of the Klansmen was the owner of the most land ... Mark Henry Csontos."

"I know the last name. I have heard stories about an old, crippled man with the last name Csontos that used to terrorize the black kids that worked in the fields with their parents. I thought that it was just an old folk tale," said Beany. She suddenly shivered.

"Apparently it wasn't such a tall tale after all. He and about four other white landowners supposedly murdered four black kids, molesting the girls and throwing them in Riddles Pond. None of them were ever convicted for the murders. Mr. Csontos made enough money to build the biggest house on Pinch Gut Road. He and his wife, Caroline, had two sons, Danny, and Frankie – and a black maid. The maid told black folks about the boys being taken advantage of by their father. And she warned the black children not to be found walking the roads alone. When

Danny and Frankie were both old enough, they built houses on Pinch Gut Road. One of the houses is still there."

"Let me guess," said Beany, "432 Pinch Gut Road."

"Bingo."

"So, what does that have to do with Tavone?" Beany asked.

"Danny Csontos, one of the sons, tried to fight his demons. He married a very nice lady and they had two boys. Danny also had one son outside of the marriage. That third child was your father."

"Tavone?" asked Beany.

"Yes. Tavone's mother was from a small town in Lenoir County ... Kinston."

"I know where that is. Kinston, North Carolina. ... Right?"

"Yes. She moved to Camden to find work."

"Okay, so my grandmother was from Kinston. ... Okay?"

"Tavone's mother was the Csontos' maid. She washed clothes and did anything that needed to be done around the house. After having the baby, Tavone's mother, Mildred McKnight, continued to work at the Csontos until she confronted his wife about Tavone being Danny's."

"Why would she do that?" said Beany.

"People who knew her said she was in love with Danny Csontos. In some crazy way, she thought that he loved her, too. I don't really know."

"So, that's why they moved to Virginia?"

"Yes, Danny must have given her a large amount of money and she left. I drove by the place in Norfolk where he grew up. I must say, Tavone lived pretty well. He even went to a private school. I also think he didn't want old man Csontos, Danny's father, your great-grandfather, to find out that his son had a baby by a black woman, especially since his father was a member of the Klan."

"So, my grandparents were a bunch of rednecks?"

Beany sat thinking hard about how she had been treating Tavone and what he must have been going through all these years. She also knew the dead children that she had been seeing from Pinch Gut Road were the children that her great-grandfather had killed years ago. She suddenly looked at the detective.

"What were my uncles' names?"

Teddy wasn't finished with his findings. One last piece to the puzzle would help Beany complete the picture she wanted to gain about Tavone.

"Beany, this is the part that freaked me out."

"What?"

"Your father had two brothers, and, as you know, they were white. One of them, they called Little Charles, was found in 1977, barbed wired to a tree and burned to a crisp. Tavone's other brother's name was ... James Earl Csontos."

"You mean to tell me that Donnie's stepfather and Tavone are stepbrothers?"

"Which meant that Tavone was Donnie's uncle ... which explains why Tavone wanted to be there with Donnie. If you read **Three Damned Lies**, you would see that Tavone was visiting Donnie and knew a lot about Stacy and the other boys."

***

Beatrice got off the phone with Teeny Baby and came into the living room.

"How are you, Teddy?"

"I'm doing fine ... and you?"

"I'm doing just great. So, did you and my daughter figure out who Tavone was?"

Beany looked at her mother.

"I think we found out more information than I want to know," Beany said. Beany asked if she could be excused. She went outside, around back, to where Beatrice usually sat. That spot was her favorite when she needed to think. She began to wonder how all of this played into what the children were trying to tell her. She knew there was even more the detective would find and that he would come to see her in the near future. Beany got up and went back into the house where Teddy and Beatrice were.

"Baby, Teddy just told me what he found out about Tavone. I'm sorry. I wish I had of known all of this. I swear I would never have even looked his way."

"That's okay, Mama. It's not your fault. How would you have known if he didn't tell you?"

"Yeah, Ms. Harold. You would have never guessed it. It took me almost three weeks to find this information, and I have a lot of resources."

"Well, thank you very much for your information. I think I'm going to go in my room and lay down. Mama, will you see Mr. Warden out for me?"

"Oh, sure. I'll be glad to."

Beany left for her room. Halfway there she turned back, glanced at her mother, and winked her eye. When she got to her room, it was cool ... a little too cool, she thought. She knew that the Shadow people had been there. She just wondered why they came while she was not present. Instead of going in her room she decided to go into her mother's room. She kept her phone by her side, waiting for Stanley to call, making sure not to miss him.

Teddy stayed and talked with Beatrice about Tavone, telling her he wasn't done with his investigation and that he wanted to find out more about the uncle that was burned to death. He wanted to look in the files and see if he could get permission from the Camden authorities to reopen the case since no one was found guilty of his murder. He recalled his father working on this case some thirty years ago, but at that time his father could not find any leads.

Beatrice wanted to change subjects. She asked him where he was from and whether he was married.

"I am from Virginia, and, no, I'm not married. I'm only married to my job."

"What happened? Wife left you?"

"Yes, she left me years ago." He paused. "I could use a good date and a nice dinner," Teddy said, hinting to Beatrice.

"Me, too!" Beatrice said, not letting his gesture pass by unnoticed.

"So, would you like to go out for dinner?"

"Are you asking me out on a date?"

"I guess that's what I'm doing," said Teddy, smiling. "Have you eaten dinner yet?"

"No, I have not," Beatrice said like she was starving to death.

"If you are ready, then I'm ready. Do you want to ask if Beany wants to go?"

"Sure," said Beatrice hesitantly.

Beatrice thought to herself that she hadn't been on a date with a man in years and she sure didn't want Beany to drag along. She was even thinking of maybe getting lucky.
She looked in Beany's room to ask if she wanted to go, but Beany wasn't there.

"In here, Mom," said Beany, "and ... yes, you can go out to eat ... and ... no, I don't want to go. Have fun."

"Breanna Latoya Harold, I hate it when you do that shit. ... Bye. ... Call me if you need me."

"You call me," Beany said laughing. Then with a more serious tone, Beany said, "Mama, you are a pretty lady. I hope I got your genes."

"Why, thank you, Breanna."

"Oh! And Mama ..."

Beatrice turned back smiling.

"What now?"

"I love you."

"Ah! Thank you, and I love you too, Breanna."

"And mama?"

"What? What? What? I got this man out here waiting."

"Please stop calling me Breanna. It's starting to make me sick."

Beatrice started to laugh as she headed back to where Teddy was waiting. She told Teddy that she was ready, and they left.

It was about seven and Stanley hadn't called. Beany was starting to get lonely and figured if he didn't call her by eight, she was going to call him. Soon after her thought, Rosa called.

"Hi, sister-in-law. We made it back home."

"Girl! Your soon-to-be mother-in-law is gone out on a date."

"With whom?"

"That detective that came over the other day."

"Girl!" said Rosemary. "I can't wait until I tell Alex that your mother has gone on a date. Where are they going?"

"I think they are going out to eat and probably to have sex."

"For real?"

"Nah, but if he asked her, she'd probably say yes. Damn! I hate to even think about my mother having sex with somebody, old as her butt is. Where's Alex?"

"He's upstairs studying."

"Tell him I said, 'Hi.'"

Beany could hear Rosemary yelling upstairs.

"Alexxx! Your sister said, 'Hi.'"

"Tell her I said, 'Hi,' and that I will call her later," Alex yelled back.

Rosemary continued with the conversation.

"Did you find out about your Bio-Pops."

"Girl! Yeah, it was a trip. He has a lot of shit with him."

Beany started to tell Rosemary everything that she had learned from the detective.

"Hold on a minute. I have a call on the other line."

"Hello."

"Hey, Baby!"

"Baby, I was thinking about you, wondering when you were going to call," said Beany.

"I figured you were. I have been so busy today. Every time I tried to call you, someone wanted me to rush off to do something. So how are you?"

"I'm doing good. I just wish you were here right now."

"Me, too. I know now that I'm not going to do this much longer. I think maybe for the rest of this year. Then I'm going to give this book thing up."

"Why?"

"Because I am missing my daughter and you are too much. This isn't what it is cracked up to be. They are so concerned with making their money back that they are saying yes to everyone that wants me for anything."

"I know, baby, but look on the bright side. Some people wish they had that problem."

"Yeah. You are right, but I'm getting tired of this. I have someone looking at turning this into a made for TV movie. My agent and a few lawyers are looking over the papers right now. I should make enough money to never have to do this again."

"Well, I hope all goes well. Oh, my gosh! I have Rosa on the other line. Hold on."

"Okay."

Beany clicked over but Rosa had already hung up the phone. She quickly clicked back over to Stanley.

"Hello."

"I'm here."

"Okay, where were we?"

"We were talking about me, but enough about me. What have you been up to?" Stanley asked.

"I found out who the Reverend Tavone McKnight really is."

Beany began to tell Stanley everything that Teddy had shared with her. They talked for three hours, sharing different ideas about what, if anything, she'd learned and what it meant. Stanley was a little surprised to know that Tavone was Donnie's uncle. Donnie probably didn't even know himself, thought Stanley.

Stanley asked about everyone. Beany told him about the date that Beatrice was on with Teddy. Stanley asked Beany how she felt about her mother dating again. Beany explained that she didn't mind and felt that it was time that her mother got out and met someone.

Beatrice eased into her room while Beany was talking to Stanley.

"I'm back," she whispered to Beany.

"Hi, Mom. How was your date?"

"We'll talk when you get off the phone," said Beatrice as she tapped Beany on the arm playfully. "And, by the way, get out of my room so I can get myself together."

Beany got off the bed, not missing a beat while talking and went into the living room. Beany and Stanley had been on the phone for so long that Beany's left arm had gone numb. She and Stanley figured that it was time to go and save some of their conversation for later that night if he or she couldn't sleep.

Beany went back into the living room and began to wonder about the people that had found their way into her life the past few years. She thought about how everyone in her life was connected to each other, somehow.

When Beatrice had an affair with Tavone, it seemed to be the basis for the connection. The book Donnie wrote names Rosemary's sister, Velma Martinez, as the last contact person he was with physically before he went to jail. Then suddenly, Alex shows up with Rosemary at the house. She knew that Rosemary even gave it some thought, but never mentioned if it bothered her. Rosa was somehow pulled into this triangle that Beany may have inadvertently webbed. Beany wouldn't blame Rosa if she had any bad feelings about her. Beany prayed that she did not have anything to do with what may happen in the future.

Alex's meeting Rosemary at school was more than just weird – it seemed to have been meant to be. When Stanley came to her house last year to ask Beatrice about Donnie's innocence and showed them Donnie's book, somehow Beany knew they would meet again. Meeting him at the Hut was an appendage. Stanley and his wife, Sandy, were still together and Stanley was still working at the prison when Stanley stopped by Beatrice's. Beany remembered coming out of the kitchen and responding.

"Yes, the book is true. It led you here to me." She then went on to explain that Stanley and Donnie were supposed to cross paths and that Stanley was supposed to inspire him to write this book. She told Stanley that he was supposed to find her, and she was supposed to tell Stanley the book is all true. Beany also told Stanley that Donnie left him clues in the book that would help set the blue birds free. Although Beany told him these things, she never knew it might have been meant for her as well. She had no idea that her mother would be seeing the man that was tearing through Donnie's conscience. The same detective that appeared in Donnie's nightmares, nightmares Beany had made, appears unknowingly. Only when she read the book did she have a clue of his existence.

Beany began to wonder if Stanley was feeling the same and not telling her. She also prayed that he didn't think she had anything to do with his wife dying or anything bad that has happened in his life. She only wanted to make him happy. She figured that she would find Tavone and see what he knew about the book and the nightmares she had been having. After the information she'd found out today, she knew Tavone was tied to what she had been experiencing on Pinch Gut Road.

Beatrice came back in the room to talk with Beany about her little dinner date. Beany talked to her about maybe contacting Tavone to talk with him. Beatrice brought up the fact that she hadn't heard from Tavone since she last saw him in Raleigh. Both Beany and Beatrice had one more day together for a while ... and then it was back to school for both.

Beatrice had to attend a meeting at Camden High School and was excited because this would be her first-year teaching. She used to be a teacher assistant, but when Harry was living, he didn't want her to work. Beany had to start back to school for her last year.

"What do you have planned for tomorrow, Mama?"

"Nothing. I thought since it was our last day before we start our busy semesters, we could do a little school shopping and catch a good dinner and a movie."

"That sounds fun. I guess I'll take my tail to bed and get ready for tomorrow."

"Me, too."

"Mama, please don't forget to remind me that my man will be on TV tomorrow night on the Larry King show at ten."

"What will he be doing up there?"

"Trying to sell that book."

"Okay, I will just program it so that it will go directly to that channel at ten."

"Okay, Mama. I'm gone. Glad you had a nice time. I told Alex about your date."

"What did he say?"

"Nothing. He's supposed to call me back, but he never did."

"Well, I'll see you in the morning. I love you."

"Love you too, Ma

CHAPTER 17

The Madness Stops

Six weeks had passed, and Beany was back at Elizabeth City State trying to balance school, her love life, and her pregnancy. She hadn't told anyone about her condition, except Stanley. She didn't know how to tell anyone else.

Beatrice was at the middle school attending staff development workshops to prepare for her first-time teaching. This teaching job was her first job in almost twenty-seven years. She and Beany were so busy that they didn't have time to pay much attention to each other or what was going on around them.

For Beatrice the relative solitude was a good thing. She had spoken with Teddy a few times. Both were so engrossed in their work for the last few weeks that they hadn't had time for each other. Beatrice got a call from Rev. Baxter reminding her this Sunday was 4th Sunday. He hoped to see her. The pastor reminded her that he hadn't seen her at church in a few Sundays. Beatrice assured him that she would be there to participate. She knew this 4th Sunday was also feeding Sunday. She also knew Rev. Baxter wanted to make sure that she cooked his favorite dish.

When Ma Elise had died, Beatrice had given up on going to church. She didn't feel like she had too much to be thankful for. Losing her husband, Harry, and her mother, Ma Elise, had been a big blow.

Unlike Beatrice, Beany made sure that she thanked God for blessing the family and looking over her throughout the years. After missing her period and taking the pregnancy test to make sure she was right, Beany often went to the church on campus and prayed to make sure that the baby ... and she ... were safe.

Beatrice got home Friday and kicked off her shoes to relax. She wasn't used to working those long hours and was more than glad for the weekend to begin. She got the idea to call up the gang to see if they wanted to attend the quarterly meeting with her. She even called Alex to see if he and Rosa wanted to come. She knew Alex wanted to come home because he tried to make it home at least once a month. Beatrice also wanted to see Teeny Baby since she hadn't talked with her in a few weeks and figured it was time for them to get together. About the time she was going to call Teeny Baby, Alex called.

"Hey! Mama, guess where we are?"

"Where?"

"We're on the way to Big Country Camden."

"Good. I was just getting ready to call you to see if you could come home this weekend for 4th Sunday Quarterly meeting."

"I was thinking the same thing, wasn't I, Rosa?"

In the background Beatrice could hear Rosemary agreeing with Alex.

"Mama," Alex began, "is Beany home yet?"

"Boy, you know I hardly ever see that girl much these days. When she's coming in, I'm usually going to bed. She really works hard in school. She's also working at the library at school."

"Why?" Alex asked in surprise. "With all the money that Stanley has, why does she need to work?"

"Well, she wants to do things on her on. I think she got that from Harry."

"Okay, Mama. I've got to go. I don't want to use up all of my minutes."

"I'll see you when you get here. Drive carefully."

"I will."

As soon as Beatrice hung up, she called Teeny Baby to see what she was up to. Beany walked in the door, slung her books on the couch and went straight to the rest room.

"Hold on a minute, Teeny Baby," said Beatrice.

Beatrice went to the back to see what was wrong with Beany. She knocked on the bathroom door and asked Beany if she was okay. Beany said that she was fine and that she had the runs.

"TMI," said Beatrice as she went back to talk with Teeny Baby.

"What? You left something on the stove?" asked Teeny Baby. Teeny could be a nosey somebody, Beatrice thought.

"No," Beatrice laughed. "Beany came in running like her ass was on fire. She said she had loose bowels. I told her that was just a little too much information."

"Yeah, that is too much information. Did she ever find out where Tavone was?"

"No. No one knows where he is. It's like he just disappeared from the face of the earth."

"No matter. He always has a way of finding his way back to Camden. Did I ever tell you about the mess Beany found on him? Girl, that man could have killed someone with all the stuff he's been through."

"Well, I'm glad he didn't."

"I see why Beany had strange feelings about him. Is she still looking for him?"

"Yep. I don't know why. I sure don't care if I ever see him again."

"Have you seen that detective?" asked Teeny Baby.

"No, not in a few weeks. He's been busy and so have I. But you wouldn't know about that? You know ... being busy."

"Girl! I work around the house cleaning and cooking for Jr. and Michael. By the way, have you seen him?"

"Seen who?"

"Michael."

"He's not around there?"

"Okay, I see him."

As Beatrice carried on her conversation, Beany was back in the restroom throwing up the lunch she'd had earlier. She knew at some point she had to let her mother know she was pregnant, but she didn't know how.

She would not have told Stanley, but she had gotten so accustomed to being naked around him and enjoying her new sexual freedom that he couldn't help but notice when her belly began to get round. He tried to convince her to tell her mother. Stanley insisted that everyone would be happy for her, but Beany was scared. She was thinking that maybe Beatrice still viewed her as a little girl and would scorn her for having sex before getting married. Maybe ... she thought ... Beatrice didn't want her to make the same mistakes that she'd made.

No matter what, the damage was done. She wanted to tell her mother about her morning sickness. She figured the only thing to do was to wait until 4th Sunday when everyone was around the house after church to tell her secret.

Beany came out of the bathroom, went to her room, and flopped on the bed. She took a cold washcloth and placed it on her forehead, and she began to look around at all the pictures on her walls. She had pictures of her and Harry, along with pictures that she drew as a little girl. Her room hadn't changed much, but she knew that she had changed. The time had come for her to take charge of her situation.

She got up and went into the room where Beatrice was talking on the phone. Her plan was to wait until Beatrice got off the phone and then spill her guts. Beatrice saw that Beany was sitting with the rag over her forehead. She got off the phone with Teeny Baby to see what was wrong.

"Girl, what's wrong with you? Are you okay?"

"Yeah, I'm fine. Just tired. I think my brain is hurting from all the stress."

"Well, you better make sure that you come to church with me this Sunday."

Beatrice looked at Beany, staring closely at her face.

"Girl, your face has been filling out a little bit. You are starting to look like a woman now. That's what happens when you start having sex."

"Who says that Stanley and I are having sex?" asked Beany as she removed the cloth from her head.

"Your mama ain't psychic like you, but she can see how those hips of yours are spreading like butter on bread. Just don't go getting pregnant until you and Stanley get to know each other and have been married for a few years."

Beany knew that it was no longer the right time to tell her mother that she was pregnant. She also knew that she would have to tell her mother sooner or later, but later seemed like the right time now.

Beatrice went on talking about church this coming Sunday: who was going to be there and how she was going to get up early Sunday morning to cook. She let Beany know Alex and Rosemary would be home in about 10 minutes or so.

Alex and Rosemary pulled up later that evening. Beany and Beatrice were waiting for them around back in their favorite spot. Because it was such a nice day, Alex and Rosemary got out of the car and sat right down with Beany and Beatrice to enjoy the evening shade.

"Rosa!" said Beany. "Look at you. You have gotten just as big as a house. And cute, too."

"Thanks ... I guess," said Rosemary. "Girl, I'm only seven months, but I feel like I'm nine and a half months."

"I hope that baby don't take his time like Alex did when I was carrying him. I thought that he was never going to come out," said Beatrice.

"I think she is."

"She?"

"We meant to keep that part a secret," said Alex. "That's our real reason for coming home. To tell you that we were having a baby boy."

"Sorry, Alex. I've spoiled the whole thing, haven't I?" asked Rosemary.

"For Mama maybe, but I already knew what the baby was going to be," said Beany.

"Hi, everybody," shouted Michael as he skidded his bike to a halting stop.

"Does your mama know where you are, boy?" asked Beatrice.

"No. I don't think they even care. They are in their room keeping up a bunch of noise, so I had to go for a ride."

"What were they doing?" Beany asked jokingly.

"If you want me to, I'll show you," Michael fired back.

"Maybe in about ten more years when you are about twenty."

"I will have me another girlfriend by then," said Michael. "Can I have some water, Ms. Beatrice?"

"It's right in the fridge. Just make yourself at home."

Once Michael was in the house, Beatrice shook her head.

"I have told Teeny Baby that she needs to pay more attention to that boy. She acts like he's grown at 11 years old."

While Alex and Beatrice were on the porch talking, Beany and Rosemary decided they would take a walk down the road for exercise. It was also a chance for Beany to tell Rosa her secret.

"Where are you two going?" asked Alex.

"We are going for a walk down the road."

"Yeah," Rosemary said. "My back is a little stiff from riding and I need to get a little exercise."

"Well, you two had better carry a big stick. Those dogs will get after you and cause you to have a heart attack."

Beatrice reminded Alex of how he and Beany used to ride their bikes and how they would get chased all the way home by the dogs. Alex laughed as he broke a limb off the tree for Beany to carry for protection. Then he asked Beatrice if she would help get Rosa's things out of the car. Beany took the branch and headed to the road.

"Can I tag along?" asked Michael, mounting his bike.

"No, I think you'd better head back home. It's getting kind of late, and I know your mama is going to be looking for you to be home."

"Okay, but don't forget that you are still my woman. I don't care about that new boyfriend you are supposed to be marrying."

"No matter who I marry, you will always be my baby."

So glad to hear Beany say that Michael got on his bike and rode off, waving goodbye.

"So ... what do you have for me, Beany?" Rosemary said as they began their walk.

"What makes you think that I have something new to tell?"

"When have YOU ever wanted to go for a walk? I was down here for three weeks and you never talked about going for a walk."

"Okay, you got me on that one. Rosa, hold your stomach," Beany said.

"Why?"

"Cause I'm probably about seven weeks pregnant."

"Oh my God, Beany! No, you are not ... are you?"

"Oh my God ... yes, I am."

"Have you told anyone?"

"Other than you ... No. Well, Stanley knows. But I do plan on telling everyone. Stanley told me I should have told everyone as soon as I found out, but I was afraid to."

"You really do need to say something so you can get started on your prenatal care."

"I know. Plus, I can't wait to get mama involved in this with me. I'm sure she will be here for me. I'm just nervous about telling her."

"So, what do you and Alex have new for me? I know you two have been up to something."

Rosemary held out her hand and asked Beany what she noticed about her engagement ring. Beany did a double take and saw that she had the band to go with it.

"I know that you and that fool didn't go out and get married without telling me. I could understand not telling Mama, but me ... your sister?"

"Girl, it's been a big deal. Shoot! when we went to see my parents in Florida, my father almost insisted that we get married. So, we just went to the courthouse while we were there and did the damned thing."

"I think Alex and I will end up sending Mama to the crazy house with all the shit we've placed at her table," said Beany with her hands on her chest.

"We are all going to be alright. That's what families do.... Have problems and get through them."

They both stopped and turned around to head back to the house. Before taking a step, Beany embraced Rosemary.

"Thanks for being a good friend and sister-in-law."

Rosemary reminded her of the first time that they'd met and how nice Beany was to her. Beany told Rosa that she could tell that she was a good person at first sight.

***

"Where is Michael, because his crazy mama has been calling for him?" Beatrice asked.

"We ran him on home. He should be there in a minute," Beany said.

Being that it had been a few weeks since the family was together, everyone felt a need to sit around and catch up on everything that had been going on in the last month or so. Alex was concerned that Beany hadn't heard from Tavone. He would usually have come by or called to see how everyone was doing.

Everything was back to normal in Camden on North River Road. They had found the two boys that had burned the straw man in Beatrice's yard. The boys swore to the police and the court authorities that they had given a ride to a man that night, on the back of their truck … and that he had wanted to burn the straw man. They had just helped him pull it off, but they hadn't meant anything by it. They could not come up with the man's name who they claimed instigated the burning.

One of the boys claimed that the white man had stood in the yard and watched the straw man burn, but they jumped back into the truck and drove off. When they described him, they said that he was an old white man. He looked to be in his late sixties and that he was dressed like someone back in the 1960's. In the end, the boys were found guilty of trespassing and setting a fire near a dwelling. Everyone in town thought the boys were trying to make something up to get out of trouble.

Everybody in Camden ... except Beany.

Beany knew who the man was ... and what was behind the statement he tried to make with the burning. She, along with Stanley, had been putting information together, trying to figure out if it had anything to do with her and Tavone's side of the family. She was hoping his past was not trying to repeat itself. The only piece of the puzzle missing was Tavone … and he was on Mars, as Beany would say.

Beany had stopped having the frequent visits from the children of Pinch Gut Road. She felt as though they had given her all the information they could give. Now, she faced the calm before the storm. As she sat and talked with the family, she wondered why Stanley hadn't called. Before long he came pulling up in the yard.

Stanley walked in and hugged Rosemary. He complimented her on how nice she was carrying the baby. He then spoke to everyone, winked at Beany, and asked Alex to come outside. After he and Alex walked outside, Beatrice looked puzzled.

"What's wrong with Stanley?"

Beany said she didn't have a clue

"He probably had something to drink in the car and wanted Alex to have a drink with him and didn't want y'all to know."

"Hell, he doesn't have to worry about me. I need one myself," said Beatrice.

"Me, too. ... I wish," said Rosemary.

When Stanley got back outside with Alex, he began to spill every bean in his pocket.

"What's up, man? What's been going on with ya?" asked Alex.

"Not much. Just trying to figure out how to tell your mother that your sister is pregnant."

"What?" Alex said, laughing loudly.

"Chill. Chill, man. I don't want your mama to hear you tripping like that."

"Does Beany know that you are telling me?"

"No. She's trying to figure out a way to tell Beatrice, too."

"Look, bro, you're not in this boat by yourself. Rosa and I got married while we were in Florida. How are we going to break *that* news to Mama?"

"Look, I've got half a gallon of Hennessey in the boot of the car. If you can get two cups and some ice, we might can drink our way to a solution."

Alex went back into the house to get the glasses.

As he walked pass Beany, he stopped, looked at her, and snickered. She swung at him, hitting him on his butt as he continued to keep the smirk on his face.

"Alex where are you going with my good drinking glasses?" asked Beatrice, knowing what was about to take place.

"We are going out to the shed to have a couple of drinks."

"Don't you get my boyfriend all drunk, Alex."

"Shit, he's grown. I ain't got nothing to do with how much he drinks."

Alex left out the door so he wouldn't be standing inside for the next hour answering a tussock of questions. By the time they came back inside the house, Alex and Stanley were about as high as a person could get without throwing up to relieve them of the poison they had consumed. They still didn't have a dry cut solution for the problems they had placed on themselves, but they also didn't have a worry in the world at the time. Alex soon left everyone in the living room talking as he went back to his room to sleep. Rosa sat around hoping that maybe Beatrice would notice the wedding band on her finger so she could break in with reasons they decided to rush and get married. Beatrice was so contented with the children at home that she didn't even pay a lot of attention to any particular person. She mostly asked about the baby and how things were going for them at school. Stanley had fallen asleep on the sofa, leaving the girls talking about him and laughing as slobber dripped from his bottom lip.

When Stanley began to snore loudly, Beany knew the time had come to take him home. On the way back to Stanley's place, Beany asked him if he'd told Alex about her pregnancy. Stanley explained that he and Alex were trying to come up with the best way to tell Beatrice about the pregnancy and the fact that Alex and Rosemary had gotten married.

"What did you come up with?" asked Beany.

"A headache."

Stanley laughed and then told Beany the story Alex had shared with him about a particular 4th Sunday in the Dirty. Alex and Stanley thought that maybe they should have their own little Sunday go to meeting, dirty south adventure. Beany didn't like the idea of everyone knowing her business, but at the same time she knew that all would know in time. Also, a 4th Sunday meeting would be a good way to get the baby a blessing before he was born.

CHAPTER 18

4th Sunday

The girls spent all day Saturday shopping, with everyone trying to find something to wear for church. This Sunday was "feeding Sunday," so the church was going to be packed. For Beatrice and Teeny Baby, it meant looking good to give others something to talk about. Beatrice also had to buy a few items so that she could make Rev. Baxter's favorite dish and do a little grocery shopping for herself. She made sure that she had her buddy to go with her so she could have someone to hang out with now that Beany and Rosemary were close. Beatrice was starting to feel left out but was happy that Beany was hanging with someone her age.

Sunday morning had rotated its way to Camden side of the earth. Beatrice was up early cooking for the church. Soon everyone was moving around, getting themselves together for a spirited day. Alex began to run around like Harry when he used to prepare for church.

"Rosa, did you pack my black socks?"

"Yes, baby. They are inside of your shoes."

"How about my necktie? I can't find it anywhere."

"Try looking inside of your suit jacket."

"Why don't you just dress him?" asked Beany.

The phone rang.

"Someone get that for me," said Beatrice. Teeny Baby was on the other end saying that she needed a ride. Beatrice yelled to Rosa, who had answered the phone.

"Tell her to get a taxi or a ride from Mr. John D."

Although Mr. John D. was 95 years old, he was still driving and would pick a person up for a little fee. That was the closest thing anyone could get to a taxi in Camden.

Teeny Baby told Rosa to tell Beatrice to call him and ride with him herself. She told Rosa that she was following Mr. John D. one day and saw him run two stop signs. She said that those signs had been at the same two intersections for the past hundred years, but he didn't see them.

Rosa laughed as she told Beatrice what Teeny Baby said.

"Tell Teeny Baby that I will send Beany to pick her up in a few."

As Beany drove to pick up Teeny Baby, she noticed a truck coming at her at a high speed. It seemed to be driving in the middle of the road. She slowed down. What was that driver going to do? As the truck got closer, it finally straightened up, barely making its way to the right side of the road. It almost ran Beany off the road. The driver of the truck turned back as he passed and stared. Beany got an eerie feeling as she looked in her rear-view mirror at the truck. For some reason, she felt like she had seen this man before.

Once Beany picked up Teeny Baby and brought her back to the house, Stanley and Chasity Taimia were parked outside waiting.

Everyone moved south towards the New Philadelphia Baptist Church. By the time they got to the church, the parking spaces were few. Everyone in Camden had decided to go to church, it seemed. They parked about a half of a mile from the church and walked.

Being that the church was packed, no one wasted time standing outside talking. They quickly moved in and found a seat. Enough spaces were available for everyone to sit with their own little clan.

Rev. Baxter was so excited that the church was almost filled to capacity that he wasted no time starting. He started by having "Children's Hour." Sandy Kite came to the front pulpit, called all the children up, and read a brief story. Then she asked the children a few questions about the story and sent them back to their seat.

Next was time for the announcements. Dorothy Mae read off names from the sick and shut-in list, and then read thank you cards from those who'd received a little money from the church.

Afterward it was time for visitors to be recognized. Rev. Baxter asked that all visitors stand to be greeted. Since Alex hadn't been home in years, and hadn't been to church in even longer, he stood along with Stanley and eight or nine others. Stanley, recognized for his work with the book, stood out a little.

They were given a blessed greeting from the church. Then they were seated.

Beany, Alex, Stanley, and Rosa all began to look at each other from the corner of their eyes. They knew what was next. Stanley, having worked in the prison and done interviews for the book, *Three Damned Lies*, was ready to talk. The time had come to confess and thank God for any blessing that you had received in your life. This part of the service usually took about ten or twenty minutes unless someone got carried away.

Beatrice was so proud to be sitting with her best friend and her children that she was the first to stand.

"I want to thank God for bringing my child, Alex, and his fiancée home to Camden safe. I also want to thank you, Lord, for keeping my family and me safe through some trying times. I thank you in Jesus' name."

As Beatrice sat down, another member of the church stood to testify. That gave Stanley and Alex enough time to get their story together. Neither Beany nor Rosa believed that either would go through with it. As soon as Ms. Nobles sat down, Alex and Stanley stood simultaneously, with Alex going first.

"I would like to give all the glory to God for bringing me and my beautiful family here today. I would like to thank you for giving my mother the strength to raise my sister and me ... by herself ... after my father died. I would also like to thank God for blessing me and my wife Rosa, with the precious gift of life, the child growing inside of my wife."

While Alex was testifying, Beatrice looked at Rosa. Rosa flashed her finger, showing off the ring. Beatrice could only wonder what Stanley had in store.

As Alex finished, he looked at Stanley to take the stand. Beatrice, sitting beside Beany and Teeny Baby, looked at Beany's finger and saw no wedding band. She then grabbed both Beany's and Teeny Baby's hands and looked on as Stanley began to speak.

"I'm not too good at this, but I do know blessings when I'm steadily receiving them. I first want to thank you God for bringing Beany into my life. I also want to thank you for blessing us with the new life you have placed upon us. I only hope that we can bring him up in the same loving arms that my caring fiancée was brought up in."

Beatrice sat crying like she was at Ma Elise's funeral. Teeny Baby began to hug her. Soon Alex, Beany, Rosa, and Stanley joined in on a group hug. Rev. Baxter took advantage of the opportunity and soon the entire church was hugging each other. The minister began to preach about the presence of God in the house and how life teaches you lessons each day.

After the service ended, no one wasted time moving to the dining area. They all wanted to make sure they got to their favorite foods before the dishes were picked over by the swarm of church folks. As the line grew, it started to look like a soup kitchen. While waiting in line, people took the chance to do a little "chit-chatting," as country folks call it.

"I was really moved today by your children, Beatrice," said Teeny Baby. "That Stanley must really love Beany. He stood right up and let it rip."

"I started to stand up and rip his damn head off for getting my baby pregnant," said Beatrice. "And that Alex had the nerve to marry that girl and didn't even let me know."

"Oh! Now, she's that girl, huh?"

"Yep. I started to slap the living daylights out of her, too. She ought to be glad she is carrying my grandbaby."

As they got close to the food, they stopped talking about the children and started talking about what food not to eat. They always kept an eye on Ms. Penny Harris. Ms. Penny could cook, but she also dipped snuffed tobacco. Teeny Baby swore she was with Ms. Penny one day when she was cooking and saw her drip about a spoonful of snuff and spit into the mixture. The spittle fell from Ms. Penny's bottom lip right into the collard greens. Since then, they always kept a look out for Ms. Penny's special dishes. After filling their plates, they went to where Beany had saved seats and a table for them.

"Where is Michael? Why didn't he come?" asked Beany.

"He wanted to go fishing with his dad. I tried to get him up to go with me, but he just lay there. I even told him that you were going to be here, but he said he didn't want to see you with Stanley."

"I am so sorry," said Beany. "I am going to call him when we get back. He really thinks he is my little boyfriend."

Soon after Beany started to eat, she began to get sick. She excused herself from the table and ran into the restroom. As the sweat beaded on her forehead, she turned on the faucet to cool off and try to pull herself together. She didn't feel the common form of morning sickness today. This sickness was not morning sickness. This sickness stemmed from turmoil and insight. She felt that something terrible was happening. She was hoping for the predictions of the dead Pinch Gut Road children were not taking place right now. She suddenly felt the need to go home. She ran back to ask Stanley to take her home. But Stanley and Beatrice were already standing outside of the restroom waiting for her.

"Are you okay, Baby?" said Beatrice, obviously worried.

"Yes. I think I just need to go home and lay down."

On the ride home Beany began to tell Stanley about the feeling she was getting, and that the feeling had nothing to do with morning sickness. She felt more like it had something to do with the safety of the baby. Stanley remembered that she'd told him about one of the spirits mentioning something about a baby boy. Stanley began to feel what Beany was feeling and monitored her closely.

When Beany got home, she lay across the sofa. Stanley put a blanket on her. Before long everyone was home. Since they were concerned about Beany, they had wrapped their plates and decided to finish eating at home.

Teeny baby got on the phone to call Jr. Ceffus to let him know that she was over at Beatrice's and that she would be home soon. Jr. asked if she'd brought something for him.

"No, I didn't. You know how funny those church folks are about taking plates with you. I will get you something from C C's Rib Shack on the way home."

"Has Michael eaten?" Teeny added.

"I don't know. I haven't seen him since you left this morning," said Jr. Cefuss. "I thought he went with you, as a matter of fact."

"No, I thought you were going fishing."

"No. Our fishing trip is tomorrow."

"Well, then, where is he?"

"I don't have a clue. I'm watching the football game. I told him I wasn't going until tomorrow," Jr. Ceffus said. "I'll go looking for him. He can't be too far."

Since neither knew just how long Michael had been gone, both began to panic. Teeny Baby started pacing back and forth, wondering what she should do. As quick as she was with the tongue, she was almost ashamed to tell anyone that they didn't know where Michael was. She would not tell anyone until she got word back from Jr. Cefuss that he had found their son or that he was home.

Only thirty minutes went by before Jr. Cefuss called back to let her know that he hadn't seen Michael anywhere. He assured her he had searched all the places Michael would go. Jr. Ceffus couldn't find him anywhere. He even talked to Lips and a few others that usually would see Michael riding by. No one had seen him all day.

While Teeny Baby's concerns turned into genuine panic, Beany lay on the sofa feeling sicker than she had ever felt in her life. She felt so bad ... that she started to cry and called for her mother. She was thinking that somehow something was trying to get to her unborn son. She tried to put together the pieces of information she'd gotten the night the spirits of Donnie, David, Maurice, Stacy, and all the children from Pinch Gut Road came to visit her. She started to play their voices over in her head, trying to pull off the layers of clues twisted in their phrases.

"He's coming for you."

"He will be home soon, and he is coming for you."

"He ... can be stopped."

"He doesn't want you. He wants your baby boy."

"He loves boys."

"Three Damned Lies *will help you find him. Secrets lie within these places. Chains still on child."*

"He's just like his father and his father's father."

"Stop him. They will help you."

"He can help you."

"He will tell you."

As she revisited what the spirits said to her that night, she began to calculate ways that Tavone was involved. Maybe he might be the one after her baby. She figured that if someone was coming for her it would be today. She just hoped the answers didn't kill her or harm her child.

CHAPTER 19
faith and hope combined

After the death of Donnie and the publication of *Three Damned Lies*, no one could find Tavone. Even his son, T.P, had not heard from him. Beany was hoping that she could find him before it was too late. She just knew that something bad was taking place. Even worse, she knew it was happening now. Beany removed the washcloth from her head and got off the sofa.

"Did you all see that?" Beany asked.

Quickly thinking, Beany sat there quietly as the shadow people stood over her. They never appeared around others, but it was almost like they wanted to be seen protecting Beany. Knowing she couldn't speak loudly, fearing all would think she was crazy, she began to ask them questions with her mind.

"Why are you all here?"

One of the elders in the group, sounding like a faded foghorn, answered. She heard his voice clearly in her mind.

"He is here, and he has your baby boy. Get your baby boy before it's too late. He will come. He will help."

The shadow people departed in silent beams, leaving Beany screaming, holding her stomach, and yelling.

"Please, God, not my baby," Beany gasped. "Please don't let them hurt my baby."

Stanley asked her who was she talking to, and who was going to hurt the baby. Beany tried to explain what she'd just seen, thinking that no one would understand what she was talking about. She began to tell anyone who would listen about the shadow people she'd been seeing over the years. She told them what she'd seen and heard a few minutes ago.

Teeny Baby could no longer hold in her secret. She burst into tears and told everyone in the house that Michael was missing. She looked at Beany like she wanted Beany to tell her where he was. Beany could only tell her what the shadow people had said about someone talking about harming her unborn child.

Stanley and Alex decided to go help Jr. Ceffus look for Michael before darkness fell. They drove separate cars through different subdivisions. They hoped to see him playing in someone's yard. They saw no sign of the boy.

Beany decided to call detective Teddy Warden to see if he could help her find Tavone and get some answers. She rose from the sofa, got the phone, and went to her bedroom. She dialed his number. For some reason he answered the phone before it rang.

"Hello!"

"Hey," said Teddy, surprised. "I was just getting ready to call you. I have some information for you, information which I found a little weird."

"What? Is it about Tavone?"

"Yeah. It was something that my father shared with me."

"That's funny, because that's what I was calling you about," said Beany. "Please tell me what your father knows."

"Remember me telling you the two brothers were white? One of them, they called him Little Charles, was found in 1979, barb-wired to a tree and burned to death."

"Yes, I remember that. I even found the newspaper clips. His name was Charles Ray Csontos. He was twenty-eight years old. What about him?"

"Well, when I visited my father, we just so happened to get on the subject of my having a girlfriend. I guess he wants me to get married again. I told him about your mother and about you and said that I had done a little research on the Csontos family."

Beany held the phone, listening to him carry on about Beatrice, wishing he would get to the point. After Teddy finished explaining how they got on the subject of Tavone, Beany began to listen in closely.

"Anyway, my father, who is now in a rest home, worked that case right before he retired. He has a memory deficiency and seems to remember more of what happened thirty years ago than what happened five minutes ago."

"Sorry to hear that," said Beany.

"Well, he's a fighter. He told me that he worked the case where Charles Csontos was set on fire. He said that after reading the book *Three Damned Lies* by Donnie, he believes Tavone had something to do with his brother's murder. But he doesn't think that Tavone actually did it."

"How did he figure that?" asked Beany.

"My father said that when they found Charles Csontos' remains, he saw grown male shoe prints by the body, along with children's shoeprints. Plus, if children did it, they would not have been able to tie the body up to the tree like that."

"How did your father come up with Tavone having anything to do with his brother's murder?"

"Because Tavone's brother was investigated earlier that year for having some boys over to his house and trying something with one of them. The girl he was living with confirmed it and left him because of it. Now, remember their father molested Tavone's brothers when they were boys, as well. He then told me to read the book and I would get the clues.

"Well, I called today because your mom called me and told me that Teeny Baby's son is missing. For some reason I feel like Tavone could help you all find him."

Beany realized she was no longer in danger. Teddy picking up the phone at the same time she was thinking of calling was no accident. She begged for Teddy to call as soon as he could determine Tavone's whereabouts.

"Okay. If I can find him, I will call you back. In the meantime, you should contact the Kelly Glass Foundation and have them do an Amber alert. Time is crucial in a situation like this."

"We will as soon as I get off the phone," said Beany.

"Why haven't y'all called already?"

"Because we were waiting to see if Stanley, Alex, or his father came up with anything first."

"Well, you guys had better get on the ball. Tell your mother I said to call me if you come up with something else."

"Okay. Bye!"

"Goodbye."

Beany hung up and went to tell everyone what Teddy had just told her. Soon Alex, Stanley, and Jr. Ceffus came back to Beatrice's. They had no idea where Michael was. They decided to take Teddy's advice and get some help from the police. Beatrice decided to call Officer Hutton to find out what steps they should take.

Once they contacted Officer Hutton, she advised them to hold still, and she would be there in a few minutes. When she arrived, she began to question Teeny Baby and Jr. Cefuss about the last time they had seen their son. Both remembered him getting up, eating breakfast, and going back into his room. Teeny explained that he spent a lot of time in his room playing with his Xbox. She was sure that's where he was when Beany picked her up for church.

Jr. Ceffus thought that Michael had gone with Teeny Baby to church, so he didn't bother to look for him when he got up. He explained that he had worked in the yard most of Saturday with Michael.

Officer Hutton said most of the time twenty-four hours had to pass before the department would issue an alert. Because of his age, she would start looking for him. She also asked if she could use their computer to start looking at other ways to get information.

After getting all the right authorities involved, Officer Hutton then asked the McDuffy's if they knew any friends, they could call to organize a group to search the wooded areas. Jr. Cefuss got on the phone and called Lips, Bucky, and a few other people in the neighborhood. They mapped out the areas they would search. They planned for an hour, gathering flashlights, and other equipment they needed to tackle the thick-brushed woods.

Beatrice asked everyone present to come into the living room. She then instructed all to gather in a circle and hold hands. She then led everyone in a prayer for Michael, letting faith and hope combined as a light that would guide him home safely.

Right in the midst of prayer, there was a knock at the door.

CHAPTER 20

Something Unimaginable

Had God answered their prayer so soon? Was Michael at the door? Beatrice excitedly rushed to open it. When Beatrice cracked the door and peeped to see who it was, she could not believe her eyes. Tavone was standing there, sweat pouring down his face.

Beany had been looking for Tavone for the last six weeks, hoping to apologize for her behavior over the years. After Teddy gave Beany the information about Tavone, she'd wanted to contact him for many different reasons. The one thing she really knew was he had answers – and plenty of them.

"What brings you here?" asked Beany, happy to see her father perhaps for the first time.

"I heard the Amber alert over the radio and rushed to see if I could help."

"Well, I think you have helped enough," said Beatrice.

"Now, Mama, please don't start."

"Damn! Look who's talking," said Beatrice. "Just a few months ago, you couldn't stand the man."

"Look," said Officer Hutton, "we don't have time for this petty stuff. We need to get the team together and start looking."

"Tavone, can I please see you in my room for a moment? I have a few things I want to talk about," Beany said.

"Beany," said Beatrice, "this is not the time to be sitting around trying to make amends with your father. We have work to do."

"I know, Mama, but what I have to discuss with him may..."

Beany stopped what she was about to say to her mother and asked Tavone to come with her.

Beatrice flushed with anger.

"If he's gonna help look for Michael, the people are ready to go. Now."

"They can go ahead. I can catch up with them."

"No, thank you," said Stanley and Alex, knowing what Beany was up to. "We can wait for y'all. There are a few different places that we want to look anyway," Alex said, trying to think of an excuse so they would not have to let Beany leave with Tavone.

Jr. Ceffus got together the rest of the helpers and moved out. Tavone followed Beany back to her bedroom. Beany closed and locked the door and then turned on her CD player just loud enough so no one could hear the two talking.

"Tavone, first I want to apologize to you for the way I've been acting all these years. I guess you could say I was hurt finding out that Harry wasn't my real father. I know that it's no fault of yours ... well, I guess some of the fault is yours. But I'm slowly getting over that."

"I, too, am sorry. There's so much I've kept secret. I wish I had someone to talk to about it. I figured after a while, you would find out about me ... and start looking for answers. I'm just sad that we had to meet like this," said Tavone. He fought the tears that rose in his eyes.

"Well, I have some questions to ask you, and they will not be too nice."

"Hey, I have some answers that won't be too nice either."

Beany told him about hiring a detective to find out as much as possible about him. She then informed him of all the things the detective had discovered and why she wanted to know more about him. She told him about the dreams that she'd been having and about the stories about the baby. Tavone felt that she had found out so much about him, that it was time he told his version of the truth and how he may know where Michael was.

"Beany, everything that you have found out about me is true. I am the brother of James Earl and Charles Csontos. Our father used to molest both. If I had been able to stay with them, I would have been in the same boat. James Earl and I were pretty close ... as close as we could get for me being his half brother and black. I didn't know that he was having those problems, fighting the demons that crawled in his blood like Charles. As close as he and I were, we weren't as close as he and Charles.

"So why didn't you want anyone to know that they were your brothers?" asked Beany.

"Because my mother made a promise after they paid for us to move to Virginia. To get the money for a fresh start, she had to promise never to discuss this situation again. That promise, along with discovering that my grandfather had been a Klansman, made me ashamed of who I was. So, I helped her keep the promise.

"But now I have to face this. When Donnie wrote that book, I knew I was in trouble. I was surprised that no one came looking for me earlier. In a way Donnie carried a sheaf of secrets to his grave. It was like he was protecting not only Maurice, but me as well. Maybe it was a way of saying thanks to us as well."

"Why?" Beany asked.

"Because of something that happened."

"What are you talking about? The murder of your brother?"

"Yes, something like that."

"I just want to know one thing. Am I or my baby in any danger?" Beany asked, shivering.

"No," Tavone answered.

Tavone then asked Beany if she could just listen and let him tell her what he thought was happening. He wanted to explain the reason they must find Michael before it was too late.

"It wasn't until later that I learned that Maurice was the one who actually killed my brother Charles. Donnie felt loyal even before the three murders that he talked about in his book. Because Donnie had chickened out …"

"Chickened out of what?" Beany asked, struggling to keep up.

"Stacy and James Earl went to hang out one night and left the boys with Charles. Being that David was the oldest of the boys, I gave him my number and told him to call me if he ever needed me. He called me and told me that Charles was trying to make them do things. The boys were young. I think David was eleven, Donnie was about nine, and Maurice was about six. I jumped in my car and drove as quickly as I could to Charles' house to get the boys. When I got there, I walked in. Charles had Donnie doing some real crazy shit. I knocked his ass out and drug him into the woods. I had the boys come with me, not wanting to leave them by themselves. I just wanted to scare him. I tied him to a tree and left him for dead, hoping something would get him while he was out there.

"A few weeks later – right on Pinch Gut Road – in the same neighborhood, Charles molested and killed Donnie and Maurice's cousin. He was sentenced to prison, but he escaped and hid out in the rural area. I hunted him down, knowing he was hiding in the same places we used to play when we were kids. I tied him up to that same tree and let Donnie and his brothers do what they wanted to with him. David, the oldest boy, gave Donnie a gun to kill him since Donnie was the one who got molested by Little Charles. Donnie couldn't do it. So, six-year-old Maurice took the gun from Donnie's hands, without Donnie putting up much of a fight, and shot Charles Csontos in the groin twice. Then they set him on fire. That's why Donnie wanted to keep his little brother out of harm's way. He tried to keep him safe ... all the way to his grave.

"When Maurice killed those three women, Donnie felt it was his duty to take the fall. Since Maurice had overcome so much to become a doctor and psychologist, and especially since Maurice was helping other young kids, Donnie thought Maurice was more valuable than he was. If Donnie learned any lesson in the military, he learned what it meant to be expendable.

"I think Maurice had a dual personality. He seemed shy and calm, until someone threatened or hurt someone he loved. He read a lot of comic books and wanted to be a superhero like one of his favorite characters. Heroic Man, a character in one of the comic books, taught that you should slay the monster that threatens or hurts your loved ones.
Maurice came home feeling proud that he had killed the monster.

"He asked his mother if he could spend the night at my house. That's when I learned what they had done to my brother. He was surprisingly calm for a boy his age. He showed no remorse. He only cared that he or his brothers would not be harmed again. He did have nightmares at times, because of the uncle he'd shot and then watched burn alive, screaming and yelling."

Tavone explained that the detective, Teddy Warden's dad, now retired, came around and questioned the boys. He probably had enough evidence to send them away for what they done, but he never turned the boys, or me, in. He applauded them and would let them, and their friends visit him often.

Beany remembered Detective Teddy Warden telling her that his father, an old man and retired detective, seventy-seven, said the boys used to come by the house. Tavone confirmed what Beany said. He explained that the detective had learned of the murder and burning of an escaped convict by putting two and two together.

"He knew that Donnie, Maurice, and David had something to do with it, but he took his feeling for the boys to heart. He had worked on other cases with my family, but no one outside of his jurisdiction would listen to him. Maybe it was because he was a black detective investigating a white family. The old man's son, however, never felt like his dad should have spent so much time with the boys, and he grew resentful. He grew up to become the detective in *Three Damned Lies*. He is the one you chose to find out about me."

Beany sat, never saying a word. She knew Tavone had more to tell her.

"My brother, James Earl, was released from prison last summer. He moved back into the house on Pinch Gut Road, not too far from where Little Charles was found burned. I lost contact with him over the years. Until the trial, I didn't know that he was doing that to those boys. I think he is still sick. I believe he may have Michael. I also think the ghosts knew he was coming back and that's why they came to you to stop him. I should have told you that he was getting out. I bought the house from those people so James Earl could have somewhere to stay while he tried to get himself back together. He promised me that he was a changed man. But if he has that boy, I want to find him before the police do and put him out of his misery."

Beany had more questions that she wanted to ask Tavone, but she knew time was precious. She and Tavone left the bedroom and went to let Stanley and Alex know that they had to go to the house on 423 Pinch Gut Road. Michael might be there, she said. Beany asked Alex and Stanley not to let anyone know where they were going unless they needed help.

Alex and Stanley both wanted to question Beany and Tavone, but there was no time for explanations. Beany told them that she would tell them as much as she and Tavone knew on the way to Pinch Gut Road. They were not to call anyone else.

Before Tavone got into the car with the rest, he went to his car to retrieve a black bag.

"We are up against something unimaginable."

Only Beany knew what he was talking about. Even she had no idea that Tavone felt so strongly about what he was facing.

As they headed north to Riddles, Beany and Tavone tried to explain why they thought Michael was at the house. Stanley remembered that when he and Beany had stopped by the house, he thought he'd seen a man standing at the door as they pulled off. Since a "For Rent" sign was in the yard, he thought his mind was just playing games on him.

Alex thought about when Dr. Milado had told him he would help save someone close to the family, and how he would be a medium for Beany. He remembered her saying his touch would guide them past the wall. Out of all the things Dr. Milado had shared with Alex, that one thing had stuck with him. He didn't know how this would come in to play tonight, but he would soon find out, he guessed.

"Beany," Alex asked, "didn't you call Michael your 'Baby Boy'?"

"Yes, I have always called him that."

"Then maybe that's the baby boy that the ghosts were talking about. And you were thinking it was your baby."

Beany thought about the Cripple Cries incantations she'd sung when she played with the children from Pinch Gut Road. She began to go over it in her head, trying to figure out if something could help them once they got to the house.

Cripple... cries

Dancing... lies

The truth shall come at... night

Lonely... walls

Tear that... falls

When guided by the light

Dead man... sick

Still he's set... free
Gonna burn you...if you cry
His blood is... yours
Under his basement floor
He's gonna get you before he dies

"He is there," Beany cried out. "He is at the house, and he is locked in the basement. There is a window, and he can see cars coming. He will see us when we drive up. We got to stop the car and walk when we get close."

"How do you figure that?" Alex asked.

"Trust me. I know. He's in there. I can even feel him crying ... and he's hurting. We must hurry! It's this thing the children and I used to sing when we jumped rope called 'Cripple Cries.' It's like they were helping me prepare for this day."

"Just like in Donnie's book of poems and when he wrote about hearing that on the plane," said Stanley.

At this point everyone's heart was pumping with excitement. A determination came over them, a will to save Michael. Their heartbeats soon turned irregular when they turned onto Pinch Gut Road.

Alex was driving well over the speed limit when the car started to slow down and lose power. The light started to go out, and Beany started to lapse into some trace-like state. She was unable to speak or to stay awake. Everyone in the car knew that they were dealing with a strong demonic spirit. They also knew they had to drive on.

Soon the car came to a squelching halt. The porch light was on at the house at 432 Pinch Gut, but something was trying to keep them from getting past. All of a sudden, everyone was staring, seeing what held them back. They had appeared – images of men...dead men... the Haints of Pinch Gut Road, wearing white robes with hoods covering their heads and hideous faces. There was a squelching sounds of tortured souls crying to be set free inside the robes of the Haints as they moved toward the car... floating above the ground. The Haints came near the car making dreadful noises and with a smell that would wake up the rest of dead. A nasty blue fog began to circle Pinch Gut Road.

Soon, the car was surrounded, the dead standing heads down and arms placed in front of them. Fifteen or more mounted not letting them pass.

This event marked the first time Alex or Stanley had seen anything of the kind, and they were scared as could be.

Alex, being Alex, and because of the dreadful smell, yelled out loudly, "who in the hell done gone and shit on them self?" he then stopped and said, "oops never mind...that might have been me."

Rev. Tavone McKnight said, "I think the smell is the gates of hell opening, around us" as he began to pray for all to be released from the circle. Suddenly, the elder of the group came out of nowhere. The group of hooded figures standing around the car began to part, letting an old white crippled man through the wall they had positioned around the car. As he got closer to the car, Tavone recognized him as his late grandfather, Mark Henry Csontos.

By now Beany was totally unconscious. While unconscious, Beany began to see visions of what had happened to little Michael, the boy that she had for years called her 'Baby Boy' and her little boyfriend."

***

Michael had gotten up early that morning, even before Teeny Baby had gotten up to get ready for church. He wanted to go down to Indian Town Creek to fish. He gathered his fishing gear and tied it to the rack Jr. Ceffus had built onto his bike. He headed out on his five-mile bike ride. He went through Riddles and down Pinch Gut Road on his way to the creek. An old blue pick-up truck came speeding up behind him and ran him into the ditch. The truck then turned around and came back, pulling over to the side of the road. James Earl stepped out of the truck and offered to give Michael a hand. Michael had no idea who he was reaching for.

"Where are you headed, little buddy?" asked James Earl.

"I'm headed to Indian Town Creek to do a little fishing."

"Trying to catch those trout going back up stream, are ya?"

"Yes, sir ... I sure am."

James Earl reached down into the ditch to retrieve Michael's bike.

"Hey! Didn't catch the name, boy."

"Michael," the boy said. "My name is Michael, Michael McDuffy."

"Well, looks like you are going to need a ride because your bike is a bit dismantled. Maybe I can give you a ride back to the house."

Michael remembered not to ride with or talk to strangers, but he didn't want to leave his bike or fishing gear as he walked back home. Being that he wasn't too far from the house, he decided to accept the ride back with James Earl. After James Earl put Michael's bike, fishing poles, and buckets onto the back of the truck, he opened the passenger door to let Michael into the car. Once in the car James Earl turned the truck around and he headed back up Pinch Gut Road. Michael suddenly felt he was in trouble. His house was in the opposite direction.

"Sir, where are we going? I live the other way."

"Boy, I know where the fuck you live at," James Earl said.

As James Earl drove towards Pinch Gut Road, he saw a car coming and pulled out his gun. He demanded that Michael pull his head down so no one could see him. As the car drove past him, he stared directly into the eyes of Beany as she drove past him to pick up Teeny Baby for church. She remembered not paying too much attention until he passed. She had started to get a strange feeling as she looked out her rear-view mirror and saw that he had turned around once more to look at her.

***

Alex didn't know what to do. With Beany passed out on the passenger side, Tavone asked Stanley to reach behind the back seat of the SUV and get the black bag that he'd put in earlier.

As Stanley reached for the bag, Old Man Csontos commanded everyone to take off their hoods. Tavone started to see people that he'd known when he was a little kid going to work with his mother at the Csontos house. They were all part of the dead Klansmen who tortured the black families and took their land. With Alex behind the wheel and Beany up front in the passenger side, Alex worried more about Beany and tried not to focus on the ghost. He wanted to make sure that they didn't overpower her or get inside her head.

When Stanley got the bag and turned around to hand it to Tavone, he noticed the ghosts with their hoods off. He saw their angry faces. Panic gripped him. He kicked the car windows and screamed for them to go away. He tried to rouse Beany. Alex told Stanley not to look at them and to think of Beany and how they could help Michael.

Tavone reached into his bag and got out his Bible. He flipped to Luke 8:26-29 and read the words:

26 And they arrived at the country of the Gadarenes, which is over against Galilee.

27 And when he went forth to land, there met him out of the city a certain man, which had devils long time, and ware no clothes, neither abode in any house, but in the tombs.

28 When he saw Jesus, he cried out, and fell down before him, and with a loud voice said, What have I to do with thee, Jesus, thou Son of God most high? I beseech thee, torment me not.

29 (For he had commanded the unclean spirit to come out of the man. For oftentimes it had caught him: and he was kept bound with chains and in fetters; and he brake the bands, and was driven of the devil into the wilderness.)

As Tavone continued to read from Luke 8 in the language of the Kings James version, the demons surrounding the car seemed to weaken....

But they were smart. Like the Devil himself, they knew what it took to confuse Tavone. Dead Old Man Mark Henry started to rip his robe down the middle and from out of his robe came Charles, his younger brother. Tavone kept reading the scriptures, trying to stay focused and get to Michael before it was too late. All the ghosts wanted was for them to put the truck in reverse and leave so that they could have Michael when James Earl was done with him.

Alex tried help to Beany. He began thinking of everything he could to make some kind of connection. Then Dr. Milado's words came back to him. She had said that all the people Beany had bonded with the family were necessary. Dr. Milado told him the circle would make them strong and that Beany would lead them through the light.

With so much happening so fast, Alex yelled for everybody to gather around Beany and to interlock fingers with each other, making the best circle they could in the car. Stanley and Tavone were asking why, but this was not the time for explaining. Crisis was never time for explaining, Alex reminded them.

Once they got in the best circle they could form in a vehicle, Beany, still unconscious, began to talk.

"Close your eyes and help me call them. They want to hear me. They want to know that I need them. They want to help save him."

Stanley and Beany had many conversations about everything she had been seeing, what they were saying, and what everything meant. He knew that she was talking about the dead children on Pinch Gut Road. The ghost-children wanted to help her. He begged Tavone and Alex to do as she said. He had a feeling that he knew what she was talking about.

As they closed their eyes, Beany started to call for help, but she could not do it alone. They tried to come, but Beany needed more help.

"You have to help me call them. You must believe that they will help us. Help me call for them. Believe they will come to help us," said Beany, still in her state of unconsciousness.

"Who do we call?" asked Stanley.

"Just call some damned body," said Alex. "This shit is driving me nuts."

They began to call on people they knew who had died on Pinch Gut Road, especially their friends. After a few seconds, they were calling for everybody they knew who had passed on to glory. They asked for their help, begged for their help. Alex, who loved rap music, started to call his favorite rappers for help: Big Papa, Tupac, Big Pun, Left Eye, and one of the Fat Boys.

"Help me ... Baby baa-baaa!"

"This ain't no time for jokes," Stanley admonished.

"I'm not joking. See. It's working, isn't it?"

Within seconds, Beany opened the car door and began to walk among the phantasmal creatures. Striving to keep the circle, Alex, Stanley and Tavone made sure that they kept their fingers interlocked with each other and around Beany. Beany advised all to follow the light so they would not get distracted. They felt the disembodied spirits touching them. The Klan spirits were unable to harm them. Instead, they could hear screams, screams that faded as if the hooded demons were being snatched away by some other force. Beany knew she was getting help from the old black folk spirits from Pinch Gut Road.

Beany stopped walking and fell to the ground, still unconscious and still unaware. Alex opened his eyes hoping that he would not see anything, trying to help Beany. The coast was clear, and he told the others that they, too, could open their eyes. They were within yards of the house. The light that led them to the house came from the basement. Tavone made sure he'd brought his bag. He didn't want to leave the one thing that he knew would stop his brother from hurting any more children.

CHAPTER 21

The Madness Stops

Since Beany was passed out, Alex asked Stanley to stay with Beany. Tavone and Alex went toward the house hoping it was not too late to save Michael. When they got to the door, Alex waited until Tavone went around to the back of the house before knocking. Tavone knew a key was always kept under a stump around back in case someone needed to get in. He tried to peep through the window, but it was dark inside. When Alex felt Tavone was around the back, he began to bang on the door, calling for James Earl to answer. No one came to the door, so he took off his shirt, wrapped it around his fist, and began to punch the glass. He reached through the broken glass and turned the door handle. As soon as he stepped inside, he was met with a shovel to the head, knocking him out cold. James Earl turned and went to the basement.

As Tavone was fumbling around back looking for the key, he noticed a freshly dug grave prepared for someone. He found the key and ran to the back door. The back door led straight to the entrance to the basement. By the time Tavone got to where Michael was, James Earl was standing over Michael, shovel raised in the air.

Tavone made a quick reach into his handbag and pulled out his chrome-plated .45, the same gun the boys had used on his brother Charles.

"Please. Put the shovel down! I don't want to shoot you."

"Why not? You let them kill our brother," James Earl spat back at him.

"This boy has nothing to do with that. It's not his fault our brother could not keep his hands off those boys. He only got what was coming to him."

"Don't matter. He was still our brother. We could have helped him."

"Funny you say that. You spent almost twenty years incarcerated, and it didn't help you any. What makes you think that he could have been helped? The bad thing was that what Charles did to those boys was the same thing that our father did to ya'll, and what our father's father did to him – not to mention what you did to those boys when they were young ... and all the time calling yourself their stepfather," Tavone said.

"When does it stop?" Tavone yelled. "When?"

"Our father paid for you to be sent away from this mess," explained James Earl. "He never touched you the way he did Little Charles and me. You never had to put your mouth on him. I hated that man. I always wished I was black like you, so he could have paid for me to be sent away. When you were born, Dad told Little Charles and me that you were our brother. That's why Little Charles loved you so much. He hated knowing that our grandfather was not only a Klansman but a pervert as well. See....We used to get it from him, too, and sometimes from some of his drunk-ass friends. And you want to know when it's going to stop?"

"Put the shovel down," Tavone pleaded, but James Earl reared the shovel back to swing at Michael's head. Tavone fired and fired and fired, hitting James Earl in the shoulders, and landing two rounds in his back. James Earl fell to the floor. Tavone stood in a daze as he watched his brother take his last breaths.

"The madness stops now ... it stops now, James Earl, my brother," he whispered, tears wetting his face.

Tavone untied Michael and started to carry him up the stairs. James Earl rose from the floor as Tavone carried Michael, grabbed the gun from the floor, and took aim at Tavone.

"Rev. McKnight!" yelled Officer Hutton.

Tavone crouched with Michael on the stairs as Officer Hutton fired six more rounds, dropping James Earl to the floor. She then helped the two up the stairs.

"Where is Alex?" asked Tavone.

"He has a little bump on his head. He's been taken to the Albemarle Hospital to be checked out," said Officer Hutton.

"And how is Beany?"

Beany walked up to Tavone and gave him a hug.

"I'm fine, Daddy. Just fine. Thanks for being here for me."

Tavone buried his face in his daughter's shoulder and wept.

CHAPTER 22

Straight to Therapy

Two years had passed since Tavone helped save Michael from James Earl. Now Tavone was considered a hero in Camden. When The New Shady Creek Baptist Church needed a new pastor, the board members requested Tavone's services. Tavone was reluctant to take the position, but when Beany and her husband Stanley asked if he would do the honors of christening their son, Stanley Deya Miles II., Tavone figured what would be better than to christen the child in his own church. He decided to take the job. He reacquainted himself with a lady he had met when he was attending Elizabeth State. Tavone felt his turn had come to have the love that had been missing in his life. He also felt God had called him back to Camden to help the community.

Tavone was entitled to more than two hundred acres of land once owned by his grandfather, Mark Henry Csontos. He felt the land belonged to the families that had suffered from his ancestors' deceit years before. If he had had a couple of mules to go with the forty acres, he would have thrown them in, too. Most of the families entitled to the land decided to pass on the offer. They feared they might see the same mean spirits that had been reported by Lucy Gray. After all, once Lucy got word of the stories about the night Michael was saved from James Earl

Csontos, she spread those stories with relish. So, Stanley decided to buy the land after Beany convinced him that all the demonic ghosts who had once roamed Pinch Gut Road were gone.

Now Riddles was as safe as any other township in Camden. Stanley understood that Riddles and Pinch Gut Road had a long history of dividing whites and blacks, so he wanted to build a recreational facility in the area. He got some of the prominent whites in Camden to help invest in breaking ground to start the building process. He figured this action would start a blending of those from different races and from different economic backgrounds. Many were relocating and making Camden their permanent residence. Of course, the new people would not know the history of the area.

Although Stanley and Beany thought building a rec center was a great idea, no one in the family believed it would work. Stanley and Beany wanted their son to grow up in a different Camden. They wanted to make sure that he didn't have to go through the things his great-great grandparents had caused blacks to suffer. They also wanted Pinch Gut Road's old ghosts to become just an old memory – a myth or a folk story.

Alex passed the bar and decided to move back to Camden to give affordable legal services to those who didn't want to use the cutthroat wacky lawyers like Willie "The Loser" Peterson. He also wanted to run for a seat in local government. The Honorable Jesse Daniel Hews was retiring in a few years, and Alex wanted to build a following that could help him win that judicial seat and put a new face on Camden justice. He made one important contribution that won him immediate respect. He remembered when he had gotten stopped in what he considered a speed trap as he traveled back and forth from college. Alex started a petition to get the speed limit changed between Camden High School and the Exxon Station. His petition worked and the limit was raised to 45 miles an hour after school hours instead of the 35-mph limit that had caught so many drivers unaware. That move alone almost assured him a seat as County Judge.

Tiffany, his two-year-old daughter, was the spitting image of Rosa. Her hair was as long as her mother's. Tiffany was the apple of Alex's eyes. Rosa was now teaching at Camden Middle School and was voted teacher of the year during her first-year teaching. She was the Spanish teacher and with all the Mexican immigrants moving into Camden, she had her hands full.

Alex was also on the board of education. He made sure that the teachers were highly qualified to teach and pushed for a higher supplement so good teachers could afford to stay in Camden.

After teaching just one year at Camden High, Beatrice felt she was not cut out to be a teacher. Instead, she thought she would do better staying at home and keeping her two grandbabies. She didn't feel too comfortable with the other teachers. Often when she would go into the teachers' lounge, other teachers would stop talking and look at her sheepishly. Sometimes, she overheard them talking about her or someone else in her family. She tried to stay professional, but when she heard the principal talking about Beany being a witch, Beatrice jumped to her daughter's defense and threatened to help the custodians by mopping the hallway floors with the principal's ass. The principal apologized to Beatrice, but the damage was done. Beatrice didn't understand how Rosa dealt with it. All Beatrice knew was that she was proud of her children and of her in-laws. She knew that Rosa and Beany were paying her way more than they should have for keeping their children. Every Christmas she would make sure that she saved up enough money from baby-sitting to buy the children special presents.

Like clockwork, every Sunday the family would meet over at Beatrice's house for Sunday dinner. Her love life was back in order as well. Teddy Warden had quit the detective business and taken on the care of his father. Beatrice made sure that Teddy was not lonely. She spent time helping Teddy with his father – and getting her back broke as much as possible. Teddy wanted to marry Beatrice, but she didn't want anyone to replace the vows that she had made to her beloved Harry. She did promise him that she would always be grateful that he'd come into her life and hoped that he would be with her to complete her journey on this earth.

Beatrice also kept a closer eye on Michael and made sure that she called Teeny Baby every now and again to make sure she was in good spirits. Teeny Baby was shaken up after Michael was found kidnapped by James Earl Csontos. She was not her usual outgoing self. She spent most of her time blaming herself and Jr. Cefuss for what Michael had gone through. Teeny and Jr. Cefuss barely talked. She would often have Michael sleep with her, fearing someone was going to sneak into the house and take him. Beatrice suggested that Teeny Baby get help. Like so many black families in Camden, Teeny Baby wanted to keep her problems within the family.

Michael had seen and been through too much. No one ever saw him without his mother. Rosa mentioned to Teeny Baby that maybe he should see a child psychologist. Teeny Baby refused. Rosa informed Teeny Baby that he was acting out at school. Michael was grabbing his private parts in front of the little girls at school and saying vulgar things to his teachers. The school tried to work with him because they knew what he had been through. Needless to say, his story was on the news. Of course, what the news didn't cover, Lucy Gray did. Even the school warned Teeny Baby that if she didn't get him help soon, he was going to get put out of regular school and placed in an alternative one. Teeny Baby swore that nothing was wrong with him and if the school tried to put Michael into an alternative school, she was going to sue. Jr. Cefuss, on the other hand, understood that something was wrong with Michael. He didn't feel as close to Michael as he once had. He called Beatrice once to ask if she could help him find somewhere to place Michael away from Teeny Baby so he could get Michael the help he needed. The problem was that every place Beatrice found required the consent of both parents. The end of the school year was near, and Jr. Cefuss knew if he could make it until the end of school, he could definitely get help for Michael before the start of the next school year.

With Beany's life in the most normal state, it had ever been, she felt sorry that Teeny Baby was going through so much with Michael and with her family. Teeny Baby had always been there for Beany when she was not comfortable telling her mother things. She felt the only right thing to do was give a party. She'd bring in a few friends to help Teeny Baby forget her problems for a day.

Beany knew that Teeny Baby's 50th birthday was coming up, and Beany wanted to give her a surprise party. After all, their parties always brought out the best spirits within the family and friend circle. Beany got on the phone and called Beatrice to ask what she thought about giving Teeny Baby a cookout for her birthday. Beatrice thought it was a good idea. She got on the phone and called Teeny Baby to see just what she had been up to.

"Hey, girl! What's been going on with you? Word on the street is that you have lost your damned mind."

"Word on what fucking street?" Teeny Baby asked. "You tell the word on the street to kiss my ass."

Then Teeny Baby hung up the phone.

Beatrice knew Teeny Baby wasn't herself. She needed tough love to get her back on her horse. That was the sixth time that week she had hung up on Beatrice. Beatrice figured the time had come to visit her buddy and make sure the word on the street wasn't a reality.

When Beatrice pulled up in the yard, Michael saw her and came running to the car. Teeny Baby was not too far behind him. She was yelling, telling him not to be running out to folks' cars. Beatrice, furious and tired of her best friend acting like a hermit, jumped out of the car.

"What do you mean, 'Running to folks' cars? What's wrong with you? You are going nuts. Now ... I am your friend, not 'folks.'"

"Well, you know what I meant. I'm not talking about you," said Teeny Baby trying to apologize and defend herself at the same time.

"Well, you need to say what you mean and mean what you say when you are addressing me. You never had that problem before. Lord! What's wrong widcha?"

"Ain't nothing wrong with me. Years ago, you used to say that I needed to keep a better eye on Michael. After what happened, I want to do just that."

"But don't you see what you are doing to him in the process? You are making him scared to trust people again, especially when you tell him he can't come running to me. He has known me his whole life, and now you are calling me 'folks' right in front of him. What kind of message is that sending him?"

"Well, if you've got a problem with it, you can get back into your car, and take your know-it-all ass back to the house."

Teeny, directed Michael into the house, went in behind him, and slammed the door.

Beatrice got back into the car. As she drove off, she left a trail of dust and rocks flying. Beatrice had always been a forgiving person and was even more tolerant of Teeny Baby. Teeny Baby knew she was in the wrong. She got on the phone and called Beatrice's cell before she turned onto the highway. Teeny Baby was pleading for Beatrice to come back so they could talk. Beatrice wanted to make Teeny Baby suffer, so she played with Teeny Baby's emotions for a few minutes.

"Girl, I wish I would turn around and go back down that dusty, pothole, dirty-ass trail! I have heard all I want to hear from your crazy ass," said Beatrice, secretly laughing inside.

"Please," Teeny Baby said. "I was just so ... Just come back. I need you really bad right now. I'm tired of this and I need to talk to you."

Once she knew Teeny Baby was torn up about what had just happened, Beatrice waited until a few cars passed, made a U-turn on the main highway, and headed back to Teeny Baby's.

Teeny Baby stood on the porch and watched as Beatrice drove back toward the house. Beatrice knew that Teeny Baby wanted to work her way out of her depression. She had wanted help over the past year but didn't know how to reach out for it. Beatrice stopped the car and got out.

"Come on up here on this porch, fool, and give me a hug," Teeny Baby said and then sobbed, "I sure could use one."

Beatrice held out her arms and Teeny fell into them. They stood for several minutes hugging and sobbing. Both took a seat on the glider porch swing, ready to talk about how they could help heal their friendship – and how they could get help for Michael. After a while, their old relationship, including the gruffness, seemed to be healed.

"First of all, Teeny Baby, where do you get off hanging up on me when I call you?" asked Beatrice, with mock severity.

"If you remember, you kept hanging up on me back when you found out about Harry and me. I tried to call you, but you played me like a football game."

"Yeah! But you HAD slept with my husband. What did you think I was going to do?"

"Okay. You've got a point there. It still doesn't change the fact that you hung up on me. How about when your mother died? I called and you never answered the phone. I left you alone until you got over it and felt like talking."

"True ... true ... but it didn't take me almost two years to get myself together."

"Well, you are here now, so how can we move on from here?"

"I think that you and I are just fine. It's your son that I am concerned about. I think that he needs some professional help. And I think that you and your husband need some help, as well."

"I know, but it's so hard to get help when this small, minded town always stays in your business."

"Teeny Baby, you can't worry about what other people say. Just look at what I've been through with Beany and her crazy psychic shit. And look at that book that Donnie wrote. The whole world knew about my family and we still persevered."

"Yeah but look at how it all turned out for you. Your children are successful, and that Beany married a millionaire. I don't give a damn if he did mess y'all up, at least at first, by publishing that book. I think he knew what he was doing."

"No matter. We got through all of it didn't we?"

"I guess you did," said Teeny Baby. "If you think I'm crazy now, if I had gone with those fools on Pinch Gut Road the night they saved Michael, I would really have lost my mind. Shit! The first time I saw one of those haint, ghost-things, Michael would have been in some real trouble."

"And we got through it with a lot of help from you. You were right there by my side with everything I went through, and you weren't judgmental. You practically helped me raise Beany and Alex. I just want to help you with your son and your family."

"Okay. So where do we start?"

"We start by getting Michael into some kind of therapy."

"That stuff is for white folks on the Oprah Show. That don't work for us."

"That's what I thought, too. But it sure helped change the way Beany and I got along."

"What? You mean to tell me that you and Beany went to see a shrink?"

"Sure did. Her little thing with seeing Harry, my mother, and all those other dead folks was starting to drive me up the wall. Remember when I told you that I was taking Beany to dance lessons?"

"Yeah."

"Well, we were dancing alright. Dancing our asses straight to therapy."

"I used to wonder why I never saw a tutu or dancing costume. That's why when I asked you about the recital, you said she didn't like dancing and quit."

"Yep. You got it ... and trust me, the therapy helped."

"But you had the money to do it. I don't have that type of money."

"See ...that's when friends help other friends. Beany, Alex, Stanley – and all the others who love you so much – and I wanted to give you and your family a party. Stanley suggested that we have it during the grand opening of the recreation center on Pinch Gut Road and maybe raise a few bucks."

"Now, I'm not trying to take any handouts, and I damned sure don't think I need to be on Pinch Gut Road trying to do anything. Don't forget that's where my baby went through that horrible ordeal."

"I know what you are saying, but this is how I feel about it. First, you have to face your fears. Pinch Gut isn't the same Pinch Gut it used to be. Beany said the children that she used to see never visit anymore. Now, when she said that about Harry, I never had anymore problems seeing him around the house. She said that they are at rest. Plus, if you think about it, they are the ones that helped Michael."

"Do you really believe that?"

"I don't know, but you should hear the stories that Stanley and Alex told."

"Well, I'll think about it and get back with you."

Beatrice and Teeny Baby sat on the porch and talked until dark, and time came for Beatrice to go. Teeny Baby went into the house and shared the suggestion with Jr. Cefuss. He wasn't too thrilled about the fundraiser event or about having it on Pinch Gut Road, but he did agree that his family needed help.

CHAPTER 23

The Michael McDuffy Youth Center

The Grand Opening of the Center was the next day, and Beatrice had yet to hear from Teeny Baby. Stanley was at the center with the inspectors making sure everything was in order. Everyone met at Beatrice's house and tried to figure out how they were going to present the money that had been raised for the McDuffy's. They didn't want to make the family feel uncomfortable by taking up money for them, yet they knew the family needed it. Finally, Alex came up with a plan. If Jr. Cefuss or Teeny Baby decided to come, they would put the money into an envelope and give it to them, without making a big fuss. If they did not come to the grand opening, all their closest friends and family would meet them at their house and make them take it.

***

The day of the opening was the most beautiful day Pinch Gut Road ever had the pleasure of experiencing since the birth of the land. New houses were springing up all over Riddles. Neighbors, blacks and whites, and a few others that had moved from the neighboring states were building at a rapid pace. Pinch Gut would surely need the center.

Balloons and a big sign that Stanley had custom made gave the building a festive look. A statue wrapped in a large blanket stood in front of the building. At twelve noon, a crowd of people started to fill the parking lot. The grills started to smoke, leaving the smell of roasted pig in the air to blend with the pine trees. The pines helped wave the aroma throughout the Riddles community, alerting the attendees that hadn't arrived that the ceremony was at hand.

Soon the mayor of Camden, Stanley, two investors, and Rev. Tavone McKnight took their seats behind the podium. Beany, Alex, Rosa, Beatrice, Teddy, and the kids made their way to the V.I.P chairs that faced the makeshift stage. Other seats on the front row also bore names: Michael, Sara May, and Jeffery McDuffy, but the McDuffy's were nowhere to be found.

Since the crowd was getting larger, Beatrice got Stanley's attention and signaled for him to start the ceremony. Stanley asked the reverend to open the ceremony with a blessing. Stanley introduced the guests and those who were responsible for making the recreational center happen. Each speaker took his or her turn praising the center and explaining why it was so important both for the community and for Camden. Then the time came to reveal the statue in front of the building.

That would have been the time for Stanley to call the McDuffys up to the stage. Stanley began to walk slowly to the podium, hoping Teeny Baby and company would appear out of nowhere like in a good movie.

"I would now like to unveil the statue. Before I do, I wanted to give you a little history behind it," said Stanley. The seated crowd had to turn their heads to get a glimpse of the unveiling. Beatrice looked at Beany. Beany stared with a smile. Rosa and Alex caught Beany smiling and knew something was about to happen.

Stanley saw Beany with the look that he'd become accustomed to seeing. Something special was getting ready to happen. He just knew it. But he just didn't know what. Then Stanley cleared his voice and continued.

"This statue that my friends and I decided to place here today was built as a dedication to a young man who, in some ways, brought us and this community together. Almost two years to this date, he was riding on his bike. He was just trying to find something to do. He was kidnapped in this very spot. He's one of my heroes. I was hoping that he and his family could be here today so they could see and feel the love we have for him. I wanted them to realize how much we all appreciate him. Since he couldn't make it here today, I would like for my wife to pull the rope, removing the blanket, especially since Michael actually wanted to marry her first."

The crowd began to laugh.

Beany left her seat and moved to the statue. Out of nowhere, a loud horn started to blow, and a blue 1975 Buick Electra 225 came flying up to the center.

It was Mr. John D. speeding to the rescue.

Jr. Cefuss' car would not start. Since Camden had no taxis, the McDuffys had to call the next best thing, Mr. John D.

When the car came to a stop, Teeny Baby and Michael rushed to the ceremony, hoping that they hadn't missed all of it. Jr. Cefuss made sure that he paid Mr. John D. Mr. John D. blew his horn again as he drove off, not understanding – and not caring – that a ceremony was taking place.

Stanley introduced Michael and asked him to join Beany.

"That's what's up," said Michael as he ran over to help. Teeny Baby took her seat beside Beatrice and leaned over.

"Girl! That old-ass man damned near scared me to death. The only stop sign in Camden – and he ran right through it."

"Who?"

"Mr. John D."

"Well, you're here safe, aren't you?" snickered Beatrice.

"Yeah, by the Grace of God," Teeny Baby replied.

"I didn't think that you were going to come."

"I wasn't, but when I thought about someone besides myself, then I wouldn't have missed it for the world."

Stanley had the crowd count down to unveiling the statue.

Ten

Nine

Eight

Seven

Six

Five

Four

Three

Two

One

Beany and Michael pulled the rope, dropping the cover. There stood the image of Michael holding a basketball. Everyone clapped and cheered. Two of the speakers loosened four more ropes, releasing the grand opening sign.

"We now present to you the Michael McDuffy Youth Center."

Stanley then broke a bottle of apple-cider to mark the official opening. A teary-eyed Jr. Cefuss, along with the rest of the family, went to stand on center stage to thank everyone who had anything to do with the center. Then they asked Michael if he had anything to say.

"Thanks," he said. "Now let's eat and play."

Without making a big scene, Stanley walked up to Jr. Cefuss and Teeny Baby while they were in line to eat and called them to the side. Teeny Baby complained that she was trying to get her grub on. She told Jr. Cefuss to go ahead and that she would save him a spot for when he came back. Like always, Jr. Cefuss did exactly as Teeny instructed him.

"How can I help you?" asked Jr. Cefuss.

"No," said Stanley. "It's how can I help you. I wanted to give you a little something that the community got together. We thought you might need it to get you and your family back on the right track. I know you went through a lot, and I hope that this can help Michael get the help that he needs."

In the envelope was a check for fifty thousand dollars and a referral to the best doctor and psychologist in town.

"I don't know what to say," said Jr. Cefuss.

"Just say that you will take care of my baby boy," said Beany, as she held her little son cradled in her arms.

As Beany continued to talk to Jr. Ceffus, she couldn't help but keep an eye on the shadow people who stood at the edge of the road on guard, waiting for Tavone to eat his last meal.

The

End

About This Story

Being that this story had to happen, I knew I would have to use my most creative juices.

I poured a cup my imagination into a bucket of verisimilitude to bring it to life. After all, what is a good fiction story if you can't believe that most of it happened.

Those of you familiar with '**Three Lies f.s.i.t.d pt 2**', will hopefully understand and enjoyed reading '**Pinch Gut Road f.s.i.t.d pt3**'. The thought process I put into this was bananas. I am so grateful that the characters took over the story and made it interesting. I also feel it's time to let you know, the wait is almost over. The next book of this trilogy will be coming. '**4th Sunday in the Dirty f.s.i.t.d pt1**'... The beginning'. And for those that haven't figured it out yet, '**f.s.i.t.d**' stands for "Fourth Sunday in The Dirty". This is the book that started it all and the story that left my fans wanting more...So until than...I'll...

See you the soon!

Kent Hughes

About the Author

Kent Hughes is a native of Camden North Carolina. He lives in Raleigh North Carolina with his wife!!

Black Frame:
Life-Inspired Poetry
by
Kent Hughes

Introduction

I decided, since **Pinch Gut Road** ends where **Three Lies** begins, I would keep with the tradition by adding a few new poems into the mix. Most of the poems you will read are about love. Either I was in love, trying find love or found love. Read closely there maybe a little story behind some of the poems, so read enjoy!!

Just Maybe

I thought by now, I would have run out of words
Wrote too many metaphors that you've already heard
And your memories of me, would be a distance blare
Or that you would read with less feelings or not even care
I thought by now I 'd fade, like sunshine does the rain
Wrote too many "your beautifuls" and you'd think I'm insane
And your memories of me, would be less joy and more pain
Or that you would read unenthused, like some sick love game
And then…
I thought…well, maybe I am just wrong,
Maybe she loves me, like lyrics in love songs
And her memories of me, made her burst into sweat
Or she
read it with feelings, hmmm, just imagine that
I thought just maybe I would be the man of her dreams
Write her so many "your beautifuls "it makes her heart scream.
And her memories of me, would make her do anything
Or that she would think she was in love and call me her King
But No matter what…its more than a fling`, since my heart is at
her place, that makes her my queen.

Note: Some of these poems a very old, over 20 years at least…but this poem
had to be first one I selected to put in here because I wrote it for my Mrs.
Tiffnii Hughes

Die Empty

I want to leave this world without you questioning if I loved you
or not…simple…I love you

I want to die empty…because I mentally gave you all the love I
have and…more

If I said it and it broke your heart, believe me, I was broken too

If I didn't say I am sorry,

I am…

And this is my apology to you.

If I held on too long

It's all because

My vision wasn't always clear

If I let you go and you did not know

It means you really didn't need me there

If I tried to help you with what I had

If you think I could 've done even better

Then I apologize as I realize

I was no match for your stormy weather

But if my existence

And presence in life

Make you feel I'm necessary

For me to exist

Here's the twist…

I want to leave this world without you questioning if I loved you
or not…simple…I love you

I want to die empty…because I mentally gave you all the love I have and…more

Explained in your Beautiful

Explained in your beautiful…

Understood in your tone…Comfort in the smile you wear

Caught in a daze…Your beautiful out weights

My heavens when…God placed you here

Hugging your rhythm… kissing your motion

You move me without taking a step

In your arms I belong…Be it right or be it wrong

Be it whatever the gods have left

Your eyes… could train my sun to shine

Your smile… my world to sing

Carrying a tone now… perfect song… and some how

In your beautiful we can do anything

A taste of wine… A Rembrandt painted perfect

You are more… to me…than just you

You are my wish as a child…My perfect smile

You're my… prayer …that somehow came true

The smile, the heart, the touch, the peace

The way your sexy flows…

Understood in your tone…Can't leave this daydream alone…

All …Explained… in your beautiful

by kh

24/7 Feels

When you ask God for anything, you also must have faith in the answer you will receive and... the answer that is intended.

I asked, if He would allow me to fall in love and show me what being in love felt like...because I really felt as though I never had that experienced before.... ever

I truly believe he sent me one of his angels (you) to have that experience with.

I believe that I connected with every emotion a man could feel and it happened without me having any control of it...I literally had to calm myself down...now I understand that...

Love and pain are not friends...I now understand what it's like wanting to be with someone 24/7 feels like...needing that person in your presences...hearing their voice...wanting them to feel what you are feeling...and most of all not wanting to ever control anything about that feeling.

And the scary part is, it left me feeling happy...small feeling, yet most important in life. I am glad that God allowed me to understand that I can love someone hold heartily and get it in return.

Thank You!!

by kh

More Silly Side

Not so much in to rebounds but I love to play defense
I can hit a ball out of the park if that makes any sense
I can run pass a cheetah waving my hand, they say I am really quick
I would wrestle a tiger, fight a bear, and can tell a butthead he's full of sh*t

Not so much into the beat down, but boy do I love the words
I can give you two minutes of crazy stuff, I'll bet you've never heard
                    Or
I am so into you that… sometimes poems can disguise themselves
I am so happy to have you in my life that I can't think of nothing else
I am so glad that you love me that even the highway can't make you on trip
I am so excited about loving you, that I can make a cripple man on ice not slip
As you figure this is a whole lot of nothing, but it flows so what the hell
As long as you know I love you. My heart is in your jail
by kh

How To Love Me

Call me for no reason…
Or because you think I need it
Gas me up when I am feeling low
My ego… sometimes feed it
Want me even in your sleep
Wake up giving me your best
Take road trips to my place in your heart
So, I can have some rest
Understand that I hold things in
Understand … yet… I am strong
Understand that I am a physical being
Understand I still belong
So, compare me to no other love
And let the world know who I am
And let them know… that I am yours
And that we don't give a damn
Until then, these are unassumingly words
If I must tell you…you already failed
They say people make time out for what most important
And … one or the other can tell
Call me for no reason…
Or because you think I need it
Gas me up when I am feeling low
My love… just keep on feeding it

by kh

Should Be

The last words should be
Beautiful
Forever
Wonderful
Meaningful
The last words should be
Teaching
Believable
Touching
Undeniable
The last words should be **beautiful** like your heart that will **forever** beat **wonderful** and **meaningful** songs into my life.
The last words should be **teaching** others that love can be **believable**, **touching** any heart until it is no longer **undeniable**…that
The last words should be… **I love you**.

by kh

November 03

It was like the wind blew in and took total control of what, I swore I would never do, ever do again. On November 03, today, I went for an ordinary guy to a man on a mission.

My mission is to continue to try and make you understand and believe that if it's not me you should love...then it is no one meant for me. Right now...if you ask me to do, I really love you...my answer is YES...if you ask me why...my answer would be why not ...there is everything about you that I love.

This is not a poem this...one month after meeting you

Love,

by kh

Never heard from her again

I have more than just deep feelings for you

 I have this thing burning in my soul

I have a craving to be touch by you

To have someone to hold

I have tears that I hold back at times

I have a crazy love for us

I have something that needs you in my life

I have a God that I can trust

He brought us both together

I have a feeling we are supposed to be

I have a love for you that is deeper

I have you and you have me…and never heard from her again…lol

by kh

With Me

If you are with me, tell me you are with me

If you are all in with my being, then make me feel whole as I should you

If you are with me, meeting me halfway is not even acceptable…if all of you want all of me

If you are with me, I want us, all the time, all the way…in heart and feelings… that's togetherness

If you are with me, expect for me to give you wholeness

If you are with me, not one part of me belongs solely to me

Because… If you are with me, there should never be a day that I feel like you are not with me...or I am not… with you... nor should you or I ever hurt that way…If You are..

With Me…

by kh

Note: She was not with me…lol

Day One

I have hugged and embraced you…and I still feel you embracing
me
I have kissed you once and it has lasted to date
I have held you in my arms…and I still feel the warmth
I have place both hands on you face to feel your smile…I still
feel your smile
I have laid my hand on your shoulders…I still smell you…yum
I have loved you from day one

by kh

Hang Up

Late nights, long talks so many words left unsaid

Smiles forever, leave you…never

Forever...dances in our heads

Crazy stories about our past, some funny, some so sad

Wishing we had each other back then

And bottled tears together to blow in the wind

Because our love is crazy mad

When we'll meet again, we both know, our bond will grow much
stronger

Smiles forever, leave you…never

We are today, forever, and longer

by kh

That Thing You Got

With that thing

You can make me glow

And sometimes…I shine even longer

With that thing, I start believing I'm superman

I can feel me shinning much stronger

With that thing

 You kill me softly

 As I slowly come back from the dead

When you go there

You're a pro there.

My heart becomes part of my head

With that thing

I will give you, your props,

Because that thing is so sexy and wild

That thing you got is a gift that's hot!

Babe…. how I love your SMILE

by kh

Dat Ain't Right

I want to tell you so badly that I love you but ...dat ain't right...naw can't be

It can't be right to feel how I am feeling because...feeling like this...dat ain't right...nope!

It ain't right that I save your picture to my screen saver and now... every time I look at my phone or cut on my computer, I see you and I think of how your lips might taste... and you know... dat ain't right...true I really do...but it ain't right

And I know it ain't right that I look at your sex and think... how sexy your smile is and...

I get that, all happy feeling, like we just danced to a love song...that you played just for me, and I am in love with that rap part you do...and ...dat ain't right...can you rap?

I want to tell you so badly that I dreamed this into existence...and you secretly love me too...but dat ain't right...well I did ask Him to send me someone like you

It ain't right that I want to listen to you breathe when words aren't spoken... and

I want to pretend that I have known you for years and do things to you like we are married.... nope...dat... dat ain't right...Naw Kent...why?

I am...doing things to your breast softly with my imagination, cuddling close to you as you sleep, tapping you and wanting you to make grown up noises with me, and thanking God afterwards...but... dat ain't right...is it...lol

I wanted this poem to be the best poem I have ever wrote and you say afterwards that you think you are madly in love with me...but dat ain't right...uh?

"Yesss babe," in my smooth voice, (remember that?) I want to tell you I love you...but I do know dat ain't right ...but

If loving you is wrong... and it would be right now...at some point I will...I' m thinking, by then, I don't want to be right. :)

by kh

Note: Needless to say, it wasn't right.

Trash Box

Some say I am unapologetic, but they know… they be lying
I have failed so many times but dang … I be trying
Done kicked myself in the ass because I knew I was right
Got butt naked and bombed out…trying to be so polite?
No…I wasn't bare; know need to go there
I'm talking about sharing my feeling, like food with a bear
I would think you'd understand, but… then who really does
When I tell you it really is, you'd say it wasn't… when it was
So… I put my Jesus, on my speakers, while you catch my buzz
My peeps around the corner shouting, "I feel ya cuzz"
I would say I am unapologetic like a black man to the fuzz
I am just saying what people thinking cause they 'knows what I luvs'
If you feel me say you feel me because some people… do
If you, don't feel me, yet you feel me, I guess I'm talking to you
Got this trash box in my pocket and I am ready to cope
Energetic, half poetic so they think that I'm dope
You… and that other, I see ya'll got that memo
You took the air out of my lungs, so… let… me… clear… my… throat…
I would say I am unapologetic but damn… I'd be lying
I was inside of me saying this trash box… man! I be trying
by kh

Like Mental

Reciprocations of love,

Like splashes of windblown raindrops smoothing that pulsating desire.

I speak you into motion,

As my emotions spread like wild roses...topping the needled gardens.

Cautiously...

I protect you with my strength as we melt in our warmth,

And the gods cradle you... with me.

These times are insightful wonders.

They are delightfully dreams, placing us into our same... space.

And we are thankful and kind...and very simple... yet so complex...

When... two, are all we need to become one.

Reciprocations of love, like mental stimulation telepathically channeled through time and space and...

Reaches us and moves us in time...

And we are time's journey

And its home is in our hearts...and now that we found us in us... we...

We have conquered it all.

by kh

Tiffnii

I can't imagine living my life without you… so I don't

If we live for a thousand years on this earth and…we won't

I would spend the majority of it serving you…because you are my Queen

And the rest of our time living this beautiful dream

I can't imagine one day passing… without hearing your voice

If we talked for a thousand hours a day…and we can't of course

I would tell you how you've changed my life… for the better

And I would pour magic into each word… and place it in a love letter.

If ain't no mountains high enough and there ain't no valleys too low

Then I guess there is a river that flows through us, that takes us where we need to go…

I can't imagine living my life without you… so I don't

If we live for a thousand years on this earth and…we won't

I would breathe you with each breath that I take and shout out to the world, that God makes no mistakes

And to the rest of the world… we should only be seen… as best friends in love… a King who found his Queen…Tiffnii

You Wished

When you are so blessed that you wished...

Everyone understood that trouble really does not last always

All knew that a bird in the hand really does beats two in the bush

You could see people in love, couples together, singles praying for that true love

When you are so blessed that you wished...

Those that doubt you, dislike you and or envy you... understand it doesn't matter ...really

You wished that everyone has a chance to experience something life changing and beautiful... right now

That when you pray, not only do you pray, but you must also believe and have faith

When you are so blessed that you wished...

You understood beforehand that, everything that happened in your life was a direct path into your life now

That you were thankful for everything, when you compare it to the worse that could have happened

All broken will be fixed and at the end of all our journeys we will find ...love, peace...and Soul train :0)

by kh

That's when life started getting really good and I wanted everyone to be blessed!!

Being Strong

The greatest minds...enjoy silence amongst chaos
The broadest shoulders need the most physical therapy
And the biggest heart receives the strongest prayers
So...what I know for sure is...
'Being' still is a gift...being strong is a state of, and prayers with
blessings are gifts from the heart knowing...
God is LOVE
by kh

Note: At work thinking on paper!

What I Know for Sure

What I know for sure...If you ever want anyone to truly respect you, no matter man, woman, or child.... you must show and give an opposite but equal amount of respect to that person. Respect is not something you are born with, it's something shown, taught, and learned into habit. Don't expect to get respect like it's your born right. And fearing you and respecting you are not the same thing...and don't get it confused with honor.... hmmm

What I know for sure...Always and Never are 100% modifiers ...Always believe and never give up...100% Living...

by kh

Intertwine

Between the reality of night and day, are visions that formulate
the moons we seek… our tomorrows
We have scanned our universe in darkness searching for that one
star to bring brightness out of our darkness… our existence
A sequence of circumstances, combined by the blessed…
untangled we are a merciful creation of … our thoughts
Life and the ability to love all, intertwines in the heavens we
created, when the impulse of life pushes us to … ourselves
We intertwine cascading amongst the scars of unbroken
tomorrows and love is introduced to …our song…and we
sung…our song
With all that has stressed our strength in love, even our
possibility of hope is relevant, but our dreams are…our dreams
Peaceful, is our friend, flowing, is our movement and faithful…
is our promise to hold, to have and to blanket ourselves with our
love as
we …
Intertwine
by kh

Note: A friend/co worker gave me the word 'Intertwine' and I came up with
this.

Never this...

Never let this time… make you regret…and

Never let tomorrow… make you forget…and

Always count the times that matter…and the ones that made you smile

Don't let that one mistake you made…not be worth your wild…and

Sometimes cry… it's often good for the soul…because

Sometimes all you really need is a … tear to make you hold on…and

If your season is me… than that's reason enough…and

If your reason brought pain and your season called your bluff… then

Just pray for the rain as if the storms aren't enough…and

Just pray for the lighting when the thunder sounds rough…yet

Never let that distance crack… be that quake in your road…and

Never let your tomorrow bare… yesterday's heavy load

by kh

Note: I sometimes write on my lunch break at work. This was a motivational PEACE for me!

Beyond Beautiful

In my mind, I have her all perfected out.... I mean she has a smile that I want to place in an hourglass and turn it upside down each hour to keep my heart timed to her beautiful.

So, I read a small part of her thinking, just to find out she doesn't have time for games or men that can't afford a date....and I thought...In my dreams I have already taken her out...I have touched the winds blowing in her hair and walked with her along the eroded shores ...she was so beyond beautiful.

In my mind, she was thinking...I have been there done that, and to her I was another frozen horny face ready to place my bid in for a...hello back...as she placed my hello in an hourglass and turned it upside down to remind herself that she doesn't need that ...she is to know and to love.

I am the beautiful one, she wrote, and I agreed quickly... but I froze, because I was not used to someone as beautiful as she and she knowing she is as well ...but I have already taken her out...I held her hands as the stars spelled out our name and the moon aligned us... than I realized she was wrong... for she was... beyond beautiful

I decided to not to say hello but to give her what she had...but beyond it... to give what maybe her heart longs for...but beyond it...

I decided to give her this poem…in hopes that it is as beautiful to her as she is …and beyond beautiful…and she said nice poem and I never heard from her again!!

by kh

Note: This was based on a lady's profile on POF…yes …I had a profile once upon a time…LOL

Just Keep Living

I have prayed for peaceful

Yet my worries were real

I have asked God for strength

yet my visions weren't clear

My trails were many, my troubles weren't few

My love was powerful but

it was only for you

I reach out for you

for so many reasons

I miss what l had, that got lost in our season

I stay strong for ours...yet I get...so

depressed

I cry in silence, yet I try my best

To hold you down...but

No matter how I try

Sorrow doesn't fade… as the days...goes by.

For you...I smile

For you... I exist

For you...I stand

For us... I kiss

The kids at night …

and each time l pray

I move forward in

The darkest of days…

And although I know times it will be tough

Living a me… without you...will never be enough

Note: I wrote this for a friend whose husband had past

One day...

You will look forward to that joke I made up out of thin air that made you laugh

You will look forward to the answer to that question maybe you already knew the answer to but wanted to see what I am thinking.

You will miss telling me that I am crazy as you rub my bald head and ask me, "how was your day and I say, "it was arite."

You will miss yelling out to me, "don't forget to put the seat down on the toilet," as I leave it up again and mumble, "I hope your ass fall in one day" ... you say, "I heard that" and I say, "I didn't say nothing" and you say, "I know what your ass was thinking."

You will miss me holding you like when I first held you and the way I stared at you with you saying, "what" knowing I think you are as fine as ever...

Ol' and that thing we do...lardy, lardy, lardy

One day...I will miss you too

I will miss that beautiful smile, and how I would be at work literally thinking about it and wondering if you could feel me thinking about you as you smiled.

I will miss writing those love poems for you; trying to say in words what I could not say that day you were upset with me over leaving that empty milk carton in the frig...for weeks

I will miss singing our favorite song, the one by the Five Heartbeats... and you thought they were really a group.

I will miss looking into your eyes, yes, your windows to my soul, and wanting to read your heart through those eyes just to see how deep your love for me is.

I will miss those oops, don't worry it slipped but mine don't stink like yours do… and all of a sudden, we have to roll the windows down in the car.

One day…

Yes! One day, and even if you never existed or don't exist right now or We haven't even met yet! When we do, I will love you and be with you until the heavens divides us and we meet again.

One day…

kh

Note: I was single when I wrote this excuse me if it goes astray.

My thought for today

We can alter our appearance, but our hearts don't lie

We can generate a smile, while inside we cry

We can show our true colors and get mad when resisted

We can be what we aren't… that's why blessings are distance

We can paint our faces with clown like colors

We alter our attitudes… to hate one another

But what we can't do is fine one simple way

To make this world a better place before the end of all days

by kh

Note…Okay Hughes!!

Basic Needs

As pure as darkness when your eyes are closed
As bright as the visions you see
Being carried by your dreams,
Your impossible is no longer unbelievable
But pre-written in your stone
You believe what is in your heart
And pray for who has blessed you…and your reality is….
Caring …Loving…God…and
Those are your Basic Needs

As strong as your words unspoken, as loud as your spiritual
whispers
As salient, as the thunder beating in the depths of your heart,
Your strength is powerful
And it flows in your veins,
It moves in the uncharted vessels within you.
And you pray for who has blessed you…and your reality is….
Peace…. Serenity…God…and
Those are your Basic Needs
With compassion
You surrender to the thoughts that feeds your soul…
with all that is beautiful about you…you are
To love… without conditions,
To care… without concerns,

To fly… without spreading your wings,

To change…without changing…

and to feel without the physical touch…that is

As pure as darkness when your eyes are closed and it...

Carries you through your life's journey unharmed

And you pray for who has blessed you…and your reality is….

Understanding… Heaven…God…and

Those are your Basic Needs

by kh

If the road leads to nowhere....... there's usually a sign saying Dead End trust the signs

The End!!